The First Dragon

Also by James A. Owen

The Chronicles of the *Imaginarium Geographica*

Book One: *Here, There Be Dragons*

Book Two: *The Search for the Red Dragon*

Book Three: *The Indigo King*

Book Four: *The Shadow Dragons*

Book Five: *The Dragon's Apprentice*

Book Six: *The Dragons of Winter*

Lost Treasures of the Pirates of the Caribbean

(with Jeremy Owen)

THE CHRONICLES OF THE *IMAGINARIUM* GEOGRAPHICA

THE FIRST DRAGON

Written and illustrated by

James A. Owen

SIMON & SCHUSTER BFYR

NEW YORK LONDON TORONTO SYDNEY NEW DELHI

For my children

An imprint of Simon & Schuster Children's Publishing Division

1230 Avenue of the Americas, New York, New York 10020

Also available in a SIMON & SCHUSTER BFYR hardcover edition

Book design by Laurent Linn

The text for this book is set in Adobe Jensen Pro.

The illustrations for this book are rendered in pen and ink.

Manufactured in the United States of America

First SIMON & SCHUSTER BFYR paperback edition November 2014

2 4 6 8 10 9 7 5 3 1

The Library of Congress has cataloged the hardcover edition as follows:

Library of Congress Cataloging-in-Publication Data

Owen, James A.

The first dragon / written and illustrated by James A. Owen. — 1st ed.

p. cm. — (The chronicles of the Imaginarium Geographica ; [bk. 7])

Summary: "To save the world, the new generation of caretakers must find the First Dragon and restore the lost lands of the Archipelago before it's too late."— Provided by publisher.

ISBN 978-1-4424-1226-2 (hardcover) — ISBN 978-1-4424-1228-6 (eBook) [1. Time travel—Fiction. 2. Characters in literature—Fiction. 3. Fantasy.] I. Title.

PZ7.O97124Fir 2013

[Fic]—dc23

2012037552

ISBN 978-1-4424-1227-9 (pbk)

Contents

List of Illustrations

Acknowledgments

I first suggested the idea of H. G. Wells having owned an atlas of maps to imaginary lands in the first of my MythWorld novels, published in Germany over a decade ago. It was a couple of years later that I wrote up a ten-page proposal for a film called *Here Be Dragons,* which I subsequently turned into a book proposal, and which, a couple of years after that, was developed into the published book *Here, There Be Dragons.* It will have been eight years between the publication of that first book and the publication of this one, and in that time readers who started the series in grade school will be finishing it in college.

The entire journey has been one of unusual synchronicities. If the magazine ventures I was involved in had not imploded, I would not have gone out soliciting movie studios and publishers to buy my personal creative work. My attorney, Craig Emanuel, connected me with the managers at the Gotham Group, who connected me with Marc Rosen and David Heyman at Heyday Films. If not for David's interest and Marc's encouragement and assistance in fleshing out the story, I may not have held on to it long enough to decide to pursue a book deal first. And if Julie at the Gotham Group had not called David Gale at Simon & Schuster Books for Young Readers, then perhaps none of these books would have existed at all.

But all of those connections happened, the books exist, and a great many people helped push this cart along the way.

Craig Emanuel, Julie Jones, and David Schmerler at Loeb & Loeb have constantly and consistently looked after my interests and made sure that the contracts went smoothly.

Julie Kane-Ritsch, Ellen Goldsmith-Vein, Lindsay Williams, and Julie Nelson played a similar role at the Gotham Group, and more than once went out of their way to make sure my bills were paid.

David Gale began all of this by saying yes to the first book, and he and Navah Wolfe made all of the books better than I imagined they could be. The rest of the team at Simon & Schuster, including Carolyn Reidy, Justin Chanda, Jon Anderson, Lizzy Bromley, Paul Crichton, Laurent Linn, Siena Koncsol, and all of the wonderful people who worked on making and selling the books reshaped my career, and I am grateful to all of them.

My friends are the ones who held me together in every possible way through the making of this series: Brett, Shawn, Heidi, Robb, George, Bill, Irene, Ray, Shannon, Dave, Daanon, Kristin, Homer and Effie, Russ and Bekki, John and Valerie, Kevin and Rebecca, Tracy and Lisa, and Tracy and Troy. My mother, Sharon, and brother Jason were also there when I needed them to be, and they all made it possible for me to do the work I do.

Lon, Mary, and especially Jeremy helped me to find my arête in my art, and in the work we do together. There would be no Coppervale Studio without Jeremy. And there would be no reason to do the things I do without my family: Cindy, Sophie, and Nathaniel drive me to be a better artist, a better writer, and a better man.

All of you made these books possible, and I can't express my gratitude enough.

Prologue

Stories have existed since the beginning of the world, and human history itself consists of little more than the stories that survived. All stories are true—but some of them just never happened.

The story of the first murder is one that is both true, and real.

There is, however, a secret part of the story about the first murder that almost no one knows, because there were only two witnesses, and one of them was bound not to speak what he knew. The other, of course, was dead. And the world where dead men speak had not yet come into existence, not really—because it was the murder itself that created it.

The first Maker was their mother, and the first Namer, their father. They were brothers, twins, although as in the way of all things, one was called the elder, and the other, the younger. It was their parents who called them such, and so they did not question it. It was only after they had grown to manhood that they were given their secret names and were told what their true purpose in the world was to be. With purpose came callings, the first of their kind in the world, and the most crucial.

One was the Imago, meant to be the protector of the world; the other, the Archimago, meant to be the bringer of destruction. One was the agent of order; the other, of chaos. Locked in a perpetual struggle, the brothers were meant to create balance in the world, but that was not what came to pass.

The elder son raised up a stone and struck the younger son a blow across the head, killing him. Thus did Cain murder Abel, in the first story that gave meaning to the power of choice in the world.

His family cast Cain out, and marked him, that the other peoples of the world would know him for what he was. Thus, he chose to become someone else and clothed himself in the stories of humanity so that he could walk among them unseen, unknown.

In the centuries that followed, the elder son wandered the world, taking a thousand names and living a thousand lives before he found his purpose again. He found it in the last life he created for himself, as a storyteller, who wrote of mystery, and murder, and solving unsolvable riddles, and the mechanics of creation itself.

In time, he tired of simply telling stories, and once more inserted himself into the affairs of two worlds. He built a house in a distant corner of the Archipelago and named it for one of his creations. There, he gathered together all those of his brotherhood who would help him to defend both the Archipelago of Dreams and the Summer Country against the darkness that was coming.

He shared many secrets with those who gathered around him, but of himself he shared very little—especially the greatest secret of them all.

Only a few personages still walking the earth knew that the first Imago and Archimago had been brothers, but what none of them knew was which one had been murdered.

One was killed; the other survived. Only he knew which he was: the agent of chaos, or the agent of order; and he had been bound not to tell. Not until the last battle between Darkness and Light, when all things would stand revealed and all allegiances declared.

On that day he would speak their secret names, and in doing so give voice to his brother from the grave, the way so many other dead men had made their voices heard there within the bounds of Tamerlane House.

On that day he would finally discover if the choice he'd made, oh so long ago, would be responsible for saving the world, or destroying it.

And on that day the elder son, also called Cain, also called Nimrod, also called Prospero, also called Poe, would discover if finally, he could lay down his burden, and rest.

Part One

The Return of the Black Dragon

". . . I miss all the Dragons."

Chapter One

Ancient Promises

"I miss Samaranth," the young Valkyrie Laura Glue said as she descended the ladder, arms laden with ancient books and scrolls. "In fact, I miss all the Dragons. They may not have always been there when you wanted them . . ."

"But they were always there when you needed them," the Caretaker named Jack said, finishing the expression all of them had said at one time or another in recent weeks.

"That's only because," Harry Houdini said, raising his finger to emphasize his point, "none of them ever threatened to roast and *eat* any of you."

Jack's colleague John, the former Caveo Principia and current Prime Caretaker, chuckled and clapped the magician on the arm. "You did ask for it, Ehrich," he said, using Houdini's given name. "Both you and Arthur. You should have known better than to step on the Dragon's tail, even metaphorically."

"I'm sure Conan Doyle did know better," said Jack, "but he was swayed by . . . *Other* influences."

"I resent that," said Houdini.

"I meant Burton," Jack said, feigning innocence. "Perhaps your conscience heard differently."

He took the bundle of documents from Laura Glue and handed them to John, who winked at him, not necessarily out of agreement, but just to give Houdini a tweak. The former members of the Imperial Cartological Society might have rejoined the Caretakers, but some of the old divisions were still present in every conversation. "These are pre–Iron Age," John remarked as he peered more closely at the topmost parchments. "They're in surprisingly good shape."

"Everything here is," Jack agreed. "Unfortunately, we're still no closer to finding anything useful."

"We must persevere," John replied. "If there is anything that can give us a clue as to how to find our friends, it will be here."

The Repository of Tamerlane House was located in the centermost room, accessible only by the master of the house, who rarely involved himself directly in the affairs of the other Caretakers, and by the Prime Caretaker, who until very recently had been Jules Verne.

There were several libraries within the walls of Tamerlane, including one that contained all the unwritten books of the world, but the Repository was different: It held the books that were the most rare, the most sacred, to the Caretakers and all those who came before who tried to make better worlds out of the ones they had been given. The Histories, written by the Caretakers during each of their tenures, were there, as were the Prophecies, which were future histories that had been compiled primarily by Verne and his immediate protégé Bert, also known as H. G. Wells, the Caretaker who had chosen John, Jack, and their friend Charles to become Caretakers themselves.

There was also the *Telos Biblos*, the Last Book, which was both history and prophecy. It contained the names of all the Dragons, which the Caretakers' enemies had used to capture their shadows and compel them to service—which led to the destruction of all the Dragons save for the oldest one. Unfortunately, since the incident that severed the connections between the Archipelago and the Summer Country, time itself had become more and more erratic. Might-have-beens and alternate histories were taking the place of pasts and futures that previously, Verne had relied on as being set in stone. But that stone, it seemed, was fluid, changeable; and so the Last Book was no more helpful to them than the books in the last case: the *Imaginarium Geographica*s of other worlds yet to be explored.

Jack looked wistfully at the case with the other *Geographica*s and chuckled ruefully when John smiled and shook his head.

"I understand, old friend," John said, not for the first time. "I want to explore them too, but our first responsibility must be to the restoration of the lands from the *Geographica* we're already Caretakers of."

"I'm just feeling the weight of it all, John," his friend replied. "No one is going to suddenly appear with a magic solution to fix everything, are they?"

"We have only ourselves to rely on, I'm afraid," John said with a heavy sigh. "We can only hope that we will prove to be a fraction as effective at keeping the evils of the world at bay as the Dragons were."

In the centuries since the *Imaginarium Geographica* was created, it had been entrusted to many Caretakers for safekeeping—all of whom had the same reaction to the legend inscribed on the maps.

It read, *Here, there be Dragons,* and to a man, every Caretaker had at first assumed this was a warning. In time, they came to learn it was not.

Here, there be Dragons was meant to reassure the Caretakers and all those living in the lands depicted on the maps that there would always be someone watching over them; someone older, wiser, and stronger than any forces who might seek to destroy the world of the Archipelago of Dreams. Since the creation of the Archipelago, when it was separated from the world called the Summer Country, there had always been a Dragon—at least one—standing watch.

That was before the coming of the Winter King, who sought to rule the Archipelago, and the Caretakers of prophecy from the Last Book, three young scholars from Oxford, who defeated him and saved both worlds. But the price was high—before the Winter King was defeated, the Keep of Time, which connected the two worlds, was set on fire and gradually destroyed, severing the connection.

Time in the Archipelago was severed from the Caretakers' base at Tamerlane House in the Nameless Isles, as well as the rest of the world, and in the process, had begun to speed up. Thousands of years passed in the Archipelago, and it was eventually taken over completely by the Caretakers' great enemy: the eternal Shadows known as Echthroi, and their servants, the Lloigor.

The Nameless Isles were spared the same fate only because of a temporal and interdimensional bridge built by William Shakespeare that connected Tamerlane House to the Kilns, Jack's home in Oxford.

With the destruction of the keep, the Caretakers also lost the ability to travel in time—something that their adversaries, led by the renegade Caretaker Dr. John Dee, seemed to have a greater facility for. Only the Grail Child, Rose Dyson, and the new Cartographer, Edmund McGee, working together to create chronal maps that could open into any point in time, could give the Caretakers any hope of repairing the damage that had been done and restoring what once was in the Archipelago.

Somehow, the Keep of Time had to be rebuilt. And the only way to do that was to find the Architect—and no one in history seemed to know his identity, or when the keep had been built to begin with.

Rose and Edmund, along with the tulpa Caretaker Charles, his mentor Bert, the clockwork owl from Alexandria named Archimedes, and the once leader of the Imperial Cartological Society, Sir Richard Burton, were dispatched into Deep Time to try to find the Architect—and the mission was a disaster.

Burton was trapped in the far future, after narrowly defeating an Echthros-possessed alternate version of their friend Jack; Archimedes was nearly destroyed; and Rose's sword, Caliburn, was irreparably broken. Only the intervention of a mysterious, near-omnipotent old man in a white, timeless space called Platonia saved the other companions. Bert was returned to Tamerlane, just in time to die and become a portrait in Basil Hallward's gallery; and Rose, Charles, and Edmund were sent more deeply into the past, to a city that might have been Atlantis.

Since Bert's reappearance and the discovery of an engraving of the city that Edmund had left inside a Sphinx for the Caretakers to find, nearly two months had passed, with no sign of the companions, and no further word of where, or when, they were.

Shakespeare, who had a gift for constructing chronal devices, had fashioned a pyramid he called the Zanzibar Gate out of the fallen stones of the keep, in order to use it to go after the missing companions. Unfortunately, it had to be powered by the presence of a living Dragon—and there were no Dragons left. Even the great old Dragon Samaranth had vanished when the Archipelago was lost—so the Caretakers couldn't even seek him out for advice, much less ask him to go through the gate. That left everything at a standstill for weeks—and when Rose, Edmund, and Charles failed to reappear, John, Jack, Laura Glue, Houdini, and some of the others at Tamerlane House began searching for other options. But even the fabled Repository of Tamerlane House had given them nothing.

"It seems there are times when only a Dragon will do," Houdini said, slamming shut another ancient tome. "There simply isn't any substitute."

"Do you need a hand with those?" Jack asked, rising from his chair as Laura Glue again descended a ladder carrying a precariously arranged assortment of boxes.

"It's all right," Laura Glue said as she carefully balanced the stack on the table. "I got this."

"Actually," Jack said, "the proper way to say that would be 'I've got this.' The way you say it makes you sound . . ."

"Uneducated? Like a wildling, maybe?" Laura Glue replied.

Jack frowned. "I was going to say, it makes you sound less intelligent than you actually are."

Laura Glue frowned back. "'Ceptin'," she said, deliberately using Lost Boy slang, "you knows I be intelligent as all that, and I knows I be intelligent as all that, so what be the problem, neh?"

"The problem," Jack said, now in full professor mode, "is that no one else who heard you speak that way would know how intelligent you really are."

She shrugged and smiled at the Caretaker. "Why should I care what anyone else thinks? I know, and that's enough."

"She has you there, Jack," John said, clapping him on the back. "Best just shut up now and help her move the boxes."

"Nah," Laura Glue said, waving one hand at them as she hefted another stack of boxes with her other arm. "Like I said—I got this."

"An' I gots some munchies," the badger Caretaker Fred announced as he strolled into the room, carrying a large basket filled with fruit. "It's midafternoon, and you missed lunch, so I thought I'd better bring something up."

"Thank you, Fred," Jack said as he selected a bunch of grapes and sat down. "Anticipating a need is the mark of an excellent Caretaker."

"Don't go quoting Jules, now," said John. "Especially regarding anticipating our needs."

"That's not entirely fair, is it?" Houdini asked as he examined some pears a moment before selecting a peach. "He hardly could have anticipated a crisis like this one."

"He seems to have anticipated every other kind of crisis," John grumbled, "including an entire alternate timeline set into motion by Hugo Dyson closing a door at the wrong time, which, as I recall, was partially *your* fault. So why didn't he anticipate this? Where's the backup plan for the backup plan?"

Jack stood and sidled around one of the tables to move another stack of scrolls and parchments, which he dropped onto the floor next to John's chair. "Perhaps we have gotten too accustomed to his being our deus ex machina," he said, sitting heavily in the wing-back chair next to Laura Glue. "We count on his always having the answers, because before we knew how many strings he was pulling, he always seemed to have all the answers. And then, even after we found out just how many events he was manipulating, we still allowed it because it always seemed to work out. It was only after something finally went terribly wrong that you took matters into your own hands and stepped into the role yourself."

John scowled. "You are referring to the role of Prime Caretaker, I hope," he said with a hint of irritation, "and not Jules's predilection for meddling with time."

"What's the difference?" Laura Glue asked as she selected an apple from Fred's basket and bit into it. "Isn't that precisely what the job be, neh?"

"That's the problem in a nutshell," John said with a sigh. "It really is, but it *shouldn't* be."

At that moment, Nathaniel Hawthorne stuck his head around the corner. Before he could speak a word, he exploded with a violent sneeze, then another, and another.

"You would think," he said as Fred handed him a handkerchief to blow his nose, "that Basil Hallward could have painted some version of my portrait that left out my allergy to dust."

Jack chuckled. "That's not how it works," he said blithely, referring to their resident artist's technique for preserving life by painting portraits of Caretakers who were about to end their natural life spans. "As you were in life, so you remain in Tamerlane House."

"That's slender consolation sometimes, Jack," Hawthorne grumbled as he wiped his nose. "You'll understand when you eventually join us."

Jack hesitated. "I . . . haven't yet decided," he finally said. "I know I don't want to become a tulpa like Charles did when he passed, but I'm not certain that I want to be a portrait, either."

"It's not so bad—as long as you don't go on vacation for longer than seven days," Hawthorne said, referring to the one limitation of portrait-extended life: They could only live as long as they were never away from Tamerlane House for more than a week—a lesson the Caretakers learned all too well when both their mentor, Professor Sigurdsson, and their once-ally-turned-enemy Daniel Defoe perished after being gone for too long.

"Time enough to decide that later," said Jack. "Hopefully decades. Was there something you needed, Nate?"

Hawthorne hooked his thumb over his shoulder. "There's some kind of commotion down at one of the beaches. I've dispatched Jason's sons to go down there just in case it's trouble, and I'm going to go have a look myself. I just thought the, ah, Prime Caretaker . . ." He paused, looking at John. "I thought you ought to know."

John waved his hand. "You're head of security," he said. "I trust in that. Let me know what you find, though."

Hawthorne winked and disappeared.

"Mebbe I should go too," said Fred, "seein' as I'm one of th' actual Caretakers now."

"Actually, we could use your help here," said Jack. "There are some cubbyholes in and around the bookshelves that are too small for us to reach, and, not to put too fine a point on it . . ."

"I know, I know," Fred said with mock annoyance. "You need a badger to bail out your backsides—*again*."

"I'll never begrudge the help of a badger," John said with honest appreciation, "especially considering that you're the closest thing to a Dragon we have left."

"That may not be entirely correct," said a breathless Hawthorne, who reentered the room in such a rush that he nearly skidded into a bookcase. "Come quickly, everyone! You must see what we've found on the South Beach."

Hawthorne's alert roused everyone at Tamerlane House, and so almost every Caretaker, Messenger, Mystorian, and creature arrived on the beach at the same time and saw the same impossible sight:

There, half out of the water and leaning slightly where it rested on the sand, was the *Black Dragon*.

Chapter Two

The Prodigal Dragon

The initial surprise that was felt by all the residents of Tamerlane House at finding the long-missing *Black Dragon* on the South Beach was quickly eclipsed by their arguing about what it meant, and more, what was to be done next.

Shakespeare, for his part, was thrilled by the arrival of the *Black Dragon*. But several of the Caretakers Emeriti, led by da Vinci, were convinced it was some sort of Echthroi trick—a Dragonship version of the Trojan Horse—and advocated burning it on the spot.

The younger Caretakers, led by John and Jack, suggested it was merely synchronicity that a Dragonship had turned up at just that point in time that a Dragon was needed, and protested that burning it would destroy their only chance of powering Shakespeare's Zanzibar Gate.

The rest were basically skirting one side or the other without taking a definitive stance, all of which meant that there was nothing but chaotic bickering right up to the point that Harry Houdini fired the cannon and silenced them all.

"Hell's bells," he said as he moved around the still-smoking cannon, which sat along one of the battlements. "I thought we kept this

. . . *Houdini and John piloted the* Black Dragon . . .

loaded in case of an attack from the Echthroi, but it seems it's just as useful in shutting up Caretakers."

"Now, see here," Hawthorne started.

"You're all forgetting," Houdini went on, ignoring Hawthorne, "that the Archipelago isn't on Chronos time anymore. So this ship didn't just leave a year ago to make its way here. It's been sailing for . . ." He looked at Twain. "I can't do math."

"Oh, uh," said Dumas, who was good with numbers. "About a . . . um, a thousand years, give or take."

"A thousand years," Houdini repeated, glaring at da Vinci. "So we know there's still a living Dragon at its heart. And as far as using it," he added, looking at John, "that isn't our choice. It's his. And we all know who the Black Dragon once was—so what he'll choose to do is anybody's guess."

"He'll do it," said John.

"You sound pretty confident of that," said Dumas.

"I am," said John, "because he's already sacrificed himself once for his daughter, and I have no doubt he'll do it again."

"Why?" asked Houdini.

"Because," said John, "I'm a father too, and it's what I would do."

"There's just one problem," said Shakespeare. "It's a Dragon*ship*, not a Dragon. I don't know if that will work to activate the portal. It may be that the only use for it is *as* a ship."

"It's all well and good," Dumas said, giving the *Black Dragon* a cursory glance, "but of what use is a Dragonship with no Archipelago to cross over to?"

"More to the point," said John, "if we can't separate the Dragon from the ship, how can we power the gate?"

"Do you really need to, though?" asked Jack. "The bridge

didn't need anything but a Dragon's eyes to work."

"I was hoping to engineer the gate to operate on the same principle as the bridge," said Shakespeare, "but that's, it would seem, apples and oranges."

"I think I understand," said John. "The Dragon eyes were sufficient enough talismans to permit us to cross between worlds . . ."

"But to traverse time, to activate the mechanism, requires a *living* Dragon," Shakespeare finished. "It's a conundrum, to be sure. That's why this new development is so thrilling—the *Black Dragon* still has within it a living, breathing Dragon . . . and that may be sufficient to activate the Zanzibar Gate."

"In other words," Jack said, grinning from ear to ear, "the Caretakers are back in the game."

"Bangarang!" said Fred.

Under Shakespeare's direction, Houdini and John piloted the *Black Dragon* off the beach and around to the small island where the Zanzibar Gate had been constructed. But proximity was not enough.

"It has to go through the gate," Shakespeare said glumly. "The Dragon has to go through first, or else it can't be activated properly." He turned to Jules Verne, who had typically taken charge of situations like the discovery of the ship—but who had instead chosen to stand back in deference to John. "Is there any way to . . . separate the Dragon from the ship? To perhaps remove the masthead?"

Verne glanced at John and Twain, then shook his head. "No method that I know of," he answered. "As far as I know, no one's ever tried. No one except Ordo Maas knew the process for making a Dragonship—and when the Archipelago was lost, we lost him as well."

"That's not entirely true," offered John. "He admitted that the *Black Dragon* wasn't one of his, remember? Someone else must know the secret, because someone had to *create* the *Black Dragon*."

Verne looked at John, eyes narrowed. "Yes," he said. "You might have something at that." He turned and tilted his head at Bert. "Someone one of us may have already met."

Bert moved quickly to Verne's side, eyes glittering. "Surely he can't still be alive?" he said, his voice trembling with excitement. "I mean, it could only be . . . He'd be the only one . . . But to still be alive, after all these centuries . . ."

"Maybe," Verne said, pulling at his beard. "It *is* possible, Bert."

"Who are we talking about?" asked Jack.

"A possibility," Verne said enigmatically. "Ordo Maas was not the only shipbuilder to construct living vessels—and the only other one we know of in history made an ancient promise that may have been fulfilled with the creation of the *Black Dragon*. And if that is so, then he may be the one who can reverse the process too."

John looked at the others, and a bit of the starch seemed to have gone out of him. "I'd forgotten," he said, slightly crestfallen. "That fellow they saved in the past. The one who owed Edmund a boon."

"And may have fulfilled it," said Verne.

Bert frowned. "We're wasting time, Jules," he said testily. "If he has actually survived since Jason's time . . ."

Verne held a finger to his lips and turned to the rest of the gathering. "I agree, time is of the essence now," he said, almost contritely. "But it is no longer my call. John? What do you say?"

The Prime Caretaker drew a sharp breath. It was the first time in the two months since their friends had been lost that

Verne had actually deferred to him in front of the others, all of whom were now watching expectantly.

"First things first," he said firmly. "Let's secure the ship in the boathouse where it ought to be. Then we must attend to other matters, such as the security of Tamerlane House. And then," he added with a tight smile at Bert and Verne, "we'll make our battle plan."

Once the ship was safely ensconced in the boathouse, John, Jack, and Bert retreated to the main house to set another part of their newly minted plans in motion.

Bert had been largely absent from the activities of Tamerlane House for the last two months, for reasons both good and shoddy. The good reason was that upon finding out he had died and was now a portrait, he also discovered that Verne had rescued his love, Weena, from the far future, and made her over into a portrait as well. The love he thought lost to the mists of time was now, here, present, and in his new life. John couldn't begrudge his old mentor that.

However, Bert had also been complicit in many of Verne's plans, including keeping the truth of many things from his protégés simply because Verne had deemed it necessary. And so when John had enough of Verne's games and declared himself to be the new Prime Caretaker, Bert also bore some of that judgment. So when an opportunity emerged for Bert to actively contribute to the plan of action, he jumped on it with relish—and possibly out of hope of a small measure of forgiveness from the Caretakers whom he had come to love like his own sons.

On the walk to the house, Bert told the others everything he could remember about the strange shipbuilder he and the other time travelers had encountered in the past—and then, together, they repeated it all to the two residents of Tamerlane House whom they could depend on to carry out their plan.

"Interesting," said Don Quixote as he nibbled on a cookie. "Don't you agree, Uncas?"

His squire climbed down from the chair where he'd been perched and frowned at the knight. "Interesting?" he exclaimed, whiskers twitching. "Sounds more like a 'mergency t' me. Finish your snicker-doodle and let's get going."

"Uh, we haven't even told you what we need you to do," said Jack.

"That's never stopped us before," said Uncas.

"What is the task?" Quixote asked, swallowing the last bite of cookie and pocketing two more before dusting off his lap. "I'm not sure where to begin looking for a shipbuilder who might have died thousands of years ago."

"You may not," said Bert, "but someone else you know does. In fact, they were well acquainted at one point."

"Of whom are we speaking?"

"The Zen Detective," said John.

"He's just upstairs, with Rappaccini's daughter," said Quixote. "Why not just go ask him yourselves?"

"Because," said John, "despite his sudden turnabout in the battle with Dee and the Cabal, the detective still harbors a lot of deep-seated and unpleasant feelings about working with Caretakers. But *you* two," he said, pointing at the knight and the squire, "are not Caretakers. And he still feels a sense of obligation for betraying you."

"And you want us to play offa that, hey?" asked Uncas. "That in't th' Animal way."

"It's the way that will work," said John. "Will you do it?"

Quixote stood and saluted. "For you, Master Caretaker, I would march alone through the gates of Hades itself."

"And I'd go with him," said Uncas.

The knight and his squire made their way through the warren of hallways and corridors to the room that had been provided to the Zen Detective, but as they suspected it might be, it was empty. Since taking up residence at Tamerlane House, he could almost always be found with one of Verne's time travelers, the assistants known as Messengers. Her name was Beatrice, but everyone called her Rappaccini's daughter, after her famous father. Her room was less a living space than it was an arboretum, and nearly everything growing in it was poisonous. This might have been a cause for concern to the detective had he not also recently been poisonous himself. Beatrice corrected that unfortunate condition, and in the most unlikely pairing possible, the two fell in love.

It took several knocks at Beatrice's door before the detective opened it in a huff. "What is it?" he said, not even trying to disguise the ire in his voice. "We're busy."

Uncas drew a breath, intending to ask what they were busy doing, but Quixote kicked him in the shin and shut him up. "Hello, Aristophanes," the knight said pleasantly. "We'd like to ask a favor, if you don't mind."

Aristophanes looked back into the room at his dark, quiet companion and snorted. "Don't insult me. The Caretakers need a favor, you mean."

"We need you to find a shipbuilder," Quixote said, ignoring the deflection. "Someone of approximately your own vintage."

"*My* vintage?" Aristophanes said in honest surprise. "There's no one living who . . ." He paused, eyes widening.

"Back in the day, he built a ship you might have heard of," said Quixote. "It was called the *Argo*."

"Argus," the detective said, shaking his head. "You want me to find Argus."

"Ah!" Uncas said brightly. "You know him!"

"I was supposed to execute him," said Aristophanes. "Plans changed. Mistakes were made. And now I'm being harassed by a geriatric knight and a talking beaver."

"I'm a badger, you—you—*unicorn*," Uncas replied before he noticed the slight gleam in the detective's eyes. He was teasing.

"So," said Aristophanes, "the Caretakers have need of finding a shipbuilder, do they?"

"Yes," the knight said, nodding, "and we need you to do so right away." He reached into a knapsack at his side and drew out a small bag, which he handed to the detective. "We came prepared," he said somberly. "Thirty pieces of silver—your usual fee, I believe."

The detective's eyes widened slightly, but he didn't answer. Instead he reached out a hand and pressed the bag back toward Quixote.

"All debts were paid," he said softly, the gruffness gone from his voice. "Tell Verne that he was as good as his word, and I have rejoined the flow of the world."

"So, do you think you can find Argus?" Quixote asked.

"Consider it done," Aristophanes said brusquely, as if trying to regain his earlier gruff demeanor. "I can take you to him now if you like."

"Really?" asked Uncas in astonishment. "That's pretty amazing."

"I'm actually very good at this," the detective said as he cast a longing, heartfelt look at Beatrice, then grabbed his hat and coat. "Also, if I'm not actually charging you to find him, then there's no point in dragging things out to drive up my expenses."

Together, the three unlikely companions crossed Shakespeare's Bridge to the Kilns, where they kept the Duesenberg. It was no ordinary vehicle—it had been modified with a special spatial projector that could transport them instantly to any number of places that were depicted on an assortment of special slides. It made missions like these a great deal easier to manage.

"Is that a new hat?" Uncas asked as they clambered into the car.

"It is," Aristophanes said, trying and failing to hold back a wistful smile. "A gift from Bea. I'm no longer poison to the touch, but I'm apparently still a unicorn," he went on, fingering his fedora, "so I still need a hat if we're going to go mingle with civilized society—or whatever passes for that where we're going."

"You're the guide," said Quixote as he started up the car. "Where to, Steve?"

"Here," the detective said, holding up a slide. "Thousands of years in obscurity, and the Caretakers have a portal that leads almost right to his door. Amazing."

Aristophanes inserted the slide, and the Duesenberg roared forward just as the portal opened up on the side of a building a few hundred yards from the Kilns. The car slid to a stop atop a grassy hill, in the bright afternoon sunlight of Greece.

"Welcome to Lemnos," Uncas said, flipping off the projector. "Where to now?"

Aristophanes pointed ahead to a fork in the road, indicating that they should drive to the right. Then, consulting a small notepad he pulled from his coat, he told Uncas they'd be looking for a seaside cottage about three miles farther along.

"This seems like a nice little hamlet," Quixote observed as they passed a number of small but tidy houses. "Hardly where you'd think an ancient shipbuilder could find peaceful refuge away from prying eyes."

"It's the standing stones," the detective said, pointing them out as the car passed between two sizable rocks that stood alongside the road. "They act as a sort of screen, keeping out the looky-loos and troublemakers. They're as good as hiding in plain sight, because someone living within the boundaries of the stones can't be found—not by the methods the Caretakers use, anyway."

"And what method do you use?" asked Quixote.

"That," Aristophanes said, pointing at the small red book he carried in his breast pocket. "With that and a stub of graphite, I can keep track of anyone I like. I just write it down."

He frowned at the look of incredulity on the old knight's face. "What?" said the detective. "Like everything has to be done with magic?"

"It's like our Little Whatsits," Uncas said, nodding in approval. "Very wise."

"Thank you, badger," said Aristophanes.

"Don't mention it," Uncas said, pointing at a small cottage. "Look—I think we've arrived."

"Please," he said. . . . "Feel free to look around . . ."

Chapter Three
The Shipbuilder

The cottage was a traditional whitewashed stone structure common to the Greek isles, save for the windows, which were stained glass that depicted ancient Greek myths in spectacular bursts of color. There were chimes outside the doorway that swayed gently in the breeze of their passing and announced the companions' presence to the occupant inside.

The shipbuilder's shop at the rear of the cottage was bright and airy and had tall, whitewashed walls that curved up into ceilings. At the center of the room, the proprietor was descending a staircase carrying a box of supplies. He paused when he saw the three visitors, then smiled and continued down the stairs.

"Please," he said, setting the box on the floor, then gesturing around the room with his hands. "Feel free to look around at my work. Much to see, more to buy, as long as the price is right."

All around the room were tables and low shelving laden with globes, clear glass jugs, and bottles, and in them floated miniature ships of various designs. Some appeared to be simple, traditional sailboats, but most were of a far more elaborate design, incorporating scrollworks and ornate carvings in the hulls. But what was most intriguing to the companions was that every ship bore a masthead that resembled an insect. Several had the aspect of a praying mantis, but most of the others were moths or butterflies with magnificent, delicate wings. As Uncas watched, some of the wings appeared to flutter with the gentle motion of the water in the bottles.

The shipbuilder was pleased to see them admiring his handiwork, and he smiled a lopsided grin. "For some reason," he said matter-of-factly, "I seem to be skilled in merging creatures that fly with craft that float."

"That's why we've come seeking you," Quixote ventured. "We understand you have had some experience with merging a ship and a larger creature—say, a dragon?"

"Hah!" The shipbuilder exclaimed. "You want someone to make you a Dragonship? Easier to ask for the Golden Apples of the Sun, or a sword made by Hattori Hanzo."

Aristophanes snorted. "Hattori Hanzo doesn't exist."

"True," the shipbuilder replied, "but that doesn't stop people from seeking out his swords."

Uncas slumped, dejected. "So it isn't possible to make ships larger than these toys?"

"Oh, it is possible, but I seldom have," Argus replied, sitting. "And not for a very long time. You don't want me, anyway. You'd be better off with my master, Utnapishtim. He's the true virtuoso for what you want."

"Utnapishtim?" Quixote said, puzzled. "I don't think I've heard . . ."

"Sorry, sorry," Argus said, rolling his eyes. "I forgot he took a different name when he'd crossed over for good. You might know him better by his Greek name, Deucalion. Or perhaps as . . ."

"Ordo Maas," Uncas finished for him. "All th' Children of th' Earth knows Ordo Maas."

Argus reached out and scratched Uncas on top of the head, which Quixote thought would offend his little friend, but oddly, the badger didn't seem to mind. "Yes, your kind would know of him, wouldn't they, small one?" he said gently. "Ordo Maas—that's who you want."

"'Cept we can't ask him," Uncas replied. "He's not findable. Not anymore."

Argus frowned. "How is he not findable? The last I knew, he had his own island in the Archipelago."

"That's exactly the problem," said Quixote. "The Archipelago is no more."

The shipbuilder's eyes narrowed. "You lie."

"Knights never lie," said Uncas. "What happened was this, see, there was a fire—"

"I don't want to know," Argus said flatly. "It's none of my business. Not anymore." He stood up as if to indicate that the discussion was over. "I'm sorry. You'll have to find someone else to build you your Dragonship."

"But, that's just the thing," Uncas protested. "We don't want'cha t' *build* a ship—we need ya t' unbuild one."

Argus turned and looked at the badger, who was all frizzy with earnestness, then up at Quixote. "I'm sorry—as I said, my master was the true creator of such things. I cannot help you."

Quixote looked at Aristophanes, who had been quiet throughout the entire encounter. The Zen Detective shrugged. "You hired me to find him, not to compel him to do anything for you," he said brusquely as he turned for the door. "If he doesn't want to help you, that's no business of mine."

Quixote sighed heavily and put his arm around Uncas. "Come along, my squire. Let's go explain to the Caretakers that their ship the *Black Dragon* is going to remain just that—a ship. And nothing more."

The sound of a glass jug shattering against the stone floor stopped the companions in their tracks. They turned back to see Argus kneeling amid the shards of glass and spilled water, gently trying to lift a Monarch ship out of the mess without damaging the wings.

"The *Black Dragon*," the shipbuilder said as he delicately installed the tiny ship in another jug. "You told me a ship—you didn't say which."

"Well, now you know," said Aristophanes. "And if you're willing to help, I'm sure you'll be well compensated."

Argus folded his arms and considered them carefully for a moment. Then he pursed his lips. "A boon," he said at last. "Your masters will owe me a boon, whatever I ask. That is my price."

"Are we authorized to agree to those terms?" Uncas asked Quixote, obviously worried. "Scowler John never said anything about offering *him* an open ticket."

"Well, it did work out the last time," Quixote whispered back, "except for, you know, the betrayal and all that."

"The Caretakers have always known *my* terms," the Zen Detective remarked, winking at Uncas, as the shipbuilder gathered his tools together in anticipation of an agreement. "I get my fee, plus expenses. And if the expenses mean agreeing to pay whatever the mark asks for, then that's the client's problem, not mine."

"I think I like your job," Uncas said. "Not much seems t' bother you. It's a very Animal way t' live."

"We need him," Quixote said simply. He turned to Argus. "I think your terms will be acceptable. We can go now, if you like."

◆ ◆ ◆

"For a moment there," the Zen Detective said to the shipbuilder as the foursome clambered into the car, "I thought you weren't going to come with us."

"For a moment there," Argus said as he took the seat behind Quixote, "I wasn't."

"What changed your mind, if I might ask?" said Quixote.

Argus paused a moment, as if the question had violated some invisible boundary of etiquette, then realized that it was, in fact, an entirely appropriate question under the circumstances. "It was the ship," he answered. "The *Black Dragon*. Any of the others would have been made by Utna—by Ordo Maas. But that one's the exception—the only one he never touched."

"How did you know that?" Uncas asked as he started the car.

"Because," Argus answered over the roar of the engine, "I'm the one who built it, as payment for a promise made . . . long, long ago. I made the *Black Dragon*, at the request of Mordred, the Winter King."

It took a few hours for the excitement surrounding the *Black Dragon* to fade away, and soon things were humming away as usual at Tamerlane House, with one exception: Nathaniel Hawthorne had doubled the patrols along the islands and the guards at the bridge, just in case the appearance of the Dragonship was somehow a precursor to another attack.

"Remember," he warned them, "discovering the Architect of the keep and rescuing our friends is not our sole concern. The Echthroi have other agents, and this ship spent a thousand years crossing from a Shadowed Archipelago. I simply want to be cautious—you never know who might also be lurking about."

John knew without asking that Hawthorne was referring to Dr. Dee and his Cabal. Dee had enlisted the Zen Detective as a double agent to locate the Ruby Armor of T'ai Shan, which was said to give the wearer almost unlimited control over time and space. But not just anyone could wear the armor—it had to be an adept; someone like Rose. Someone the Histories referred to . . .

. . . as the *Imago*.

The problem was, Dee had just such a personage: a boy, a distant descendant of Rose, who had been rescued from the Archipelago and taken into the past, where he was then kidnapped by Dee's agent, the traitor Daniel Defoe.

Defoe put the boy prince, called Coal, into a might-have-been, a possible future, for safekeeping. But he made one mistake: Defoe gave the boy a watch—an Anabasis Machine, the time-traveling device all the Caretakers carried. And, being an adept, the boy figured out how to use it on his own and spent a lifetime learning how the world worked. And finally, when Dee pulled him out of the future and gave him the Ruby Armor, the boy Coal, now grown, revealed he had been hiding in plain sight as one of Verne's Messengers, calling himself Dr. Raven.

Then, in the crucial moment when the adept could have turned the tide against either the Caretakers or the Cabal, he instead gave himself a new name and disappeared. Moments later Dee, his house, and the entire Cabal also vanished. Ever since, the Caretakers had been on guard, waiting, watching for the attack they believed was inevitable.

"Understood," John said to Hawthorne. "Keep me posted, and keep your silver sledgehammer at the ready."

• • •

As they waited for news from Uncas and Quixote, John, Jack, and a few of the Caretakers Emeriti accompanied Shakespeare back to the smaller island, to assist him with some minor adjustments he wanted to make to the Zanzibar Gate. As the poet-inventor worked, the Prime Caretaker examined the still impressive stone structure.

"You've become quite the creator, Will," John said in honest admiration. "I think you missed your calling in life. You ought to have been an architect."

"Thank you," Shakespeare said gravely, bowing to the younger Caretaker, "but I think I am responsible for too much stress and strife already, and all I've built was that cursed bridge."

"If it wasn't for that bridge, sirrah," said Twain as he stepped across the path and joined the others near the gate, "none of us might be here now."

"That somewhat resembles my point," said Shakespeare. "So much of this is my fault."

"Responsibility, you mean," said Twain.

Shakespeare shrugged. "What's the difference?"

"That answer," said Twain, "is what makes you a good Caretaker."

"No," said Jack. "That answer is what makes him a good man."

Shakespeare blushed, and bowed his head to acknowledge the compliment. "That is exceeding gracious of you to say, Jack," he said, "but my responsibilities now are less than those of others. I cannot fathom how, as the current Caretakers, you grapple with the care of the world. It is so much larger than in my time."

"I'm just happy that we aren't expected to do even more than we are," said Jack. "I have enough trouble just running the Kilns—"

"Ahem-hem," said John.

"Ah, that is, Warnie and I have enough trouble running the Kilns," added Jack.

"And Mrs., uh, Whatsit," John said helpfully.

"Her too," Jack admitted, "or rather, her mostly. My point is, I could never run a university, much less a city. And heaven forbid that I'm ever given my own country. I think I'd go mad—probably just lock myself in a tower and shut out the whole world while I stay in my room and read."

"And that's different from what you do now, how?" asked John with a smirk and a wink at Twain.

"Oh, shut up," said Jack.

At that moment, they all turned to see Dickens walking purposefully across the path toward them. "Blast it all, Samuel," he said as he drew near. "Are you going to tell them or not? Time's a-wasting."

"I was getting to it, Charles," Twain said. "Nothing is as urgent as exchanging pleasantries as gentlemen ought, before going to business."

"What business?" said John.

"The major has summoned us to the Kilns," Dickens replied, looking at Jack. "Your brother says that our agents have returned and are bringing a guest."

"The shipbuilder?" asked Jack. "I hope."

"This is Quixote and Uncas we're talking about, remember," John said as the group followed Dickens back to the small ferryboat that Twain piloted. "For all we know, they've brought back the Four Horsemen of the Apocalypse."

"Don't," said Jack, "even *joke* about that."

The Caretakers crossed over Shakespeare's Bridge fully armed, and prepared for any contingency. Warnie, Jack's brother, was already waiting for them, as were Quixote and Uncas. The detective and the new arrival were still in the Duesenberg, but as the Caretakers approached, Aristophanes climbed out, tipped his hat at John, and moved over to join Warnie, who kept glancing at the detective's skin tone as if it were a trick of the light.

A smaller, wizened man stepped from the other side of the car and placed his hand on the hood, taking in the heat radiating from the engine. "It's warm," he said admiringly, "almost like a living thing. I should not be surprised if one day someone chose to become one with a machine such as this."

"We brung, uh, bringed . . . ah, we got the shipbuilder," Uncas said, gesturing at Argus, who nodded his head in acknowledgment. His expression was grave, but a bemused smile played at the corners of his mouth.

John sized up the shipbuilder. "I must beg your pardon, but you don't appear to be several thousand years old."

"You have it," Argus replied, "but considering you sent a purple humanoid unicorn, a talking badger, and a Spaniard who can't drive to fetch me, I'm surprised you place such an emphasis on one's appearance."

"He's smarter than the average mariner," Warnie commented to Aristophanes.

The detective nodded. "You have no idea."

"How far can we trust him?" Hawthorne asked. "After all, we have only the detective's word he is who he says he is."

"Why would I lie to you now?" Aristophanes sputtered. "I live at Tamerlane House!"

"You did betray us to Dee," said Hawthorne. "You were a double agent."

"Triple agent," said Warnie. "He betrayed Dee and joined you lot after all."

"Thanks," said Aristophanes.

"Don't mention it," said Warnie.

"But," Hawthorne argued, "we still lost the Ruby Armor."

"We would have lost it anyway," Dickens interjected, "so that really isn't Steve's fault."

"Who is Steve?" Argus asked Uncas.

"Th' detective," the badger replied. "It's his preference."

"If I had known," Argus said slowly from the relaxed position where he was leaning against the Duesenberg, "that you people would be this entertaining, I would have agreed to come far more easily."

"It's him," said a voice from the back of the group. "I only met him a couple of months ago, remember? And I know his face. This is Argus."

The Caretakers parted to allow Bert to move to the front, where he peered more closely at the shipbuilder. "Do you remember me, Argus?"

"I remember," Argus replied, "that when we last met, you and your companions saved my life. But also that you were much more accepting of who I was and what I claimed to be able to do. After all, you are the ones who sought me out, and not the other way around."

"I'm sorry, I'm sorry," Jack said, taking the role of host and rushing around the others to shake the shipbuilder's hand. "We've had some security issues around here lately and need to be careful."

"I understand," Argus replied. "Thankfully, however, tolerance and patience can be bought."

Warnie cleared his throat and looked pointedly at Jack and John, then tipped his head at Argus.

John sighed and frowned at the other Caretakers. "I suppose since we've already made one deal with the de—"

"Hey, now," said Aristophanes.

"The detective, I was going to say," John continued, scowling, "then I suppose we must take this fellow at his word that he is whom he says he is."

"Not at all," Argus replied before any of the Caretakers could comment further. He smiled down at Uncas. "Child of the Earth," he said gently, "do you have a scrap of paper I might borrow?"

"Soitenly!" Uncas exclaimed. He popped open his Little Whatsit, deftly removed a small blank sheet from the pages at the back, and handed it to the shipbuilder.

Argus made no comment but simply began folding the paper over and over, his fingers moving too swiftly to follow, until he had fashioned a small paper dragon. Then he knelt and looked at the ground around him until he finally spied what he was looking for in a patch of grass.

Carefully he reached out and picked up the small black wasp by the body, and again, his fingers swiftly manipulated the folded paper.

When he had finished, he held out his creation. There in his outstretched hand was a miniature Dragonship, with wings and, somehow, the living body and head of the wasp.

The wings fluttered and caught air, and the tiny Wasp-Dragon took flight and disappeared into the trees.

Argus turned to the astonished Caretakers. "Any questions?"

No one moved, or spoke a word.

"Good," Argus said. "Can we go see the real Dragonship now? We're old friends, and I'd like to say hello."

. . . not all the aspects of the Dragon had been shed . . .

Chapter Four

Arête

Verne led the group to the large south boathouse, where the *Black Dragon* had been housed—or rather, imprisoned—for many years, and was once more, but without the locks, chains, and magic wards that had made it a prison.

The ship sat in the berth, rocking gently with the swells of water that rose and fell from the bay outside.

"I never had quite the same knack for it that my master had," Argus said as he examined the *Black Dragon,* perhaps rushing forward a little more eagerly than he'd wished to do in front of the Caretakers. "I could build the vessels, but he had the greater affinity for binding them with the beasts. And I just never cared as much as he about the Children of the Earth. No offense," he added, looking down at Uncas.

"None taken," said the badger. "If you ever smelled what one of us is like when we gets wet, you'd have given up on th' idea of letting us on boats altogether."

The *Black Dragon* seemed to rise up in the water at the shipbuilder's touch, almost as if in recognition. This was an encouraging sign to the Caretakers, since, as a ship, only Burton had ever really been able to handle it. But that was also before they learned who the Dragon had actually been before it became merged with the ship.

"The wing plates were my favorite innovation," Argus said as he ran his hands along the hull. "It was something I discussed with my friend Pelias back during our quest for the fleece, but I never quite worked out how to do it properly. Not until I put my hands on her."

"Him," said Fred. "The *Black Dragon* is a he."

The shipbuilder chuckled. "I suppose it could be, little Child of the Earth," he said, not taking his eyes or hands off the ship. "I never asked Mordred, and he never offered details. Although how he managed to tame such a fierce Dragon into willingly being bonded to a ship is beyond my understanding. I wasn't given much choice in the matter myself."

John raised his eyebrows in surprise and looked at the other Caretakers. "He doesn't know? He really doesn't know who the Dragon is, or rather, was?" he whispered behind his hand. "Don't you think we ought to tell him?"

"Let it be, for the nonce," said Bert. "We don't even know if he can do as he says he can. I certainly never saw any proof of it when we met—we simply took him at his word. No need to complicate matters by bringing up old grudges. And besides," he added, "if it *does* work, he'll know the way the cows ate the cabbage soon enough."

"So," Argus said, straightening himself and turning to look at the Caretakers. "What is it you ask of me?"

"You told Quixote and Uncas that you built the *Black Dragon*," said Bert. "Now we need you to, uh, undo that which you hath done."

Houdini rolled his eyes. "We need the Dragon," he said matter-of-factly, "separated from the ship. Can you do that?"

Argus shrugged. "Of course."

"It seemed a simple enough thing to do with a wasp," Houdini said, drawing up alongside the shipbuilder, "but this is a serious matter. Don't say you can do something you cannot."

Argus looked at John. "This is a Caretaker? They're more skeptical than they used to be."

"Not really," said John. "He's just very results-oriented, and skeptical by nature."

"Building the ship itself was the hard part," Argus said as he gestured for the others to give him room to work. "Binding something living to it was much easier."

"Even with Dragons?" asked Fred.

Argus chuckled. "Especially with them, little Child of the Earth. Because binding with a ship is about choosing one's arête—which means to achieve excellence, to reach one's highest potential. I simply help guide them in the process."

"Then how is it reversed?" asked John.

"It's just as easy," Argus said, turning to face the masthead. "I simply have to persuade the Dragon that its arête as a ship is done, and now its arête is to once more be a Dragon."

The shipbuilder bowed his head and placed his hands on the Dragon's chest, where it merged with the wood and iron of the ship. Murmuring ancient words of power, or perhaps, simply a prayer, he flexed his arms, and suddenly a glow began to emanate from the Dragon.

The hull began to crack and splinter apart. For the first time, the Caretakers could see some of the manner in which the living

Dragon had been merged with the structure of the ship. It was almost more of a spiritual blending than a physical one. The head, neck, and arms were only semi-attached, as if they were part of a sculpted masthead; but the wings were attached to part of the structure of the hull, and seemed to separate from it with more force.

Argus's murmuring became more fervent, and his arms and neck were dripping with sweat. The process was generating a great deal of heat, and so much light that the others had to shield their eyes.

Suddenly the light flared, and a thunderclap echoed deafeningly through the boathouse as Argus flew backward, hitting one of the pilings. Several of the Caretakers rushed to his side, concerned that he had been injured.

"Are you all right?" Jack asked as he and John reached under the shipbuilder's arms to help him to his feet. "Did you—"

"Look," Argus said, pointing. "It is done."

The two Caretakers turned to see what had already rendered the rest of their companions utterly speechless. There, where the shipbuilder had been working, standing amid the splintered remains that had been the fore of the Dragonship, was Madoc.

His beard and hair were overgrown and tangled, but there was no question it was he. Instead of emerging from the binding with the ship as the Black Dragon, as everyone had fully expected, he had emerged as the man he had been before he had accepted the calling, and risen from apprentice to full Dragon, and thence to Dragonship.

However, he was not entirely unchanged from the experience: his right hand, once severed and replaced with a hook, was now whole again. And while he was once again in the form of a man, not all the aspects of the Dragon had been shed with the ship—two great, black wings rose from his shoulder blades and stretched out behind him like sails.

No one spoke, or moved, until Madoc's eyes fluttered closed, and he started to fall. Then John, Jack, Houdini, and Hawthorne all rushed forward to catch him—but it was the Valkyrie Laura Glue and the badger Caretaker Fred who moved the fastest, and caught their friend's father before he fell.

"It's all right," Laura Glue whispered through the tears streaming down her face. "Rose wouldn't let you fall, and neither will we."

As the rest of the group at the boathouse gathered around the newly reborn Madoc, Verne, Bert, and Twain simply watched—because they were also watching the reactions of two others: Argus and Aristophanes.

The shipbuilder's response was easier to parse—it was that of near-total surprise. Short of just being told beforehand—something he might not have believed—there was no way for him to have known that the Black Dragon he had bonded with the ship, at the request of Mordred, the Winter King, was in fact Mordred himself, in his true persona of Madoc. The dragon already existed, and at the time, not even Mordred knew that the Black Dragon was a future version of himself, who went back in time to become the *Black Dragon*. So in a way, even as the act of releasing Madoc closed a great circle, it was understandable for the old Greek to be surprised.

Aristophanes's reaction was more enigmatic: He showed fear. Of the three Caretakers watching him, only Verne really knew the detective to any degree, but he was certain that Madoc and Aristophanes had never crossed paths. So why was his response a fearful one? It was, Verne decided, something worth investigating, but later. For now, there was a more important agenda to focus on.

Fred and Uncas were helpfully offering a drink of water to the weakened shipbuilder. The retransformation process he claimed would be "easy" was anything but, and the effort had taken a toll.

"Thank you," Argus said, handing the tin cup back to the badgers as John approached. "Well, Caretaker? Are you satisfied with my work?"

John nodded, smiling. "What was your price?" he asked. "Quixote was authorized to bargain in good faith."

"I told the knight I wished a boon."

"Whatever we owe you, then," John said to the shipbuilder, "has been more than earned. Name your price."

Argus responded by turning to look at the newly released Madoc, who was being borne up in blankets by the Caretakers for rest and recovery at Tamerlane House. The shipbuilder's face twitched as he watched, and his eyes went glassy, as if he were immersed in a long-buried memory. Finally he turned to John and extended his hand.

"There is no cost," he said. "Long ago, I myself promised to grant a boon, and that debt has now been paid—twice over, I think. No more need be said about it. I'd just like to return to my work."

John took his hand and shook it firmly, then again. "Fair enough," the Caretaker said, not certain whether he ought to question the old man further. "Even all, then."

"I would make one request," the shipbuilder said, "not as

payment, but simply a favor, if it is one you'd be willing to grant."

John spread his arms. "You have returned to us dearest blood, and given us the only chance to find our lost friends," he said in reply. "Ask what you will."

"As I said, I'd like to continue my work—but I would like to do so here."

"Here?" John answered, surprised. "At Tamerlane House?" He stroked his chin in thought, before replying further.

"You must understand," he said slowly, "that save for the connection to Jack's house, those residing here are all but prisoners. The Archipelago . . ."

"I'm not as naive or as uninformed as your agents seemed to think," said Argus, "and the detective keeps secrets less well than he believes. I know—a little—of what's happened. But I have been a virtual prisoner myself on Lemnos for a very long time."

John frowned and fingered his lip. "A prisoner? I had understood that you were a free man."

"A private one," said Argus, "and those conditions do not always mesh." He made a broad gesture with his hand. "I saw the rune stones as we crossed the bridge—I kept myself hidden in Lemnos in a similar manner. I could even be of use to you in assisting with your security, beyond what work I can do in the boathouse."

"But," John said, puzzled, "it seems as if you're merely trading one jailhouse for another. What can you do here that you could not do on Lemnos?"

"Be myself," said Argus. "The easiest and hardest thing a man can do."

The Prime Caretaker considered this a moment, then nodded

his head. "As you wish." He turned to the badgers. "Uncas, will you see to it that Master Swift arranges for a suite of rooms at the house?"

Argus placed a hand on John's arm and shook his head. "That won't be necessary," he said, gesturing with his other hand at the fractured hull of the Black Dragon. "I will be more than comfortable here. This is where I belong—and where I think I shall be content."

John agreed, and with another handshake to bind the deal, he and the badgers left Argus, who was already stroking the ship and whispering words of quiet power as a smile spread slowly across his face.

"Indeed," Argus said to no one in particular. "My conscience is finally clear, and I have at last come home."

The elder members of the Caretakers Emeriti crowded at the open door to look in on Laura Glue's patient. It was startling to see Madoc as he must have been in his youth, unbearded and unscarred by the world. But it was equally startling to see, there on top of the quilt, his right hand, whole and unblemished. That alone was unusual enough to them that they could nearly overlook the great, leathery wings that were folded along the headboard behind him.

"So," Twain said softly, "he is the Hook no longer, but fully a man again, our Mordred is."

"He is more Madoc than Mordred, I think," said Dickens. "He is, at last, perhaps once more the man that he set out to be."

Laura Glue sat next to the bed, facing this strange young man whom she had met only once before, when he was older, and weathered by the events of his long life. In a way, it felt like another first meeting to her. She wiped his forehead with a damp cloth, watching as his breathing became more regular, until he finally opened his eyes.

"Hello there," she said.

"Rose?" he asked, propping himself up with the pillows. Then his vision cleared, and he realized his nurse was not his daughter. After a moment he added, "I'm, ah, Madoc."

She giggled. "I know that. We have met, you know."

He reddened. "I remember. It's just . . . more like a dream now. It's been so, so long."

"Only a year for me, since we saw you in London."

"Which was a century before I gave myself over to my other self to become the *Black Dragon*, and then over a thousand years since that," he said, more awed by the reality of it than anything else. "And now here I sit, in this body that I remember having centuries earlier, before I . . ." He paused.

"Before you became the Winter King."

Again, he blushed. "Or at least before I became Mordred, at any rate." He stopped and looked away, out the window. "I still remember those things too, girl. I still remember the choices I made. And . . . I don't regret them. I'm sorry, but it's true."

"You must have been capable of making some good choices," Jack offered from the doorway, where he, John, and Fred had crowded past the other Caretakers. "Otherwise, you'd never have become the Dragon's apprentice."

"Mmm," Madoc answered noncommittally. "There have been times I almost regretted that particular choice too," he said, "but when I was in the presence of my daughter, it all seemed to have happened for a reason. It seemed necessary."

"Everyone makes mistakes, Madoc," said Jack.

"Not everyone was the son of Odysseus and was offered the whole world as his kingdom," Madoc replied. "But I was, and I still made many mistakes."

"So was your brother," Jack suggested, "and he had more opportunities than you did to choose a direction for his life, but for my money, he didn't turn out any better than you did. Uh, I mean worse," he corrected quickly, after a poke in the ribs from John. "Uh, sorry."

Madoc shook his head and grimaced. "I don't know. Perhaps if I had chosen a better teacher . . ."

"Better than Samaranth?" asked John.

Madoc's face darkened. "No," he said. "A . . . different teacher. Samaranth, I should have heeded more. But then again," he added, looking around the room, "Myrddyn is nowhere to be seen, and I am here—again. So that should say something, I think."

"It does," said Jack. "Truly."

"We know you've made many sacrifices," John said, "but we need your help once more—as a Dragon. As the only one left."

Madoc exhaled heavily and swung his legs to the side of the bed. "All right," he said. "Tell me what . . ." He paused, finally noticing he carried considerably more bulk than before.

He flexed his wings, which filled the small bedroom. "Well, these are new."

"Yes," Laura Glue said. "And your eyes," she added, moving closer and turning his head to the light. "They're silver."

"Silver is nothing but dragon's blood," Madoc said. "It has healing properties, and sometimes manifests itself during a transformation." He flexed his wings again, and the Caretakers could see that the leathery black was shot through with veins of silver. "I suppose I didn't expect it to leave a permanent marker."

"I like them," she said, looking at his eyes. "I liked them when they were violet, and I like them now. The wings, too. They make you look . . . imposing."

"Yes," Jack whispered behind his hand to his friends, "because he was such a shrinking violet *before* the wings."

"And I like that you are a good and compassionate person, and very forgiving, much like my daughter," Madoc said, glancing past Laura Glue to the others crowded into the room. "Is Rose here? I was hoping to see her."

Before John could respond, Fred moved closer to the bed, whiskers twitching. "That's why we done this," he said nervously. "That's why we brung, uh, brought you back, ah, sir. We need your help. Rose needs your help."

Madoc looked at the small mammal a moment, then stood up. "All right, Caretakers," he said, addressing all of them at once. "I haven't eaten in more than a thousand years, so what say you find us something to fill our bellies while you tell me why my daughter needs an old apprentice Dragon's help."

PART TWO

The Last Flight of the Indigo Dragon

The path was well lit with lanterns . . .

Chapter Five
The Zanzibar Gate

The part of the garden at the Kilns where the bridge was located was not visible to passersby, but the driveway where the Duesenberg had been parked was. Precautions had been taken to ensure that no one passing through Oxford would notice anything out of the ordinary, but then again, usually no one was looking—it was what made the Kilns a perfect entry point to Tamerlane House.

No one, that is, except for the two men sitting in the black Bentley across the street. They were looking, and they saw a great deal. Warnie had noticed the car parked there earlier, but thought little of it—the enemies he had been warned to watch out for didn't drive automobiles.

Thus it was that no one, not even Warnie, seemed to take note when the two men emerged and crossed the road. Focused as they had been on taking Argus to see the Black Dragon, *the Caretakers had simply crossed over the bridge, sealing the portal behind them without ever looking back. There were guards posted, and magic runes protecting the entry to Tamerlane House and the Nameless Isles . . . on that side of the bridge. But no one considered that if both sides were not protected equally, then both sides were equally vulnerable to their enemies. But no one was looking for enemies in Oxford.*

If someone had been looking, he might have noticed the near-identical black coats and bowler hats the two men wore, and the round black glasses that hid the dark orbs that occupied the places where their eyes should have been.

If someone had been looking, he might have noticed the identical black pocket watches both men carried, which chimed at the same moment.

"It is time, Mr. Kirke," said one.

"Indeed it is, Mr. Bangs," said the other.

In hindsight, John thought, that was the Caretakers' greatest mistake. They should have been more cautious. They should have taken better care. If they had, then perhaps things would have gone differently when the two men knocked on the door at the Kilns.

In the dining hall, Alexandre Dumas and the Feast Beasts quickly put together what Dumas referred to as "a light dinner," which nevertheless consisted of enough food to have stocked the Kilns for a year. Madoc kept refilling his plate and eating as the various Caretakers took turns explaining what had been happening in the Archipelago. He made no comment, only nodding occasionally and grunting. Shakespeare was last to speak, and he explained how he believed the Zanzibar Gate would work, and why it required a Dragon.

"The question is," Madoc said as he wiped his mouth with the back of his hand and belched as a courtesy to Dumas, "am I still in fact a Dragon? I still have the wings, but I feel more like a man again."

"It is an office, not merely a descriptive term," said Bert. "One is not a Dragon until a Dragon calls you to be one. And once you have become a Dragon, a Dragon you shall remain until a Dragon says otherwise. And," he added, "seeing as you're the only one left, I don't anticipate that happening anytime soon."

"And if we do this, and somehow find the Architect and convince him to rebuild the keep, the Archipelago will be restored?"

"There's no way to know for certain," said Verne, "but this is the first necessary step to finding out."

"And the *Imaginarium Geographica* is of no help to you in this? Or the Histories?"

"The Histories that record the future are little more than unfulfilled prophecies," said Twain, "and the *Imaginarium Geographica* was unmatched as a travel guide, but, I'm sorry to say, sorely lacking as a time travel aid. Anyroad, Rose, Edmund, and Charles have it with them, whenever they are."

"We know the Archipelago itself *can* be restored," John said, indicating the open facsimile *Geographica* on the table in front of them, "because all the maps were still there in the original. When the Winter King . . ." He looked at Madoc and swallowed hard. "Sorry. When, um, *you* first tried to conquer the Archipelago," John continued, "and the lands were covered in Shadow, they vanished from the *Imaginarium Geographica*. But they're all still here, so there must be some way to restore them."

"Not all," Fred said quietly. Laura Glue moved closer to him and put a reassuring arm around the little mammal's shoulders. "Avalon isn't there, and neither is Paralon."

"I'm sorry, Fred," said John. "I didn't forget."

"Some of the lands are missing?" Madoc asked in surprise. "I thought they weren't Shadowed."

"Not Shadowed, as you remember it," Jack said quietly. "Destroyed, by the Echthroi. The rest, according to what Aven told us before she . . ." He swallowed hard. "The rest were somehow removed, and taken elsewhere by Samaranth. Where he went, I cannot say.

But it's a moot point if we can't reestablish the connection between worlds by restoring the keep."

"Well," Madoc said, standing, "either it'll work, or it won't. So let's go see what Master Shaksberd hath wrought."

Most of the company at Tamerlane House left to walk to the ferryboat Twain would pilot over to the island where the gate stood. Washington Irving and the half-clockwork men they called Jason's sons stayed behind with Dumas to guard the bridge, and the Elder Caretakers, having wished Madoc and the others good luck, stayed in the house.

Also remaining behind at Verne's insistence were the Zen Detective, Aristophanes, and his escorts, Uncas and Don Quixote. The detective protested, claiming foul play, until Twain judiciously let slip what they had originally done with Daniel Defoe after he had defied the Caretakers. After that, Aristophanes was more than content to wait things out in the comfort of the house.

As the companions walked across the expanse of sand and stone to the boathouse, Poe watched from seclusion high above. John caught sight of him out of the corner of his eye and gave a plaintive wave, which, after a moment, Poe returned before closing the drapes.

"So, this enemy, the Echthroi," Madoc said as they clambered into the ferryboat. "They are a constant threat?"

"Mostly through their agents," Bert said with a sigh. "The shadow-possessed servants called Lloigor."

The Caretakers were almost relieved when mention of the Lloigor caused Madoc to shudder. He had, after all, been one of them—the one the Echthroi once considered their greatest weapon.

"I'm sorry," said Madoc. "Sometimes, when you live long enough, you don't realize what kind of life your choices have culminated in. It is a path of a thousand steps—but the first step in the wrong direction can change it all. I let my bitterness determine my choices, and I was swayed by having followed the wrong teacher. For what it's worth, I'm sorry for my part in it all."

"You've more than made amends, Madoc," Laura Glue said, looking not at him, but to John, for reassurance. "You have already done more than we could have hoped."

"At least there haven't been any more incidents with some of the fouler creatures who used to serve the purposes of, ah, the man you were," Jack said, shuddering at the memory of their first encounter, long ago, with the creatures called Wendigo.

"Ah," Houdini said as he raised his hand to speak, then cleared his throat, "that may be in large part because most of those creatures were in the Archipelago when it was cut off, and thus our adversaries lost access to them. They were not, however, the only creatures at their disposal. Of that, you can be sure."

"How sure?" asked John.

"Sure enough," Houdini said, reddening slightly. "I cataloged most of them myself at Burton's request."

"I will surely burn for recruiting that man," Dickens lamented. "Burn, I tell you."

The sun had set fully by the time the company of Caretakers made their way to the Zanzibar Gate. The path was well lit with lanterns, which John noticed seemed to give the whole area an unearthly glow. He mentioned this to the others, and Jack shook his head.

"I don't think it's just the lanterns," he said, pointing at

Shakespeare's construct. It was radiating with a pulsing light that grew stronger the closer they got.

"Is it working somehow?" John asked Shakespeare. "Did you manage to—"

"Not my workings," the Bard replied, cutting him off. "His."

He was pointing at Madoc, and suddenly the others realized Shakespeare's guess was correct—the mere presence of Madoc was powering the Zanzibar Gate.

"How does it work?" Madoc asked. "It looks as if it was made of the same kind of stone as the keep was."

"The very same, in fact," said Shakespeare, "minus the wooden structures that made the keep, ah, well . . . burnable."

Madoc's expression darkened a bit at that, but he said nothing.

Shakespeare stepped forward and indicated the series of markings engraved on the inner ring of the gate's aperture. "These runes represent numbers in Chronos time, and can be set for up to seven different decimal places," he explained, "giving the gate a possible range of a million years or more. For this trip, we only need to set six."

He showed them a display of crystals on a pedestal that had a mirror-image duplicate on the other side. "This is the mechanism that controls the settings," he said. "Each crystal corresponds to a rune carved into the gate. As you enter, the inner ring will shift and lock into place. When all seven are locked, as they are now, all that remains"—he turned to Madoc—"is for a Dragon to step through and pass from this time into that one."

"I'd like to point out that just this sort of thing was attempted once before," Houdini harrumphed, "by the Imperial Cartological Society, and as I recall, you were so put out by our efforts that you burned it to the ground."

"Your efforts were commendable," said Twain, "but your motives were suspect, my dear magician. You, or more specifically, Burton and Dr. Dee, were trying to re-create the keep in the service of, and for the purposes of, the Shadow of the Winter King. Now, however, you serve a higher purpose."

Houdini rolled his eyes and looked at Madoc.

"I understand," Madoc replied. "That sounded like so many fewmets to me, too."

"The gate should exist in both times," Shakespeare explained, "and much like the keep did, it will persist into the future, and carry you forward. The portal will close once you've all passed through, but you should be able to open it again from the other side."

He gestured at a rectangular indentation at the top of the control panel. "This is where the plate with the destination should be inset," he explained. "The exact location, as well as the specific time you arrive, are largely intuitive, much like going through the doorways of the keep. This is important," he cautioned. "If you aren't focused, if you allow your minds to wander and drift as you enter, it might override the settings and place you somewhere you didn't plan to be.

"If there is some need to go elsewhere, or, ah, elsewhen, rather," Shakespeare continued, "Edmund should be able to create a new destination plate to use. After that, simply repeat the process as I've explained it to you, lock the settings, activate the gate, step through, and then you'll be home."

Madoc stepped toward the gate, which brightened visibly at his approach. Impulsively, he reached out and put his hands on the stone.

The world seemed to shift out of focus for a moment, before coming back to clarity in a wave that spread outward from the gate.

The air underneath the arch shimmered as if it was heated, and it took on a nearly reflective quality.

"It's quite an accomplishment," John said, smiling broadly. "With this gate, and Edmund's natural talents, we practically have a replacement for the keep right here at our doorstep."

At this, Shakespeare stepped back from the other Caretakers and wrung his hands in frustration. "I'm not the Architect who built the keep," he lamented. "I'm sorry, but as adept as I have proven myself to be, I simply don't have the skills to re-create something with the . . . ah, duration of the keep."

"What are you saying, Will?" John asked. "Will it work, or won't it?"

"Oh, it shall, I'm certain of that," Shakespeare replied, glancing over at Madoc, "now that we have a viable power source. But only thrice. That, and no more."

"*Thrice?*" Jack exclaimed. "Three times? That's not ideal, but it isn't terrible, either. If we don't find them the first go-round, we'll have two more tries to get it right."

The Bard shook his head and strode purposefully to the gate, where he motioned for Madoc to step away. Immediately the light from the gate dimmed.

"That's what I'm trying to explain to you," Shakespeare said, wringing his hands in frustration. "The gate will allow three trips, in toto. Once out in any direction, past or future; once back; and then . . ."

"Once out, with no return trip," Verne said heavily.

"Or two trips out, and then one home," Jack offered, trying to be helpful. "If we find our friends—"

"Ahem-hem," said Twain.

"Uh, that is, *when* we find our friends," Jack corrected, blushing slightly, "if they haven't yet found the Architect, we can pool our resources and try one more time before coming back."

"No one is going anywhere," a voice stern with authority rang out. "Not using the gate, anyroad. Not now, and maybe not ever."

Almost by reflex, the Caretakers turned to look at Verne, but he was already looking at the man who had spoken . . .

. . . *John.*

"We can't use it," he said, stepping around Will to stand in front of the gate, as if to emphasize his point. "It's a great idea, and may be the first step on the right road, but with a limited number of uses, it's simply too dangerous. I don't want to risk losing any among our number. One would be too great a loss."

"How is it any more risky than anything else we've tried?" asked Jack.

"You're forgetting one of the rules of time travel," John said, casting a rueful glance at Bert and Verne. "Every trip into the past must be balanced by one into the future. There won't be two trips out and then one home. At most, it would be one trip out and one back, because to go out again . . ." He let his voice trail off when he realized he couldn't speak the words. But Madoc could.

". . . means those travelers will not be returning," the Dragon said simply. "Ever."

"Yes," John said, this time looking at Jack. "It's too high a price to pay, when we don't know how the story will end."

"We tell stories for a living, John," Jack said testily, "and I believe we write the endings we choose."

"Not this time, Jack. I'm sorry."

Madoc and the other Caretakers simply watched as Jack struggled to contain what he really wanted to say to his longtime friend. This was not merely an argument, but evidence of a deeper division, one that had perhaps been growing longer than any of them realized.

"We've made our lives here ones of risk taking," Jack said, his fists clenched but his voice measured and even, "and I don't see why this is any different."

"It's different," John replied, "because every other decision was made by a different Prime Caretaker." His eyes flickered over to Verne, who was standing resolute, watching. "I'm not so willing to be reckless with the lives of our friends."

"And what about Rose and Edmund and Charles?" Jack replied, a bit less measured. "Who is looking out for them?"

"We will," John replied. "Somehow we'll find a way. But for now, we simply need to make certain the option we choose is the best one. And this one," he added, glancing apologetically at Will, "is not that option. Yet."

He started to say something to Jack, but his friend had already spun on his heel and was striding back to the ferryboat. A hand on John's shoulder stopped him from following after.

"No," Madoc said. "Not now. I'll talk with him later, but don't buckle. If you are indeed the Prime Caretaker now, you did exactly as you were supposed to do."

"Betray my friends?" John said bitterly.

"No," Madoc said again, looking at Verne. "Make the hard decisions—and then stand by them."

John cast one more rueful glance at his departing friend, then turned to Shakespeare. "That's my final word, then," he said, his voice firm but laced with sadness.

"No one will be using the Zanzibar Gate to go anywhere. We'll simply have to find another way."

Chapter Six

The Hot Young Turks

"We're going to be using the Zanzibar Gate," Laura Glue said in a whisper as she and Fred walked along the docks at Tamerlane House. "There simply is no other way."

The Caretakers and their companions had adjourned back to the main island to discuss what options they might have for creating an alternative to Shakespeare's gate, but the young Valkyrie was having none of it.

"We've been looking through every library in the house," she muttered, as much to herself as to the badger, "including every nook and cranny of the Repository. We've considered every device that has ever been used to travel in time, including a few completely imaginary ones. I tell you, Fred, Will's gate is the best chance we have—and time is running out."

"Not that I disagree with most of that," Fred replied, "but isn't time exactly what we have the most of?"

She shook her head and pulled him to one side of the grand porch at the main entrance. "If they were simply lost in time, then yes," she whispered, "but we are also trying to outmaneuver an enemy who is better at time travel than we are. They know more than we

Shakespeare . . . looked at the small company.

do. And I don't think they've spent the last couple of months just waiting on us. I think they've been busy. And that means we have no time to waste."

"So what d' you want t' do?"

She looked around to make sure no one else was in earshot, then leaned in close. "Tonight, meet me at that place where we hid that thing that one time," she said as she pushed open the door. "We're going to sort it out."

"So, how are we going to sort it out?" Houdini asked John as he diplomatically maneuvered the Prime Caretaker away from the front door and toward one of the side yards.

John realized the magician was simply trying to make sure he didn't stride right into another confrontation with Jack, and he felt more relieved by the gesture than manipulated. "I don't know," he answered honestly, "but I simply can't risk trying something that leaves us worse off than we already are. Rose and Edmund together could travel into Deep Time, and now, with Madoc, we may be able to as well. But if we lose him, we're two steps behind again."

"Two steps behind Dr. Dee, you mean," said Houdini, "but I would dare to disagree. The boy prince could have chosen sides at the battle on Easter Island, and he didn't. I think that's why Dee hasn't acted yet—his trump card is still an indecisive child."

"An indecisive child with the power over time and space," John replied, "who may yet take John Dee's side."

"Maybe," a voice said from just ahead of them on one of the paths from the west end of the house, "but we have Will Shakespeare on our side. And," Kipling added as he reached to shake John's hand, "they don't."

Twain, Dickens, Verne, and Byron were just behind Hawthorne and nodded in agreement. "That's one security we have," said Verne. "They can't duplicate what Will is able to do with his constructs. As far as I know, their watches have no greater range than ours do."

"You're forgetting two things," said John. "One, they have the Chronographer of Lost Times. Dee. His *Imaginarium Chronographica* marks far more zero points than anything we know of, so they can move about in time more freely. And," he added with a grimace, "Telemachus, and the Ruby Armor, is still a wild card here. If he doesn't cooperate, couldn't Dee just kill him and take the armor to use himself?"

"No," Verne answered as they rounded the west wing and walked toward Shakespeare's shop, "or else he'd have already done so. The armor can only be used by an adept, and there are only two we know of for certain—Telemachus and Rose. And anything else Dee could try would require cavorite, and that's not so easy to come by."

"I thought the Nameless Isles were made up almost entirely of cavorite," John said, shading his eyes to look at the surrounding islands. "Couldn't someone else just sneak over the bridge, mine some of the ore, and start making their own gate from scratch?"

In answer Hawthorne grabbed a large sledgehammer from Shakespeare's tools and strode over to where a boulder of cavorite was protruding from the scrubby lawn. Grasping the handle with both hands, he swung the hammer in a high arc and smashed it down on the stone. It impacted with a loud thunderclap of metal on rock, and the hammer shattered as if it were porcelain. The stone looked as if it had never been touched.

"Been suggested, been tried," he said, slightly breathless from the effort. "Cavorite is harder to mine than adamantium, harder to mine than unobtainium. It takes almost infinite geologic patience. More than exists in a man's lifetime. So it is, in point of fact, a far easier prospect to recover cavorite that has already been used in some capacity.

"If it had not been that the Watchmaker already had shaped cavorite, in quantity," Hawthorne went on, "then Will could not have lived long enough to mine it himself."

John frowned. "That's not the best of news," he said. "What you're saying is that the pieces we have can be reassembled into new configurations, but nothing new can be shaped. Not entirely new, anyway."

"Yes," said Verne. "The gate really is the best option we have, John. Perhaps the only one."

"We'll resort to last options when I'm convinced there's nothing else to try, and that the risk is worth it," John said flatly. "Until then, I expect every man at Tamerlane to abide by my decision."

When night fell on the Nameless Isles, Fred and Laura Glue met up at the place where they hid that thing that one time, and, making certain they weren't being followed, she then led him someplace else.

There were very few areas in Tamerlane House that were not well lit at all times—but children have a way of finding all the hidden corners. "It's very simple," Laura Glue explained to Fred as he followed her through the hallways to the secret room. "All you have to do is imagine that the longbeards—the grown-ups—have hidden some presents that they bought you, then imagine where they'd hide them, and just go there."

She pointed down the dark corridor at the northeast corner of Tamerlane House. "That's how I found this place."

"By imagining someone bought you a gift and hid it?"

"Not imagining," she said, pointing at her aviator goggles. "These were supposed to be a surprise gift from Mr. Twain."

The badger was about to respond, but the Valkyrie shushed him. A light was approaching the corner from the other end of the corridor. They both held their breath until Quixote and Uncas rounded the corner.

"And that's how I found this place," Uncas was saying, gesturing with one of his prized possessions—a copper spyglass. "It was s'pposed t' be a present from Scowler Irving."

"Well met," Quixote said as Laura Glue opened up an almost invisible door into a small room. The walls were covered with drapes, and there was no furniture. Fred and Uncas set their lamps down in opposite corners, so that the shadows would cancel each other out.

"Can't be too sure," Fred said. "At least we know no one can find us here."

As one, all four of them jumped as someone rapped "Shave and a Haircut" on the door.

Laura opened it and was crestfallen to see Jack enter the room.

"Hello, Laura my Glue," Jack said gently. "You be up to something, neh?"

"Neh," she said, answering him in the slang she'd learned among the Lost Boys, so long ago. "How did you know?"

"It wasn't me," Jack said. "Somehow Poe knew you were planning something, and he asked me to check in on you. Oh, don't worry," he rushed to reassure them. "He didn't tell anyone else." Jack looked around at the four of them. "Is this your whole band of conspirators, then?"

"Not quite," another voice said from the corridor. "For good or ill, I must be included amongst their number."

Jack moved aside so Shakespeare could enter the room. "They needed someone to program the gate, and I'm afraid at present, I'm the best qualified, like it or not. Also," he added, "I'm as anxious to help our lost friends as anyone. It was in part because of following my counsel that they've become lost."

"That wasn't your fault, Will," said Jack. "If not for you, we'd have no chance at all to restore the Archipelago."

"Are you going to go with us, Scowler Jack?" asked Fred. "It'd be a mighty comfort to have you with us."

"I wish I could, more than anything," Jack said, his eyes heavy with honest regret. "But I cannot. With John having taken the role of Prime Caretaker, I am essentially the new Caveo Principia, and there are too many responsibilities here than I can leave at present—not the least of which is trying to talk some sense into my erstwhile colleague. I want nothing more than to be of help to you, and go along—but fortunately, I'm not the only one who knows about your plan."

On cue, another face peered around the door. "What's all the racket?" Kipling asked. "I thought this was supposed to be a secret mission."

His face still bore the burns and scars from the evacuation of the Hotel d'Ailleurs two months earlier, and he moved slowly, his limbs still stiff from his injuries. He was a tulpa, and he would recover, but it would take time.

"How did *you* know?" Laura Glue exclaimed.

"I'm head of Caretaker espionage, remember?" said Kipling. "Plus, the secret missions are always the most fun."

"Fun?" said Fred.

"Yes." Kipling nodded. "I'm going with you. I'm a tulpa, and so I can actually be away from Tamerlane as long as is necessary. Plus, you'll need some kind of adult supervision."

"I beg your pardon!" said Quixote.

"Ah, that's right," Kipling said. "Sorry, Uncas."

He turned to Shakespeare. "You realize your helping us is going to really, really tick off the Prime Caretaker, right?"

"It can't be helped," Shakespeare admitted. "Not trying the gate is the wrong decision. This is our Hail Mary, to borrow one of the old Cartographer's favorite expressions. Our last play. You are going to be our emissaries into the eternities, to find a needle in an endless ocean of hay, and I cannot in good conscience send you out without having equipped you with every advantage I can."

"When you put it that way," said Kipling, "I don't know if I want to go anymore myself."

"He's kidding," Jack assured them. "I think."

"Well, that's everyone," Laura Glue began before she was interrupted by a clattering of hooves in the hallway.

"Not quite," Jack said. He opened the door and Argus filed in, followed by two goats.

"These are Verne's two best goats, Coraline and Elly Mae," Jack said, scratching the goats' heads. "They're also going with you."

"His war leader!" Laura Glue exclaimed. "And the one who bites. We be in some deep trouble, we takes them with, Jack."

"I'll explain it to Jules later," Jack said soothingly. "He might be irritated, but he'll be happy that you have some extra protection for your journey."

"If it helps you feel better," Argus said, raising his hand, "I'm not going with you. I just helped with your transportation."

Laura Glue groaned. "This was supposed to be a secret mission," she complained, "but it seems like everyone at Tamerlane House already knows about it!"

Uncas patted her consolingly on the arm. "That's how these sooper-sekrit things tend t' go, in my experience."

"Don't worry, young Valkyrie," Shakespeare said. "Argus knows how to keep a confidence. And more than that, telling him was necessary," he added, pulling back the curtain at the end of the room, "so we could do this."

Through the window they could see the flickering lights scattered across the decks of a ship—the *Indigo Dragon*. But this was not the *Indigo Dragon* that the Caretakers had used—it had been altered by Shakespeare and Argus to be used for this specific mission.

It was shortened, bore a smaller sail that could be converted into the balloon used for flight, and now had wheels. And it had been outfitted with a harness that was just the right size for two goats.

"It's essentially an all-terrain vehicle," said Argus, "even if there's no terrain at all."

"Are the goats supposed to just sit in the crow's nest when we fly?" asked Fred. "It is primarily an airship now, after all."

"No," Kipling replied. "They're here to work.

"I once had the opportunity to visit the Saint of the Northern Isles, back when I first became a Caretaker," he said as he reached into his coat pocket, "and he gave me these. I've been saving them all these years for just the right occasion to use them."

The others looked at his outstretched hand. There in the palm were a dozen kernels of corn.

"How long was he in th' fire?" Uncas whispered to Quixote.

"Hush," said Laura Glue. "What are they, Rudy?"

"Magic seed corn," he replied. "If you plant them, they grow into a crop of corn that, when eaten, ensures that you have only good dreams when you sleep, and never bad ones. I have often been plagued by night terrors, and considered planting a little garden out back. But I'm glad I saved them, because they have one other use.

"If you feed the seed corn to any creature with cloven hooves, it will be able to fly. The Christmas Saint used them on reindeer, but they'll also work . . ."

"On goats," Laura Glue finished for him. "That's brilliant!"

"Meh," said Elly Mae.

"I've already aligned the mechanisms from the Zanzibar Gate," Shakespeare explained as the other conspirators got settled aboard the *Indigo Dragon*. "I've set it to go to the same place Bert said that the others were going to, and I have faith it will work. But after that," he added, choking back a sob, "you'll be on your own."

"How can you set the device to the right time and place?" asked Laura Glue. "I thought only Rose or Edmund could do that without a trump."

"Actually, it's because of Edmund that I can," said Shakespeare. He showed them the bronze plate he planned to insert into the mechanism of the gate. "We know from what Bert told us that they are no longer in the future, but in the past," he told them, "and Edmund found a way to tell us where.

"When Jules asked me to examine the time travel possibilities of the Sphinx that Poe had in the basement," he explained, "I opened it and found this plate. I didn't know what it meant then, but I know now. And it will take you to them. This I believe."

"There's one more thing," Jack said. He handed Fred a box wrapped in oilcloth. "It's the Serendipity Box. Laura Glue has never used it, nor has Quixote, or Kipling. It's your fallback, for when you are in real trouble. But," he added, "I hope you won't need it."

It took only a few minutes for them to sail the *Indigo Dragon* to the outer island where the Zanzibar Gate stood, and only a few minutes more to prepare for the crossing through time. Shakespeare installed the bronze plate on the control device, then stood back with Jack and Argus and looked at the small company. A Valkyrie, a badger Caretaker, his father the squire, the legendary knight, and Kipling. "That's everyone, I think," Jack said.

"Not quite," said Laura Glue, looking around in the darkness. "Where's—"

"I'm already here," Madoc said as he stepped out of the trees and climbed onboard the ship. As he approached, the gate began to glow.

"I wasn't sure you'd do it," said Quixote. "You seemed very supportive of the Prime Caretaker's decision."

"I learned the art of diplomacy in Alexandria," said Madoc, "and I know when to use it. But there is a time to talk, and a time to act. And we are going," he finished, winking at Laura Glue, "to get my daughter."

"You're the best of us all," Jack said to the small company as his eyes welled with tears, "and you are the last children of the Archipelago. Be strong. Be brave. And never forget . . ."

"Believing is seeing," Fred said as the small craft lifted up into the air. "Don't worry, Scowler Jack," he added as the ship disappeared through the gate. "We got this."

The speaker was sitting on a dais at the center . . .

Chapter Seven
The City of Jade

It was the first city that was, and as such, it had no need of a name—but things that are made must also be named, for that is the way of the world. And so, as travelers came from the distant parts of the earth, to seek knowledge, and trade, and in some cases, redemption, they named the city, and carried those names back with them when they returned home.

To the younger races, it was called Atlantis. To the Children of the Earth, who had assisted in its construction, it was called the Dragon Isle. Some named it for the builder who first deigned to create something great in the world, and they called it the City of Enoch, but it was not his city they saw, not truly—and those who had created and named everything else the city is, was, and would yet become simply called it the City of Jade.

When the Cartographer Edmund McGee drew the city on parchment, to use as a chronal trump for himself, Rose Dyson, and the Caretaker Charles, and later, when he duplicated the drawing as a bronze engraving to leave in the Sphinx for the Caretakers to find in the future, both renderings were based on descriptions and memories provided to him by the legendary Gilgamesh. The great king had seen the city in his youth, and his recollections of it were strong enough that Edmund could duplicate it in line with great fidelity. But as fine as the renderings were, there was simply no comparison between viewing a simple drawing and being in the presence of a city that had been designed and built by angels.

The place where Rose, Edmund, and Charles had appeared was a grassy hill on the other side of the estuary that separated the island where the city stood from the mainland. A conversation with a passing angel called Nix had some unusual results: First, Charles was mistaken for a Seraphim, which was not necessarily a bad thing; and second, when they asked for further information about the city, and the summit that was to take place there, Nix instructed them to seek out what he referred to as a minor angel with the unlikeliest of names.

"Samaranth?" Charles said for the umpteenth time. "That just can't be a coincidence. It can't be."

"I agree," Rose said as they walked down the path taken by Nix, but at a discreet distance. They had decided that following someone who was attending to official city business would be the most direct route into the city, but they preferred not to arouse his suspicion any further than they already had. "He may be the reason this is a chronal zero point. After all, the trump could take us to the city, but something else had to influence the reason we arrived at this specific point in time—and Samaranth's presence might be it."

"We had some help, remember?" Edmund interjected. "The old man, in Platonia. He has involved himself in things before, to help you out. He must have known."

"He knew something, that's for certain," Rose answered as

they approached the bridge. It was made of the same glowing green material as the city and was several hundred yards wide. At both ends and at several points across the width of the entrance were guard towers manned by watchmen who were paying scant attention to most of those crossing—almost all of whom seemed to be boylike angels like Nix.

As the companions approached, Edmund and Rose whispered back and forth about what possible ruse they could use to pass, but the guard in the nearest tower simply looked up, nodded at Charles, then went back to his other work.

"Interesting," Charles murmured as they passed. "I would have at least expected to be stopped and questioned."

The guard overheard this and leaned out of his tower, shaking his head. "You are Seraphim, are you not?" he asked.

"Er, ah, yes," Charles said hesitantly. "I am."

"Then you are Named," the guard replied, "Naming is Being, and there is no need to ask about your business."

The three companions walked past, and for a moment, it seemed to the guard as if the girl's shadow was moving independently of the person casting it. He watched a moment more, then shook it off. After all, there were no shadows in the City of Jade that the Makers did not intend to be there—not even those that moved of their own accord.

"Back there, on the hill," Rose said to the others as they crossed the bridge, "when Nix asked if you were Nephilim, and you said you were Seraphim . . . You *Named* yourself, Charles."

The Caretaker and the Cartographer both nodded in agreement. "I think you're right," said Charles. "Somehow, how I identified myself is reflected in my countenance. It's probably a good thing I didn't identify myself as an editor or an author. We'd probably have been taken prisoner and put to work in a labor camp somewhere, just out of compassion."

There were no other guards, and no gates to pass through on the other side of the bridge—simply open boulevards between massive buildings and towers, all of which were buzzing with activity. There were angels like Nix walking to and fro, all focused on whatever was on the tablets they carried. Above their heads were other beings the companions assumed were also angels, but these creatures had wings and were flying between the great towers.

Also walking the streets were humans, who were distinguishable from the angels by the fact that they were more elaborately dressed and carried the burden of aging more obviously.

Humans could grow old, it seemed. Even in Atlantis.

Another personage paused and turned to look at the companions as they passed. He was tall, taller than anyone they had yet seen in the city. He was silver-haired and wore a silver tunic that was shot through with a streak of crimson that matched the glowing red of his eyes.

In response, Rose took both Charles and Edmund by the arms and led them around a corner, out of his sight.

"What's wrong?" asked Charles. "Who was that?"

"I've met him before," Rose answered, still hurrying them along, "twice. The first time, he said he was a star named Rao, and he had been banished to a Ring of Power on an island past the Edge of the World. And the second time," she added, unable to suppress a shudder, "was when he destroyed Paralon and revealed himself to be a Lloigor in service of the Echthroi."

• • •

Having avoided a possible confrontation with the future renegade star, the companions realized that there would be no way to locate Samaranth without asking for help. They tried asking some of the passing angels, all of whom responded politely as soon as they noticed Charles, but waved the question away as basically meaningless the moment Samaranth's name was mentioned.

"I thought he was the most respected creature in the Archipelago," Edmund said, "and everyone we've approached has mentioned his being among the oldest angels here. So why are they so quick to dismiss him as irrelevant?"

"It's the way of the world," Charles lamented. "Youth never trusts or respects the wisdom of age and experience until they are aged and experienced themselves, and by then, it's usually too late."

"Not every culture is like that, surely," said Edmund. "I was raised to respect my elders."

"So was I," said Rose.

"The exceptions that prove the rule," Charles said. "Let's go ask that fellow, there."

He was indicating a tall, finely dressed man who was writing with a stylus on parchment instead of using one of the tablets the angels all seemed to carry.

"Why him?" asked Rose.

Charles shrugged. "It's just something about his countenance."

The man listened politely as they explained whom they were seeking, and as opposed to the angels' deference to Charles the Seraphim, seemed more taken by Rose.

"Yes, I can help you," he said when they'd finished. He turned and took a few steps into the street. "There," he said, pointing at a broad, squat building in the distance. "All the minor guilds are ensconced there, in the Library. It keeps them out of the way of all the others, who are certain they are doing more important work."

Charles caught the hint of derision in the man's voice and couldn't help himself. "What work do you believe is more important?"

The man smiled wryly. "You have the countenance of a Seraphim but the manner of a scholar. The work of a scholar is to seek after knowledge—and there is always something new to learn."

He turned to Rose, more serious now. "The summit is coming to an end soon, and changes will be coming. Find your minor angel, and then leave. The City of Jade may not be as welcoming to you tonight as it was to you today."

The man spun on his heel and began to walk away. "Good luck to you, scholars," he called back. "Hermes Trismegistus wishes you well."

The Library was easy enough to get to, but impossibly large, which required a few more inquiries. Eventually the companions were directed to what was essentially the basement, where a large door separated in the center and slid open at Rose's touch.

"Come in, if you must," said a thin tenor voice, "but please make haste. I have a full schedule of Naming today, and a thousand and one things must be recorded for the book if I'm to be allowed into the summit."

The companions entered the vasty, tall room and gasped at the size of it. They knew that it was a lower level in the Library, but to all appearances it seemed nearly endless inside, and there was no ceiling, save for distant abstract geometric shapes set among a field of twinkling lights.

"Yes, yes," the voice said again, "it is small and rather cramped—the Guild keeps all its unfinished concepts here, and they take up more room than you'd think—but there's space enough for me to do my work, and that suffices."

The speaker was sitting on a dais at the center of the room, working on one of the tablets all the angels seemed to carry. That much was not a surprise. What was a surprise was that Nix had described the angel before them as being one of the oldest among all those in the city—but the face that peered sideways at them as they approached was that of a young man, barely out of school.

He blew a wayward strand of reddish hair out of his face and scowled at the visitors. "Well? Are you going to tell me what business you bring, or do I have to Un-Name you to get your attention?"

"Well," said Charles, "that sure *sounds* like Samaranth."

"Of course," the young man said primly. "I am he. I am Samaranth. Who," he added, eyes glittering, "are *you*?"

The companions stared at the angel with undisguised shock. This was not what they'd expected to see, and this small, twitchy, suspicious, childlike creature bore almost no resemblance to the great, regal Dragon they had known. No resemblance, save for . . .

"His eyes," Laura Glue said softly. "He has Samaranth's eyes."

The angel snorted. "Of course I do. Am I not Samaranth?" He stood and stepped down from the dais to approach them. He was barely as tall as Rose, and several inches shorter than Edmund. "I am the fifth assistant Namer from the nine hundred and second Guild of Namers, of the fifty-first Host of Angels of the City of Jade."

"Nix said he was one of the oldest of them," Rose whispered to Charles, "but he doesn't appear to be any older than I am, if that."

"Not to put too fine a point on it," Charles whispered back, "but as I recall, you're fairly advanced in years yourself, even though you don't look it."

"Oh, I am one of the eldest of the Host," said Samaranth, who apparently could hear just fine. "At least, among those assigned to this world. And," he added thoughtfully, "I might actually be younger than you, ah, what did you say you are called?"

"I'm Rose," she said, "and this is Charles, and Edmund. Just how old *are* you?"

Samaranth answered without hesitation. "According to the Chronos time established by Sol when this world was set into motion, I am approximately two billion, three hundred seventy-nine million, one hundred fifty-two thousand, four hundred and ninety-seven years old, give or take."

"Give or take?" asked Edmund.

Samaranth nodded. "It's difficult to figure precisely, because of a few things that have already been Named and Placed, like the 'Mayan conundrum' and something called a 'leap year.' It makes the calculations especially difficult, because we don't even have a name for the process of, ah, figuring yet. It involves numbers, but that's as far as I've gotten."

Charles sighed in sympathy. "I can relate. Trouble with math is one reason I became a writer."

"Hmm. Math," said Samaranth. "I like that. That could work." He jotted down a note on his tablet. "Math. Yes. Very good. You could be a Namer yourself, you know. If you weren't a Seraphim, that is."

"Ah, yes, about that," Charles began before Edmund elbowed him in the ribs.

"Don't say it," the Cartographer hissed. "If you can Name yourself, who's to say you can't Un-Name yourself just as easily?"

Hearing this, Samaranth turned his full attention to them for the first time, and his expression was dark.

"That is not something to be spoken of in the City of Jade," he said softly. "Things that are made may be Named, and sometimes, may also be Renamed, when they must choose a different path. But to be . . . to be Un-Named is something entirely different."

He set aside his work and stepped closer to Charles. "You are not Seraphim, are you? You bear the countenance, but I sense you are also Other."

"He is a Caretaker," Rose said quickly. "That is the most important job there is."

Samaranth considered this as he walked back to the dais. "A Caretaker, you say? Hmm. Someone who Takes Care. Yes, I understand. That is good." He made some notations on a tablet. "I shall remember that, thank you."

A chime sounded in the air somewhere above them, and the angel's expression suddenly changed. "Oh, by the Host—it is nearly time. I must prepare to finish here so I might attend the summit." He looked at the three of them as if they'd just walked in. "Have you been fed?"

"Please, Samaranth," Rose asked, "can you tell us what this summit is about? Everyone in the city seems to be involved somehow."

"Everyone *is* involved," he replied. "There is nothing more important than what will be determined here today, after debating for so many years. The younger principalities believe that almost everything that *can* be created in this world *has* been created, and in this, they are quite nearly correct. However, they also think that now there will no longer be a great need for Makers, there will also be no need for Namers either."

"Namers like yourself," Charles noted drolly. "Just saying."

"I speak to be understood, not out of vanity," said Samaranth, "and they believe they will have little need of me, even though there is still a tremendous amount of work to be done. There will always be some need for Makers—but Naming is far more valuable, because to Name something is to give it meaning. Simply being created is not enough."

"Everything has been made?" Edmund said, gesturing out the window. "Even there?"

He was looking to the west, toward the Archipelago—or at least, where the Archipelago should have been. But there was nothing except darkness there. And not the storm-cloud darkness of the Frontier, but the darkness that Rose had seen only once before, when she and her friends sailed past the waterfall at the Edge of the World and into the darkness beyond, to find her father.

Samaranth looked at him in surprise. "That is the Un-Made World," he said as if his visitors should have known already, "and it remains Un-Named, until the Word chooses a time and a place to make it and Name it. There is nothing there except darkness, and stone, and . . ."

"And the keep," said Edmund. "The Eternal Tower. Isn't that right?"

For the first time since they'd arrived, Samaranth actually looked frightened. "*Are* you Nephilim?" he asked, his voice steady, but the fear still evident in his expression. "Have you come to Un-Name me?"

"No, we aren't Nephilim, and we haven't come to Un-Name anyone," Rose quickly assured him. "Why would you ask that?"

"Because," Samaranth replied, "only a few among the Host, the eldest of us, even know the tower exists. We have traveled to it. We know how to use it. And of us all, I alone deduced how important it is to this world and the Un-Made World both. They were not always severed. And someday, they may be made whole again. This is the secret we have kept for eons. The secret worth . . . killing for. So, I must ask you again—have you come to Un-Name me?"

An elderly man . . . led the procession . . .

Chapter Eight
The Steward

"*They did what?*" John exclaimed, incredulous. "You helped them to do *what?*"

"Calm down, John," Jack said soothingly, "and I'll explain everything."

"Calm *down?!?*" John sputtered, almost too furious to speak. "You've just betrayed everything we believe in!"

Jack scowled. "No, I haven't," he said as calmly as he could manage. "We just believed that—"

"We?" John exclaimed. "You mean there were . . ." He stopped, thinking, then spun around, pointing an accusing finger at Shakespeare.

"I'm surprised at you, Will," John said. "They could not have done this without your help. You should have come to me."

"That's the rub of it," Shakespeare said, moving around the table to stand in solidarity with Jack. "We don't think you made the right call. The gate was the only viable option we had."

"You've betrayed your oath as a Caretaker, Jack," John said, shaking. "And you've betrayed me."

"Well, as regards the former," Jack said, his voice becoming steadier as he grew bolder about confronting his friend, "I disagree.

I swore an oath to protect a book that is lost somewhere in Deep Time, and an Archipelago that has disappeared to heaven knows where from a world that is dominated by shadows. So there really wasn't much to betray except my own best judgment, which I used. And as to the latter," he continued, "if that's really how you feel, oh Prime Caretaker, why don't you fire me?"

It was spoken in the heat of the argument, but Jack's statement nonetheless shocked the older Caretakers. Verne and Bert stepped in to try to calm tempers on both sides.

"Focus on what moves us forward, not what moves us backward, John," Verne said, laying a hand on the younger man's shoulder.

"Don't patronize me, Jules," John said, rebuffing Verne's calming words and comforting hand. "Besides, wasn't it your man Burton who taught us that time moves in two directions? They've gone back in time, and we couldn't even check in on them if we wanted to! We'll have no way of even knowing if they get into trouble!"

"We actually may have a way," said Verne. "It's something I'd been working on with Burton ages ago that I think will come in useful now."

John glared at Jack a few seconds longer, then tipped his head at Verne. "All right. Show me."

Verne ushered the Caretakers into a large, circular room in the northernmost wing of Tamerlane House. There was an immense round table in the center. It was made of some kind of stone, more ancient than marble. It was crisscrossed with various alchemical symbols, and a hexagonal shape, inset into the middle, was polished to an almost mirrorlike finish.

"This is the table that Arthur used to conduct séances," Verne said, gesturing at Conan Doyle. "What he didn't understand at the time, and what Ehrich spent a lot of time and energy trying to debunk," he added, winking at Houdini, "is that Arthur wasn't making contact with the spirit world, but with the past.

"This table," he continued as the other Caretakers took their seats around the circle, "is one of the few artifacts that survived the destruction of Atlantis. It is possible, if that is where our friends have gone, that we will be able to observe them, and possibly even send messages as well."

"Send messages?" John said, still fuming from Jack's announcement. "If there was the possibility that this would work, then they never should have risked using the gate."

"We don't know that it *will* work," said Verne. "In fact, it never even occurred to me as a possibility until last night. You see, Arthur always assumed he was communicating with a spirit in real time. What he was actually doing was communicating with the past, with someone who, from their own point of view, was still living. Burton is the one who figured it out."

"Actually," Conan Doyle admitted with a touch of embarrassment, "that's part of the reason Burton was able to so easily recruit me into the ICS. He had already been told a lot about me by his own right-hand man, who had been speaking to me for years via the table."

"Burton's right-hand man?" John said, frowning. "What does he have to do with all this? I don't understand."

"It is attuned to the craftsman who made it," said Verne. "Arthur knew him as Pheneas, a man of Arab descent who supposedly died thousands of years ago. In fact, the maker of this table was considerably older than that. He was known at points in his life as Theopolous, and earlier still as Enkidu. But Burton, who knew him best, simply called him the End of Time, and when he introduced us, I knew I had found the first, and perhaps the best, of my Messengers. As you know, he died at the hands of an Echthros in London, but he may be able to serve us still."

"What must we do, Jules?" Jack asked. "How does it work?"

"He always seemed to appear in answer to my questions," Conan Doyle replied. "He seemed never to age, but sometimes he couldn't recall earlier discussions. I think it's because I was going further and further back along his timeline. It functions in a manner similar to the trumps—intuition plays a part."

"As does belief," Houdini interjected. "You believed, and I didn't, Arthur. That's why you saw him."

"Believing is seeing," said Shakespeare. "We should give it a go."

"All right," John said, still reluctant, and more than a bit put out that he hadn't been told about the table earlier. "How do we do this?"

"Join hands," said Conan Doyle. "There are just enough of us here to make it work. Seven seems to have been the best number for making it operate. More, and there were too many competing thoughts; less, and there wasn't enough concentration to keep a clear focus."

Jack took Shakespeare's left hand and Houdini's right. Conan Doyle sat between Houdini and John, with Bert to John's left, and Verne completing the circle.

"What question should we ask?" said John.

"The simplest one, I suppose," said Conan Doyle. "Where is the *Indigo Dragon*?"

Together, the men gripped one another's hands and focused their will and thought on the question and the table.

Nothing happened.

"If Charles were here," Jack said after a few minutes had passed, "he would be asking if we needed to invoke some sort of incantation or magic spell."

"Abarakadabara," said Houdini. Still nothing.

"Is it plugged in?" asked Bert.

"Maybe it needed a Dragon, like the Zanzibar Gate did," Shakespeare began to say, and in that instant an unearthly glow began to emanate from the center of the hexagon.

"Ah," said John. "Well done, Will."

"Thanks, but I haven't the slightest idea what just happened," said Shakespeare.

"You focused your thoughts on a living Dragon," said Verne. "Life flows to life. We simply asked the wrong question."

"Quiet, all of you," John said as the light rose from the table in a column that began to alter and shift, forming a three-dimensional, almost holographic image. "Something is beginning to appear."

On the downward slope of a gigantic sand dune, the air shimmered and hummed, and suddenly the Zanzibar Gate came into view, becoming more and more solid as the seconds passed.

Almost instantly, the *Indigo Dragon* slid through and onto the sand, coming to rest with a slight lean about twenty feet down the dune.

"Meh!" said Elly Mae.

"Mah!" said Coraline.

"Is it over?" asked Fred. "That went pretty quickly."

"Just like walking through the doors of the keep," said Madoc. "That Shaksberd is quite the talented fellow. If I'd have recruited him instead of Burton—"

"Don't," Uncas said sternly, "even *joke* about that."

Quixote had already removed his helmet and breastplate. In the heat, the armor would be almost unbearable. He wiped his brow and looked to the horizon. "There," he said, pointing. "I think we've found the city."

Indeed, off in the distance the companions could see the magnificent outlines of the City of Jade, but the view was obscured by something so much more massive that at first, what it was failed to register with any of them. It was Madoc who understood it before the rest of them.

"The giants," he breathed, shading his eyes to look as high into the sky as he could manage. "The Corinthian Giants have formed a living wall between us and the city."

It was true—the great giants of legend, who had once saved the Caretakers from an aspect of Mordred called the King of Crickets, were standing shoulder to shoulder from the western edge of the desert that met the ocean, to so far to the east that they faded from view in the distance.

All along the perimeter formed by the giants' feet were encampments of people. Thousands upon thousands of tents, and caravans, and wagons, and what might have been a million people of every creed and color. Every culture of the young world seemed to be represented, and none of the encampments seemed to be temporary. Flocks of sheep and woolly cattle were corralled at spots along the line, as well as flocks of fowl, and animals of labor of every stripe: camel-like creatures with great humps, small horses covered in fur, and great catlike creatures that were large enough to be ridden by three men.

"It looks as if generations of people have lived here, waiting for something," said Quixote.

"Or being kept from something," said Kipling.

"Or waiting for something t' happen," said Uncas. "Turn around."

In the other direction, to the north of the Zanzibar Gate, was a sight equally as stunning—not because it was as overwhelming as the sight of the massive giants and enormous encampments at their feet, but because each of them intuitively knew what they were looking at.

Not half a mile behind the gate was a gigantic ship. It was perpendicular to their position, so they had no way of judging just how broad it might be, because it was so long they could barely see the ends.

Kipling let out a low whistle. "That has to be . . ."

"Several miles long, end to end," said Madoc. "I can't see how wide, though."

"I'll take a look," Laura Glue said, unfurling her Valkyrie's wings and leaping into the air.

"Laura Glue, no!" Kipling yelled, just a moment too late. She rose sharply into the air before she understood her mistake and dropped back down to the *Indigo Dragon*.

"Uh-oh," said Fred. "I think we're about to have some company."

A group of people had indeed seen Laura Glue's brief, ill-advised flight and were making their way over to the Zanzibar Gate to investigate—but not from the encampments. The procession was coming from the huge boat.

An elderly man, dressed in desert garb, with a long gray beard streaked through with white, led the procession of women, children, and, the companions were surprised to see, a large contingent of animals.

He raised a hand in greeting as he peered curiously at Laura Glue and Madoc in turn, taking particular care to look over their wings. In response, and perhaps as a bit of a challenge, Madoc flexed his shoulders and opened his wings to their full, impressive glory.

Kipling stepped forward, expecting to address the old man, but Fred and Uncas beat him to it, throwing themselves to the sand at the man's feet. "We greet you, oh Ancient of Days," they said in unison. "Now and forever, we serve thee, Ordo Maas."

The old man chuckled and helped them both to their feet. "That's all well and good," he said, a cheerful expression on his face that bespoke earnest affection for everyone in their group, "but there's no point getting sand in your clothes, now, is there?"

"Ordo Maas?" Madoc said, dumbfounded. "*You* are Ordo Maas?"

The old man nodded. "The Children of the Earth—the animals—named me thus back in the days when all of them spoke as these two fine badgers do," he said, scratching at Uncas's head, which the badger would have hated anyone else doing, but which he seemed to love in the moment. "In my old kingdom, back in the Empty Quarter, I was known as Utnapishtim. But here, among the people of this great exodus, I am simply known as Deucalion."

"Deucalion, the son of Prometheus," said Madoc, "who built a great ark and saved all the creatures of the earth from a deluge that covered the world."

"You're mostly right," Deucalion said. "My father was Prometheus, and I have built a ship. But it hasn't rained here in decades. Water is growing scarce. And my reputation is more that of a fool than a king or savior of animals."

"Just wait," said Fred. "I think things are about to change."

"Why were we brought here?" Kipling wondered aloud as they followed the shipbuilder back to his tents in the shade of the great boat. "I thought we'd end up closer to the city itself."

"Remember what Will told us," Laura Glue reminded them. "Intuition plays a part in how the gate is guided. If we were brought to this place, it's in part because this is where we needed to be."

"Perhaps the giants have something to do with it," said Madoc.

"You may be right in that," said Deucalion. "The Corinthian Giants have prevented anyone from reaching the city who did not specifically have the Mandate of Heaven. It has been thus for generations."

"'Generations' is certainly the word for it," Quixote said, straining backward to look up at the huge ship.

"This wasn't built overnight," Madoc said with real admiration in his voice. "How long have you been working on this vessel, old one?"

"From the time I was warned about the cataclysm to come, and my wife and I fled my kingdom to come here, it has been one hundred and forty years," Deucalion said as he gestured for his sons and their wives to serve water to his guests—first to the goats, then to the badgers, and then to the rest. "We began our family with the birth of my eldest son in the same year we began constructing the ship, a decade after our flight into the desert. And now we are nearly finished, just as my youngest son, Hap, is reaching manhood.

"But enough of family histories," he said, turning to Uncas. "What is it that brings you to my tent?"

"Some friends of ours have gone missing," Uncas said, "and we've come looking for them."

"How come I can never explain our goals that simply?" Kipling whispered to Quixote.

"Poetic license," the knight whispered back. "It's a privilege, not a right."

"I see," said Deucalion. "And I take it from what you said earlier about expecting to find yourselves in the city that you hope to find them there?"

"We do," said Uncas.

"You may be right, but without the Mandate of Heaven, you'll never know," Deucalion said. "Nothing living can get past the Corinthian Giants."

In one fluid, graceful motion, Kipling rose to his feet. "I think that's my cue. I'm going to go have a look around," he said jovially. "I'll see if I can't get the lay of the land, so we can make a game plan for finding our friends."

The shipbuilder started. "You want to go into the city?"

Kipling bowed. "That is where, it seems, all the action is. And I am a man of action."

"We could all try to—," Quixote began before Kipling cut him off with a gesture.

"Alone would be best," he said. "Just reconnaissance, I promise. I'll be back as soon as I can manage."

"Is that wise?" Laura Glue asked.

"I'm head of the Espionage Squad, remember?" Kipling said, feigning hurt feelings. "I'm just going to go have a look around. And besides," he added, glancing from Madoc's wings to Laura Glue's, "I'll attract a lot less attention than the rest of you will."

Deucalion sighed heavily. "Man of action you may be, but it is impossible. As I have told you, unless you have been given passage into the city by an emissary, the giants will permit no one living to cross the boundary."

"It shouldn't be a problem, then," Kipling said with a wink as he exited the tent, "since I actually died some time ago."

Deucalion looked at Fred and Uncas for an explanation, but the Caretaker merely shrugged, and the knight's squire stifled a chuckle.

"It's kind of hard to explain," said Laura Glue, "but trust me, he's alive enough to do what he must."

This time it was the shipbuilder's turn to smile. "As are we all, my child. God willing, as are we all."

Part Three

The Summit

. . . Kipling . . . started the long trek to the distant city.

Chapter Nine

Messages

The Echthros watched, and waited.

It was in the house because of the Binding it wore, and so, when it was called upon, it was forced to serve the master who had fashioned it. But in between those summonings, it was still a creature of will, doing as it pleased. And it pleased the Echthros to be here, watching these little things play at the machinations of the world as if they were gods. No—as if they were the only gods; as if they were all the little gods there were.

It had played a part in the choices they made, partly in service to the Binding, and partly because it found the events taking place to be interesting. Once, in service to the Binding, it had even killed someone who had spent thousands of years doing little more than helping others.

And once, very recently, it had spilled one of its master's secrets, perhaps the most important one. The Echthros claimed to have done so because of a covenant it had made oh so long ago—a covenant made almost at the same time it had been bound, when it was not yet an Echthros, but a free creature, who walked unafraid through the streets of the City of Jade.

The covenant did not compel servitude as the Binding did. Maybe that was why the Echthros chose to honor the request and offer help to the Caretakers' friends.

Or maybe it was simply another aspect of its service to Shadow. It didn't know. But soon, it might find out.

Samaranth's question hung in the air for a long moment before any of the companions chose to answer. Rose opened her mouth to speak.

"We are not here to Un-Name you," she said again, slowly and carefully. After all, Samaranth might have seemed afraid in that moment—but he was still an angel. There was no way to know what that might mean in terms of the power he could wield if he felt threatened . . .

. . . or felt the need for retribution.

"We have come a . . . very long way, to ask for your help," said Edmund. "We have no desire to interfere with you, or your summit, or anything to do with the city. We simply want to ask you a question."

Samaranth already seemed calmer, something that might have been due more to his curiosity about these strange visitors than to their soothing words. "All right," he said, having decided that whatever these creatures were, they were no threat. "What do you want to ask of me?"

"The Keep of Time," Rose began. "You say that you know how it works, and that you understand how important it is to both this world and the one out there. What we want to ask is if you have also discovered who built the keep."

The angel immediately shook his head. "That is the one question we have never been able to answer," he said, "although it is an answer I have sought myself, in secret, because unless that answer is discovered, nothing we do here will be of any value whatsoever."

"Why is that?"

"Because it is damaged," Samaranth answered, "and unless it is repaired, it will someday vanish altogether, and the connection to this world will be destroyed. And when that occurs, there will be nothing to prevent the Un-Namers from sweeping over the face of the earth."

As Kipling expected, passing the line of Corinthian Giants was spectacularly easy. His state of being as a tulpa, a living thought-form that possessed the aiua, or soul, of Rudyard Kipling, apparently made him a different enough kind of creature that the living monoliths paid him no heed whatsoever. They remained impassive, and immobile as stone. He was still human enough, however, to attract the attention of several among the refugees encamped along the living wall—and several of them, seeing how he passed successfully, attempted to do the same.

He watched with a bemused expression on his face, wondering just what method the giants would resort to for repelling the invaders—but an instant later, the smile dropped off his face.

The first two refugees had just reached the narrow isthmus between two of the giants' feet when a horrifyingly loud booming horn sounded in the sky, and one of the giants looked down. A beam of light erupted from the giant's cowled face, incinerating the refugees to ash.

Sickened, and berating himself for not being more careful, Kipling fashioned a turban out of his jacket to protect his head from the hot sun and started the long trek to the distant city.

"It stands to reason that he wouldn't know," Charles said to the others. "If he had known, surely Bert, or Verne, or *someone* back home would have discovered the identity of the Architect years ago."

"Not necessarily," said Rose. "He wasn't tame when we knew him, you know. And there were times he did deliberately conceal information so that we'd have to discover the answers ourselves."

"Also," Edmund put in, "if he is the oldest of all his kind here, then it's not very likely that anyone else in the entire city would know more than he does."

"Age does not equal knowledge," Samaranth said. He turned to Rose, scowling slightly. "Did you just call me 'tame'?"

She blushed furiously and changed the subject. "I'm sorry we bothered you, Samaranth," she said contritely. "I hope we haven't interfered too much with your work."

"You seem to know a great deal about who I am," the angel said, giving them a look of appraisal, "and I still know nothing of you. Where did you say you hailed from?"

"There is only so much we can share," Rose began in answer to Samaranth's question, "without risking terrible damage to our own future. And yours," she added quickly. "I can only ask that you trust us, and that you try to believe that our intentions are good."

The angel considered her words and pursed his lips. "I don't have to try," he said finally. "Your countenance bears out your intentions, and I can read you like a book.

"My concern now, and the concern of all those who are eldest within the City of Jade, is in continuing the Naming of all that has already been made, so that all those who reside here may continue to live here in peace. One world should be sufficient enough to share, even among the principalities."

"There are some who disagree?" asked Charles.

"This is the reason for the summit," Samaranth said as he put away his tablet and began to tidy up his workspace—which, Rose noted, was already almost unspeakably tidy. "The principalities have fashioned a proposal to appeal to the Word to make the Un-Made World, and to Name it, so that they may claim it for their own. They wish to leave this world, which they have long been neglecting, to the peoples who have spread across it."

"Hmm," said Charles. "That doesn't sound too unfair."

"It would not be, had the principalities not used this world up in the process. They have benefited from it, and prospered, and now that it seems to be dying, they wish to go elsewhere. But," he added, "unless the Un-Made World is connected once more and fully to this one, it will perish as well."

"You keep saying 'principalities,'" said Edmund. "Forgive my ignorance, but what does that mean?"

"Gods," Samaranth said simply. "This summit is a gathering of all the gods of the earth, large and small. Some are gods who began as men, and rose to the calling out of will; and some are those who fell to earth and were worshipped for the talents they carried with them, and so were declared to be gods. And if what they have proposed is not opposed . . .

". . . then both this world and the next shall fall into utter ruin, and perish."

It was a more difficult trek to the city than Kipling had anticipated. He was actually tired. That hadn't happened often in the years following his death, but, he reasoned, it was still bound to happen sooner or later. That wasn't important, though, because he had a bigger problem. Getting past the giants was one thing. Gaining entry into the City of Jade itself was another kettle of fish entirely.

There were two bridges on the northern side, and both of them were lined with watchtowers manned by guards who were giving at least a cursory glance to every personage who crossed them. Kipling wasn't certain that he wanted to try an end run, which might attract attention, so he decided to sit and observe for a while.

After an hour, something significant sparked his attention. A number of people who had crossed the bridge with virtually no attention from the guards at all had one thing in common: They all had some kind of unusual markings on their foreheads. The most common was a circle surrounded by four diamonds.

Kipling considered his options a bit more, then shrugged in resignation. "When in Rome," he said, taking a pen from his jacket. He leaned over a shallow section of the estuary some distance from the bridge to use the water as a mirror, and drew what looked like a fair approximation of the tattoos he'd observed.

Thus prepared, he walked straight toward one of the watchtowers—and, to his delight, the guard did nothing more than glance at his forehead and wave him on.

"This may be the easiest espionage job I've ever taken," Kipling murmured to himself.

"Or," a shockingly familiar voice said from too close behind him for comfort, "at least, the last one you ever take."

He whirled around to face the speaker. It was John Dee.

"Greetings and salutations, Dr. Dee," Kipling said.

"Say good night, Kipling," said Dr. Dee. And suddenly the Caretaker was plunged into pain, and darkness, and as he fell into unconsciousness, he realized that Dee was very probably right.

"I want to ask," Laura Glue said, once they had eaten from the food provided by Deucalion's family, "why did you decide to build this giant boat out here in the desert, where there's no water at all?"

"Actually," Uncas said, correcting her, "it's a ship."

"Boat," said Laura Glue.

"Ship," Uncas insisted.

"Actually, it's an ark," Deucalion said pleasantly. "And it wasn't so much a decision as it was a responsibility."

"How so?" asked Madoc.

"Come," Deucalion said, rising to his feet and gesturing for them to follow. "I will show you."

He led them through a connecting passage into another tent, which was guarded at the entryway by two of his sons, who regarded their visitors suspiciously, even though the guide was their own father. Inside, another son, Hap, stood guard over a pedestal.

"This is where we keep those objects sacred to us," Deucalion said as his son stepped back and the companions circled around the pedestal, "so that we carry with us the reminders of the work we are to do in the world."

On the pedestal was an ornate box made of a black wood with a latch made of bronze. The shipbuilder opened the latch and pushed back the lid. Inside, they could see several items: a brooch, a small dagger, three scrolls, and a simple, cream-colored note card on what appeared to be paper of twentieth-century manufacture. Deucalion removed the note card and closed the box.

"This is the reason I have done the work I have," he said pointedly. "Were it not for this, I would never have conceived of building the great ship, nor pursued the animal husbandry in the manner that I have. Although," he added, smiling and scratching Uncas behind the ear, "I have always favored the Children of the Earth above man, and thus, the work I have done only pleases me more."

"I can't read it," Laura Glue said bluntly. She looked at Madoc. "Can you?"

He shook his head. "It is far older than I, and of a language I never learned at Alexandria."

"There are few who can read it," Deucalion said, "but you already know the content of it—it is a warning about the Great Deluge to come, and a plea to gather all the Children of the Earth into a great ship, so that they may be taken to safety in another world, and to take all the knowledge necessary should the world need to be rebuilt. It was such an expression of madness that I would never have given it credence had I not also known and trusted he who wrote it."

"Who is that?" asked Madoc.

Deucalion smiled and tapped his chest. "*Me.*"

He explained how he had been approached at his court by someone who appeared out of thin air and seemed to be able to predict the future. This strange visitor was the one who delivered the note, which had apparently been written by Deucalion himself, to himself, in his own hand. Thus, the shipbuilder explained, the man must have been a prophet of some kind, and after consulting with his sons, Deucalion left his land and journeyed to the City of Jade, where they began their work in earnest.

"To be honest, were it not for him, I might not have been so welcoming of you," Deucalion said bluntly. "Even here, in this land, you are strange personages."

Madoc frowned. "Then why did you trust us?"

"Because," Deucalion answered, gesturing at the pocket watch Fred wore, "our strange visitor carried a device just like the one you wear."

Laura Glue sighed and looked at Madoc, who was rubbing his forehead and flexing his wings in agitation. "Verne," he said, sighing. "Sometimes I don't know whether to be grateful for him, or wish that someone would get fed up enough with his meddling to seal him in a tomb."

Deucalion gave her a strange look. "Verne? No, that was not his name. He called himself something more in the manner of my own people—Telemachus."

The companions all felt the same thrill of fear at hearing that name. Laura Glue looked again at Madoc, who shook his head slightly, as if to say, *Now is not the time or place.* However, as had often been the case, the humans' discretion was completely overridden by the badgers.

"That's the name of th' boy prince we lost and then found again," said Uncas. "He might be evil, though."

"Or not," said Fred. "The last time we saw him, he was still thinking it over."

"Well, he apparently made his choice," said Deucalion, "because he left something for you, too."

"For us?" Quixote said in surprise.

"The badgers, specifically," said Deucalion. "He and I share an affinity for talking animals, it seems."

At the shipbuilder's urging, the badgers peered into the box, and there, underneath the scrolls, were two more envelopes, one addressed to each of them.

"Great!" Uncas exclaimed. "I *love* t' get mail."

"What does yours say, Fred?" Laura Glue asked as he broke the seal and removed the note. It read:

You are a Caretaker, and thus, also a Namer.

Name Madoc as a Nephilim, and you may pass through to the city. Look for your friends in the center, under the great celestial dome. Good luck.

"Nephilim?" Deucalion said with a start. He looked askance at Madoc. "Are you Nephilim? I would not have thought one such as yourself would care to keep company with Children of the Earth."

"Why?" asked Madoc. "What is a Nephilim?"

"One of the Host," Hap replied, stepping closer to his father, "but one who sees Shadow as being equal to the Light, who serves the Void while still claiming to serve the Word."

"Ah," said Madoc. "I see. I will never fully lose who I once was, it seems."

Deucalion put a hand of support on Madoc's shoulder. "Naming is not Being," the old shipbuilder said, "and anything that is Named may still be Renamed. The choice as to whom you serve is always yours."

"I just want to find my daughter," said Madoc.

"Yes," Quixote said, "that is why we came, but I'm afraid we now have a clock on it."

"What do you mean?" asked Madoc.

"This," Quixote said. He was holding the note that had been addressed to Uncas. "It's hard to make the message any more clear."

The companions crowded around the knight to read the small note, which bore only a few words:

The flood is coming.

Leave. Now.

Chapter Ten

Order and Chaos

Kipling came to consciousness and found he had been bound hand and foot to a very uncomfortable chair that was sitting in a very uncomfortable room. It had the appearance of a glass conservatory that aspired to be a skyscraper, and stood along a glass-and-stone corridor that appeared to be lined with similar rooms.

"It's the same room, actually," an ornately dressed man said from his seat on another of the uncomfortable chairs, which sat in the opposite corner. "We've been having some issues with duration, and every so often it gets stuck."

Kipling didn't reply, but simply focused his attention on waking fully. He remembered being struck from behind, but other than that, what had happened after he saw Dr. Dee was a total loss.

The man was sitting facing an immense glass case, slotted with narrow vertical shelves. He was sliding thin slabs of marble that had some kind of writing on them in and out of the slots.

"Proximity matters," the man explained without looking away from his task. "Some of the scripts change others, so I have to make sure that those in close proximity are compatible; otherwise some significant meanings might be lost completely."

Enkidu was . . . staring directly at the Prime Caretaker . . .

"What are they?" asked Kipling.

"I suppose you could call them Histories," the man said, "but since some of them haven't and may never happen, that may be erroneous."

"Who are you?"

"Hermes Trismegistus," the man replied, again without turning to look at his captive companion. "I suppose you could say I am your friend's teacher."

Kipling scowled. "Who, Dee?" he snorted. "He is *not* my friend."

"He's very intelligent," Hermes replied. "Almost like a god, but without any followers."

"Only fools would follow someone like him."

Hermes looked at him like he was a child. "You'd be surprised at how effective appearing to be a god really is."

"He's evil," said Kipling. "That's all I need to know."

"Hmm," Hermes said, rubbing his chin. "I think that's one of the more recent concepts. I don't know if it has even been recorded in the book yet."

"Why are you keeping me here, Hermes?"

"Hermes Trismegistus, please. And I'm not keeping you here," he said pointedly, "*he* is."

Kipling turned and saw Dr. Dee enter the room, then kick the door closed behind him, which seemed to annoy Hermes. Dee was carrying several of the tablets, which he placed on a table next to the shelves. "Those are the last of them," he said. "That should be sufficient, at least for . . ." Dee turned and saw for the first time that his unwilling guest was awake.

"What are you doing, Dee?"

"I am a scholar, on a scholar's quest," Dee answered, "and as much as it pained me to inconvenience you, I cannot have you interfering." He paused and furrowed his brow. "How did you get here, anyroad? You were not traveling with the Grail Child and her cohorts."

Kipling ignored the question. "Why are *you* here?"

"This is the only place and time in history where I could find a codex to the language of the angels," Dee said as he walked back toward the door and swung it open. "There are runes and markings and even a manuscript written in their manner of speech, but nothing that remained after this time that could tell me how to translate them. And that was essential."

"Why do you need to understand the angelic languages?" Kipling asked. "What possible use could that be to you?"

"If I understand the language," said Dee, "then I can speak it correctly. And if I can speak it, then I can call an angel by his name. And," he added as he closed the door behind him, "if I know an angel's name, then that angel . . .

". . . can be *bound*."

The notes inside Deucalion's box were taken just as seriously as the one he had been given that had instructed him to build the ark. The companions watched somberly as he called his family together and instructed them to begin gathering the animals together in preparation for the long-anticipated flood. It was to their credit, Madoc thought, that not a one among them hesitated or questioned their patriarch in the slightest. He had raised them to believe what he told them, and they trusted him implicitly.

"You are not of this world, are you?" the old shipbuilder asked the companions as they left his tents to make their way back to the *Indigo Dragon*.

"Of this world, yes," Quixote said primly. "Of this era, ah, no. Not exactly."

Deucalion nodded. "I could tell as much. You have the smell of Kairos about you."

"Sorry," Uncas and Fred chorused. "We got a bit wet when we were watering the goats," said Fred.

The old shipbuilder smiled. "I think the smell of wet badger fur is more pleasant than the smell of a rose garden," he said.

"Y'see?" Uncas said to Madoc. "*That's* why ev'rybody loves him."

Madoc laughed. "I'm starting to understand that."

"Uh-oh," Fred said as they approached the spot where they had left the airship and the Zanzibar Gate. "You know that whole 'don't meddle with history' thing the Elder Caretakers are always nattering on about? Well, I think we've just meddled."

The airship, which resembled a boat enough still that everyone who looked at it completely ignored it as another one of Deucalion's desert follies, was still sitting in the sand where they had left it. But the Zanzibar Gate was drawing a considerably larger amount of attention.

Craftsmen from all the tribes had formed a perimeter around the gate and were constructing their own replicas of it. Even just a cursory glance among the works-in-progress showed that pyramid-like structures from all the great cultures of the world were being sculpted: the Egyptian, and the Maya, the Chinese, and even the latecomers of Mesopotamia.

"Maybe it's just a coincidence," said Quixote.

"Not likely," said Madoc. "This is the First City. No one else on earth has built anything like a pyramid before, and suddenly one just appeared out of thin air in the middle of the desert. That's too significant a happening to be ignored."

"Well, at least we finally know the answer to the question as to why there are nearly identical pyramids in every culture around the world throughout recorded history," said Fred. "They were all inspired by the work of William Shakespeare."

Observing from the circle of Caretakers seated at Conan Doyle's table in Tamerlane House, John tightened his grip on his colleagues' hands when he saw a child moving among the sculptors who were making the replica pyramids.

"There," he said, hardly daring to breathe. "That boy—isn't he . . . ?"

"Yes," Verne said, his voice barely more than a whisper. "In this time he was Enkidu, friend of Gilgamesh. But when he grows older, we will know him as the End of Time."

"Theo," Jack whispered. "It's good to see you again."

Almost as if he had heard, the boy stopped and cocked his head. He wiped the sweat from his brow and then ran back the other way, moving closer to the companions and the Zanzibar Gate.

Deucalion had moved past the others to examine the *Indigo Dragon*. He knelt next to the hull and ran his hands along it. "A fascinating vessel," he murmured, "of impeccable construction."

"Don't let's be patting ourselves on the back too hard," said Laura Glue.

"What?"

"Never mind her," said Fred, frowning at the Valkyrie. "It's a good ship, and she's taken good care of everyone who's sailed on her."

"She's been through a lot," Deucalion said, noting the scars in the wood, "but I have no doubt she'll continue to serve you well."

He turned to Madoc. "Something you ought to know," he said as the companions reharnessed the goats to the airship. "This is not, in fact, the First City."

That froze all of them where they stood.

"It *isn't?*" Quixote said, dumbfounded. "But isn't this *Atlantis?*"

Deucalion chuckled again. "Atlantis is among the oldest cities, and it is certainly the grandest, but it is not the first. My own city, in my own kingdom, predated it by several centuries. It was far humbler, but older nonetheless."

"Oh, dear," said Uncas. "That in't good."

Deucalion knelt, a look of concern crossing his features. "If your friends are in the City of Jade, does it matter if it is the oldest?"

"It might," said Fred. "That will affect what it is they came here to find. If this isn't the First City, then there's little chance they will find the identity of the first architect."

"Is that all?" Deucalion said in surprise. "I can tell you that right now."

Again, all the companions stopped doing whatever they were doing and focused their full attention on the old shipbuilder.

"Seek my great-grandfather," Deucalion said to Fred. "He left this world long before I came into it, but if any man was ever the kind of architect whom you are seeking, it would be him. He built a city. . . ." He paused, glancing around in sorrow as the enormity of the imminent destruction hit him once again. "He built the *first* city," the shipbuilder continued, "and in the beginning, before the names the younger races ascribed to it, before anything in this world had a name, it was named for him. Seek him out, and perhaps you will find the answers you seek."

He rummaged around inside his robe and withdrew a bronze disk that bore the likeness of a man on it. "Here," he said, handing it to Fred. "This was made long ago, and is said to be the best likeness of him, made by someone who knew him in his youth, before the city was built. If it will be of some help to you, you are welcome to it," he said, scanning the horizon with a visible anxiety. There were no clouds, no signs of rain, but it was clear the notes to the badgers had unnerved him more than he had let on.

"One way or the other," he said with finality, "I will have no more use for it myself."

With no farewell but a head scratch for the goats, a squeeze to the neck for the badgers, and a polite but curt nod to all the companions, Deucalion strode away to his ship.

"I don't know my mythology, uh, my history as well as you do," Quixote said to Madoc. "Who are we going to look for?"

"Enoch," said Madoc. "The city Deucalion mentioned was called the City of Enoch, and if it truly was the first, then I think he's who we have to find."

"First city, second city, or fifth city, this one is about to be covered in water," said Laura Glue. "There's no more time to waste—we have to go."

"Will the gate be safe while we go into the city?" Uncas asked. "Maybe one of us should stand guard."

"It's a pyramid built of almost indestructible stone that is older than dirt," said Laura Glue. "What can possibly happen to it?"

"The mechanisms are breakable," said Madoc, "but I would trust in Shaksberd's construction. It'll be fine." He turned to Fred. "All right, little Namer," he said. "Name me."

"Okay," Fred said. He'd been thumbing his way through the Little Whatsit, looking for the proper way to Name a Dragon as a Nephilim, but incredibly, that bit of knowledge was nowhere in the book. He shrugged and tucked it away. "You're a Nephilim," Fred said bluntly. "Congratulations."

"There's something to be said for ceremony, you know," Quixote said as the goats took a running start and the ship lifted into the air.

"Sorry," said Fred. "I'll work on that."

The airship rose into the sky, and a great hue and cry rose up from the thousands of people living in the encampments. It was not unprecedented in a world where angels walked among men and animals talked and gods rose and fell with the seasons, but it was a thrilling sight nonetheless. As the *Indigo Dragon* flew closer and closer to the impenetrable line of Corinthian Giants, every human within sight was watching its progress. Every human, that is . . .

. . . save for *one*.

Enkidu was standing away from the throng, not watching the flying ship but instead staring directly at the Prime Caretaker sitting in the circle at Tamerlane House.

"This is as far as I can take you, O spirit guides," the boy said. "I have tried to be where I felt you needed me to be, so you could see the things you hoped to see, but I can go no further. I must prepare for what is to come. And so must you."

With that the images projecting from the table vanished, and the room was plunged into darkness.

"Good Lord!" John exclaimed, jumping up from the table. He was almost choking on his own words. "Wh-what was *that,* Arthur? What just happened here?"

"I'm sorry," Conan Doyle said as he and the others also rose. "I thought you understood—it's not simply remote viewing. We are almost physically with him. That's not a hard, fast rule—none of this is set in stone—but he knew we were present the whole time we were watching. And somehow, he understood it was necessary."

"And, it seems, done," said Jack. "How are we to follow them now? We don't even know if Rose, Edmund, and Charles are in the city!"

"Yes, we do," said a voice from the doorway. It was Poe, the master of Tamerlane House.

In the hierarchy of Caretakers, Poe occupied a unique position somewhere above that of Caveo Principia, and even above Jules Verne when he was the Prime Caretaker before John took over the role. According to Bert, Poe had a unique understanding of space and time, and supposedly could manipulate both when it suited him to do so—but in John's experience, he rarely involved himself in whatever the Caretakers were dealing with unless it was a serious crisis. His appearance here was both good and bad.

"The *Telos Biblos* was written in Samaranth's own hand, from the time before the Archipelago itself was created, and there are accounts in it we have never understood until now."

He held up the book, so devoid of color that the pages appeared cold, and promptly ripped it in half.

Before any of the shocked Caretakers could react, Poe continued to tear the pages loose from the binding, then threw them into the air. They swirled about him like leaves in a storm, and then they began to slow, emitting a strange, unearthly glow.

Gradually the pages flowed past Poe and over to the table, where they reassembled themselves in order, and then began to expand until they filled the entire impression inset within the table. The light emanating from them grew stronger, and as the Caretakers again took their seats, images began to form in the light, and faint sound could be heard coming from the pages.

"Look and listen," Poe said, still standing near the doorway, "and see how the world you have cared for came into being."

"The Jade Empress," Samaranth said . . .

Chapter Eleven
The Oldest History

"What do you think?" Rose asked the two men as Samaranth readied himself to attend the summit. "Should we go with him?"

"I don't know," said Edmund. "It's history—whatever's about to go on has already happened, and I'm loath to get involved and possibly mess something up."

"We already *did*," said Charles. "Didn't you hear him? The keep is damaged—that means it hasn't fallen just in the future, but in the past as well. If we leave things as they are and try to go back, we may find our own history has been irrevocably changed."

"You've been spending too much time talking to Uncle Ray," Rose said, "but I think you're right. That's exactly what we'd be risking. So I don't think we have anything to lose by trying to learn as much as we can while we're here."

"I agree," Samaranth said. It was still unnerving to all three of them that this youthful man-child had the eyes of the wise old Dragon that they knew.

"Whoever you are, it is obvious to me that you understand more about how the world works than most of the principalities," he said as they left the Library. "If you listen, and learn, it may help you to better . . . take care, of your own world."

"That's pretty much exactly what we had in mind," said Charles. "Lead on, Macduff."

"Samaranth," the angel corrected. "Your memory needs work."

"Sorry," said Charles.

The great and spacious building where the summit was being held was less an amphitheater than it was an enormous ballroom—and in all the significant ways, that was exactly what it was. Staircases rose from the floor below, which was several hundred feet lower than the entrance, and connected a series of platforms that extended almost to the ceiling, which was so far above them that clouds had formed inside the room. There were fountains that fed streams of mingled light and water flowing through the air from platform to platform at varying levels. Everything was glass and marble and solidified light, except for the huge circle of fire in the center, and the dais above it, which stood at the far end of the chamber. Atop it was something familiar to all three of the companions.

"The ring of flames is the Creative Fire," said Samaranth. "It is where all things are made, and thus, this is where all things are decided. The high seat above is . . ."

". . . the Silver Throne," Rose said, breathless with awe.

"Hmm," said Charles. "Your father—uh, Mordred, that is, once said he was older than the Silver Throne. I think he was indulging in a bit of puffery."

"Obviously," said Edmund. "It's all still awfully spectacular, though," he added, gesturing at the grand spectacle with a sweep of his arm.

"It is indeed," Samaranth said, leading them to one of the staircases. "It was built by—"

"Magic?" Edmund suggested.

"Yes, that is the word," said Samaranth. "Magic. Or was it Will? I always get those two confused."

As they descended the stairs, Samaranth indicated that he was uncertain where he was expected to go, since he had not in fact attended any session of the summit before. The companions were about to ask why he had been excluded when Rose recognized someone on a nearby platform.

"Excuse me, ah, Nix?" she said to the angel. "Can you help us, please?"

Nix frowned—which Rose had noted, when they met before, was his default expression—and consulted his marble tablet. "I don't know why you weren't ordered when you arrived," he complained. "You are minions of a Seraphim, and—" He stopped, having noticed Samaranth for the first time. His eyes widened slightly. "I beg your pardon. I did not realize the elder was also with you." He consulted the tablet again, then pointed down at the floor level. "There should be some space for you there, if you hurry. The adversaries have claimed most of the upper platforms, and the principalities have claimed everything else."

"Adversaries?" said Charles. "I'm not sure I like the sound of that."

"It is the final session of the summit," Samaranth explained as they moved past several other youthful but apparently elderly angels and located an out-of-the-way corner at the lowest level of the room. "Matters of such importance that all the principalities have been invited, including our enemies."

"What are they called?" Edmund asked.

"One cannot identify one's adversaries by name," Samaranth

explained. "One can identify them only by their actions, and then act accordingly in return. And if they demonstrate that they no longer serve the Word, then, and only then, may they be Named as Fallen, and cast out."

"Cast out to where?" asked Rose.

"You really don't want to know," said Samaranth.

"So," said Charles, "all those above us, uh, so to speak, are gods?"

"Many of them," Samaranth answered, "but most above are of the angelic Host. Seraphim, Cherubim, and," he said, darkening slightly, "Nephilim. There are also the elder of us who serve in lesser capacities, but all who have a hand in guiding the course of the world are numbered among the principalities. Since the moment this world was divided from the Un-Made World, the younger races also began to splinter, and they grew and developed into their own distinctive cultures," he said in a matter-of-fact way. "As they flourished, they lost their connections to the Word and began the development of their own deities, whom they called gods. We, the Host, came here to build this city to try to reconnect the peoples of the world with the Word. But," he added with a touch of sadness, "the execution of that plan has fallen somewhat short of the aspiration.

"There," he said, pointing at a delegation several levels above. "That's one of the younger groups of gods, from a place called the Fertile Crescent. They are crude in their mannerisms, but effective. And there," he said, pointing to the left of the first group. "Those call themselves Titans. In truth, they bear many similarities to the Host—but their view is limited. Except," he added, "for that one."

Toward the bottom of the delegation a red-haired man was watching the angels just as intensely as Samaranth was watching him, only occasionally turning away to speak to another god, who carried a staff of living fire.

"He is the offspring of one of the Titans," Samaranth explained. "They call him Zeus. I expect great things of him, as well as the one he is with . . . Prometheus, I think."

Samaranth continued pointing out deities around the great room, and it was all the companions could do to keep up. "Loki, there," the angel said, "and his father, Odin, and Odin's father, Bor. And there," he continued, gesturing to a broad platform speckled with fountains, "the twin goddesses, Mahu and Mut, who represent two-thirds of the land masses of this world."

"What of the angels?" Charles asked. "Where are they?"

"Scattered throughout," Samaranth replied. "The Seraphim, like, ah, yourself," he added with as close an expression of mirth as any of them had yet seen, "are primarily of the Makers' Guilds, and constitute the bulk of the Host. The Cherubim," he went on, "are primarily Namers, and are those here on the lower levels with us."

"Have all the elder angels been excluded thus far?" Charles asked. "That hardly seems fair."

"Some of the older angels among the Seraphim would have allowed me to participate sooner," said Samaranth. "Sycorax is not much younger than I, nor are Maelzel and Azazel. But Iblis," he added, pointing to a tall, regal-looking angel near the top of the room, "is older still, and refused all my entreaties to become involved. He is more accepted among the younger members of the Host—why this is, I cannot say. Perhaps it is because he is more permissive than others among the principalities."

"It seems wrong," Rose fumed, "that those with the most experience aren't allowed any say at all in what happens."

Samaranth turned to her, eyes glittering. "You misunderstand, Daughter of Eve. We are not allowed to participate in the debates, but in the end, we most certainly do have a say.

"The oldest of a kind dictates the actions of all," Samaranth continued quietly. "It's one reason we are given work of little importance—so we are given as little influence as possible over the events of the world, until a decision has to be made—and then it is up to us to choose, so that in the end the responsibility, or blame, is entirely ours."

He spun around to point out a passing angel, apparently eager to change the subject. "That one, with the golden skin, is Telavel," he said. "He is a star-god who actually serves as the liaison between the Host and the stars. Some among us have even said he serves the Word directly, although there is no way to know for sure."

"Begging your pardon, Samaranth," Edmund said, "but do you mean these people you've been naming are the *representatives* of certain stars? Sort of like delegates?"

"No," the angel replied. "They *are* the stars themselves. Here, in the City of Jade, Naming is Being—and so even the stars may walk freely among its streets. In fact, in this case it was necessary, because the responsibility of this world's star is being called into question. It has even been rumored that the eldest star, Rao, has aligned himself with the Nephilim," Samaranth added. "That would be very, very bad."

"Why is that?" asked Edmund. "Aren't the Nephilim angels too?"

"They are," Samaranth admitted, casting a worried glance around them as if he were afraid someone might hear, "but they commune with Shadow and heed the call of the Word less and less frequently.

"If the Nephilim side with the stars, then there may be a split among the Host," he explained, "and the Seraphim are generally opposed to conflict, which means all that will stand between the Word and the principalities will be the Cherubim. If that is the case, the speaker for the Cherubim will have no choice but to declare the Nephilim as Fallen, and then Name them as such."

"Gosh," Charles said, craning his neck to look around at the other Cherubim. "What sorry so-and-so has that awful calling?"

"That would be *me*," said Samaranth. "Now please, be quiet. The final discussions of the summit are about to begin."

In his time with the Imperial Cartological Society, when he was acting as a double agent for Jules Verne, Kipling learned a great many things, and this was not the first time he had been held captive by an enemy. One of the things he learned was how to tell when he had been tied up by an amateur, and while Dr. Dee might have been brilliant in many ways, he was not a man of great physical prowess: The knots were loose.

"He wants to bind an angel," Kipling said, hoping that discussion would distract Hermes Trismegistus from noticing that he was trying to loosen his bonds. It might not have been necessary, though—Hermes was fully engaged in the work he was doing, which seemed to involve a series of pipettes, tubes, and glass spheres that were hovering around his working area.

"It is ambitious, to be sure," Hermes replied without turning around, "but hardly unprecedented."

"You don't seem to be very sympathetic toward them," Kipling countered, "even though you are a guest in their city."

"I see it differently," Hermes said. "I am not a guest in their city—they are guests on *my* world. And what is a single city compared to an entire world?"

"I'm starting to see why you and Dee get along," said Kipling. His left arm was starting to come loose from the bonds. "You have similar ambitions."

"As all gods ought," said Hermes.

"Gods?" Kipling exclaimed. "John Dee is not a god, he's just an alchemist with delusions of grandeur."

"That," said Hermes, "is *exactly* how it starts."

Rose, Charles, Edmund, and the angel Samaranth watched solemnly as a door irised open high up in the room, and a regal, impossibly dressed woman floated through and took a seat on the Silver Throne. Her flowing gown draped the dais for almost a hundred feet, and even when she was seated, the long sleeves of her robe continued to float as if suspended in water.

"The Jade Empress," Samaranth said under his breath, "and the last real connection between the city and the true peoples of this world."

"How old is she?" Edmund asked.

"Unlike us of the Host," the angel replied, "she truly *is* as youthful as she appears. She was a crippled beggar, living on the outskirts of the city, when it was discovered that she was the granddaughter of one of the four great kings of the East. And so she was welcomed here, and made empress, so that men would have a say in the fate of the world."

"That sounds awfully familiar," said Charles.

"Because we've heard the story before," said Rose. "The Jade Empress is T'ai Shan."

"Ah," Samaranth said, surprised. "You know her?"

"We have mutual friends," said Rose. "Look, something's happening."

The ambient light throughout the great room began to dim, and several glowing rings of varying color and intensity began to spread throughout the space, aligning themselves over each of the largest platforms. The rings separated into two, and each set began to oscillate, revolving in different directions. A brightening of a particular set of rings indicated that those on the pedestal below had permission to speak.

Samaranth's expression remained placid as the first rings to brighten were high above, on the platform of the Nephilim.

"I am Salathiel," the angel began, "of the first order of the ninth Guild of Diplomats of the second Host of the City of Jade, and I speak for all the Watchers."

There was a murmuring throughout the assembly, as if something very unorthodox had been spoken.

Charles glanced around at the Cherubim, all of whom were commiserating and whispering to one another. Something about Salathiel had disturbed everyone at the summit.

"What did he say?" Charles whispered. "All I heard was an introduction, but everyone is acting as if he'd just spit into the soup."

"He has Named himself and the Nephilim as Watchers," said Samaranth. "That has not been done before."

"What does that mean?"

"The Watchers," Samaranth explained, "are mostly Nephilim, and some Seraphim, all of whom are of the Diplomatic Guild. They were meant to have direct contact with the peoples of the world—and there are many among the Host who believe they did their job either very poorly, or far, far too well."

A look of astonishment spread over Charles's face as his old studies came back to him and he finally understood what Samaranth was saying.

"They had offspring with the Daughters of Eve, didn't they?" he asked. "The angels had *children*."

"The giants," Samaranth said, nodding. "Even now, they stand guard outside the city, to prevent the Sons of Adam and Daughters of Eve, and all the other Children of the Earth, from entering the city, or even from reaching the seas beyond. This is the great injustice that we hope to change today. The world, both worlds, were meant to be shared, for the prosperity of all, not just the privileged few."

"We wish to appeal to the Word," Salathiel continued, "to make and Name the Un-Made World, so that we, our children, and those of the principalities of this world may cross over, and build it up as we have done before."

Two more rings began to glow, farther down on one of the Seraphim's platforms. "And when you have used up that world," the angel said, not bothering to identify himself, "do you plan to abandon it as well, and move on to another? And another? And another after that? At what point do you actually become the stewards we are meant to be?"

"There are limits to stewardship, Sycorax," the Nephilim answered, scowling at the challenge, "and limits to responsibility."

"Only when you lay down your burden, Salathiel," the angel Sycorax replied. "It is not worthy of you. It is not worthy of the Host."

"The worlds have been severed," another of the Nephilim said, "through no fault of ours. The connection is broken, and none living know how to repair it. We should save what we can, and leave the rest to the mercy of the Word."

"There is a way," a slight voice said. "There is a way to save this world, without abandoning it."

It was one of the stars who had spoken—a slender, nervous being with golden hair that flowed upward like living flame and matched his glowing eyes.

Before he could speak again, another star, larger, older, stepped in front of him. "That is not going to happen, Sol. I will never permit it."

The star Sol stood defiantly in the face of his elder. "We must," he said, voice trembling with emotion. "We must ascend, Rao. It is the only way to save this world. Both worlds."

"I will not," Rao answered. "The planet of my own system is flawed, and I would not ascend to save that, so why would I possibly agree to save this little world by doing so? In any event," he continued, "it is not necessary. I have made a pact with the Little Things—"

"You mean the Sons of Adam and the Daughters of Eve, don't you, Rao?" Sycorax asked.

The star frowned, but continued speaking. "I have made a pact that will ensure prosperity for this world, if the empress will support the Watchers' proposal."

To confirm this was so, he raised a hand to the Jade Empress, who nodded once. Again, the room was filled with murmurings and whisperings among the assembly.

"So," Rao said, "as the eldest star, I formally endorse the

Watchers' proposal, as do the majority of the principalities. I would like to call for a vote of sustainment."

"Pardon me," a voice, quiet but firm, rang out into the great hall, "but I think this is a mistake."

Every angel's voice could be heard with equal clarity at the summit, so any angel who spoke could be heard. The shock and surprise that the words evoked was not because they were spoken, but because of who spoke them.

"It is a mistake," Samaranth said, "and not according to the plan. It should be reconsidered."

Chapter Twelve

The Tears of Heaven

It took Kipling only a few minutes more to loosen up the ropes that bound both his arms, and fortunately for him, Hermes Trismegistus was too sufficiently wrapped up in his work to pay any attention to John Dee's captive. In a few moments more, he had loosed the ropes around his feet as well and swung around, leaping to his feet and hefting the chair to use as a bludgeon in one fluid motion.

Hermes simply continued to work, completely ignoring him.

After a moment, Kipling lowered the chair, realizing that his odd companion really did care as little as he seemed to.

"If you've finished freeing yourself," Hermes said without looking up, "would you mind setting the chair out of the way so I don't trip over it? There's a good fellow."

Dumbfounded, Kipling rolled his eyes and headed for the door. "You're lucky no one was witness to this, Kipling," he muttered to himself, "or they might take away your spy card."

"Kipling?" Hermes exclaimed, dropping a tablet, which hit the floor with a loud clatter. "Did you say your name was Kipling?"

"Yes," the Caretaker replied, hesitant to confirm much of anything. "Why?"

The Watcher Salathiel lifted a huge, curved golden trumpet . . .

"This," Hermes said, actually focusing on Kipling in full for the first time, "is for you." He stood and handed the Caretaker a small, cream-colored envelope. It bore his name, and nothing else.

"Oh, my hell," Kipling said. He started at the envelope for a moment, then tore it open and read the note inside. He glanced up at Hermes, who was still showing a marked interest, especially compared to his earlier detachment.

"A god who wore the armor of a star gave that to me," Hermes said, wringing his hands with curiosity, "and warned me to save it for Kipling, that you would come for it someday. What does it say?"

"It says that it's the end of the world," Kipling answered, "which happens more often than you'd believe."

Before Hermes could ask anything further, Kipling spun on his heel and rushed out the door. He didn't look back.

No rings had been dispatched to cover the Cherubim, because no one had expected any of them to speak, so Samaranth spoke in the twilight glow that emanated from the walls.

"This summit has been ongoing for almost a century and a half of Chronos time," said Samaranth, "and the Un-Made World has remained so the entire time, because we have not yet earned that stewardship.

"The Watchers and their children," he continued, "seek to claim it for themselves, and that is not part of the plan given to us by the Word. It was meant to be connected to this world, to be used by all, but we have failed. This world is dying. And to abandon it would be unconscionable. It would not be"—he glanced at Charles—"Taking Care."

"It is not our failure!" Rao exclaimed. "When the Adam was given responsibility to govern this world, he divided the responsibility equally between the Imago and the Archimago. And we have all seen how that turned out.

"But," he added, "in one thing you are correct. It *is* a divided world. We seek to do the same as you advocate, and unite it again."

"By allowing this world to perish first, and for your own purposes, Rao," Samaranth said, "and not to serve the peoples of this world, who will live or die based on what we decide here today."

"There is another way," a new voice said, which silenced the entire chamber. The Jade Empress had spoken. "There is still a chance to save this world, to end the drought that has plagued it and restore it to the state it was in at the time of the Adam."

She reached into one of her sleeves and withdrew a single, perfect red rose. On it were three dewdrops that shone with a light so brilliant that it reflected through the entire room.

"No!" Rao hissed at her. "Not now!"

Once more the assembly erupted in whisperings and murmurings over what was a clear violation of protocol.

"What is this . . . ?" Samaranth murmured. He and Sycorax exchanged bewildered glances, and both looked back to the star, then again to the empress. Rose followed their glances and realized that underneath the flowing robes, T'ai Shan was wearing armor. The Ruby Armor.

"Ah," Samaranth said. "I think at last I understand." He closed his eyes and bowed his head, and a wave of energy seemed to ripple outward from him, touching every attendee of the summit, including Charles.

"Rao gave the empress his fire," he whispered to Rose and

Edmund, "just as in the story Lord Winter told us in the far future. She used the star's fire to forge the armor that she needed to find the talisman—a rose—that held the power to end the great drought. I think," he added, "that the wheels are about to come off the apple cart."

"You have no jurisdiction over our children, Samaranth," one of the Nephilim said brusquely. "Not while you reside in the City of Jade. Only here, within these walls, may you dictate what will or will not happen. Out there, we—and our offspring—are free."

A hue and cry rose up from the rest of the Nephilim, led by Salathiel, followed by equal cries of outrage and fervor from the principalities.

For his part, Rao had already begun dashing up one of the stairs, focused entirely on the Jade Empress. She watched him advancing, and the look of sadness on her face was wrenching. He had nearly reached the dais when she stood . . .

. . . and dropped the rose, and the dewdrops, directly into the circle of flames below, which exploded with light. In seconds, the entire room erupted into chaos.

The Watcher Salathiel lifted a huge, curved golden trumpet and sounded a note that rang out so loudly that it seemed as if the walls would shatter.

"Og! Ogias!" he called out. "Gog and Magog! Orestes and Fafnir! All you who are the grandsons of the Fallen angel Samhazi! I summon you to my side! Aid us, my children!"

"Fallen!" Samaranth exclaimed. "They have Named themselves as Fallen! This changes it all! We have to leave, now!"

◆ ◆ ◆

As the note had promised, Naming Madoc as a Nephilim did indeed allow the *Indigo Dragon* and all its passengers to pass by the wall of giants unmolested. But the relief the companions felt was short-lived, because as they flew past the immense limbs, the giants suddenly turned and began to stride purposefully toward the city.

Decades of dust and decay that had built up on the motionless bodies of the giants suddenly scattered and fell, forming a dust cloud that filled the air for hundreds of feet, and which stretched for fifty miles.

"What did we do?" a horrified Laura Glue said as the shadows of the giants covered them, and Madoc and Quixote both moved protectively closer to her and the badgers.

"I don't think we did anything," said Madoc. "They aren't focused on us, they're focused on the city itself."

"Well, whatever is going on," Fred said, shading his face to look up at the giants, "I bet Kipling has something t' do with it."

The great building where the summit had been held was a madhouse of frantic activity. Of the empress, there was no sign; Rao and the stars were also gone, as were several of the principalities. Only the Nephilim and certain of the Seraphim remained where they stood, as if waiting for something.

"The giants are coming for them," Samaranth said numbly. "They intend to go to the Un-Made World to try to Name it before the destruction comes."

"What?" Charles said, startled. "What destruction?"

"The empress dropped the Tears of Heaven into the Creative Fire," Samaranth replied, still in shock for reasons the companions still did not fully understand. "Everything is about to change now!"

"Because of a single rose?" asked Edmund. "I don't understand."

"Everything that is made is conceptual first," Samaranth explained as he led them back up the stairs, which were crowded with other angels also trying to leave. "Then we . . . create the thing to be made. We give it form, and substance. But then, to put it out into the world, the made thing is placed in the Creative Fire, and from then it multiplies."

"So we'll have a lot of roses to deal with," said Edmund.

"You don't understand!" Samaranth said, whirling about and grabbing the young man in the first physical act the companions had seen him perform. "That flower contained three dewdrops, but not of just any water! They were the Tears of Heaven, and they will multiply a millionfold, a billionfold. More. More."

"Oh dear," said Charles.

"Yes," Samaranth said. "Within the day, the entire world will be covered with a great flood, and there is nothing any of us can do to stop it."

A brilliant light burst upward from one of the largest buildings in the center of the city, briefly illuminating everything around Kipling as he ran. Something was afoot, and he suddenly realized that he might have very little time left to accomplish his task.

He stopped and leaned against a wall, panting. It gave him a moment to both catch his breath and consider what he was being asked to do. It made sense, in some twisted way, but he still was not certain he could trust what it said. At least one person he knew of—one of Verne's Messengers—would die in the future because of what he was being asked to do now. But it also made sense.

It was, in the grand scheme of things, logical. And, he was a bit ashamed to admit, it appealed to his sense of gamesmanship.

It meant that he might never leave the city—but it also meant that he might give the Caretakers the means to defeat not just Dr. Dee, but the Echthroi as well. And in the end, that was what mattered most.

Looking over the angelic script in the note for the umpteenth time, Kipling screwed up his courage and once more began to run. If he timed it properly, the Cherubim would be somewhere near that explosion of light, and in the confusion that was beginning to spread outward into the streets, it would never be missed until Dr. Dee found it.

"The Great Deluge," Charles sputtered as Samaranth led them back to his Library. "The flood. The destruction of the world. It's really happening, isn't it?" He took off his glasses and rubbed his forehead.

"Have you got a headache?" asked Edmund.

"No," said Charles. "Tulpas don't *get* headaches, but I think one would actually make me feel *better* right now."

"What are we going to do?" asked Rose. "What can anyone do?"

"There are hierarchies of the Host of Heaven," said Samaranth, "each with its own set of responsibilities. The stars are given the task of shaping and preparing the worlds that revolve around them, but have little concern for the creatures who evolve, live, and die on those worlds. The angels are given the task of creating and Naming the higher aspects of the world, to allow the creatures on it to develop and ascend themselves. But there is an office between the two that is rarely called upon, and rarely chosen, because it carries the responsibility of directly overseeing the welfare of all the living creatures on a particular world."

"Why is it rarely chosen?" Rose asked.

"Because," Samaranth answered, "as you witnessed, the stars are reluctant to take so much responsibility upon themselves. They prefer the bigger-picture things, like the formation of mountains and the rise of oceans. The concerns of the Sons of Adam and the Daughters of Eve, and the affairs of the Children of the Earth, are of little concern to them, and so they will almost always decline the choice to ascend."

"But our star, Sol, wanted to ascend," said Edmund. "Why couldn't he?"

"Because other stars would have also needed to do so," said Samaranth, "and Rao is oldest among them, so his decision binds them all. It takes the complete commitment of one's heart, and aiua, to ascend," he continued, looking now at Rose. "You know this. I can see it in your countenance."

"Then this world may truly be lost," Rose said despairingly. "If the stars will not ascend, what is left? What can be done?"

"Just because Rao has abandoned the care of this world does not mean the world is without its . . . Caretakers," Samaranth said. For the first time, his voice seemed to be breaking with an emotion that none of the angels in the city had displayed. "There are none here in the city willing to ascend—but the elder angels can still descend to the office necessary to look after this world. We can still choose," he finished, his words more of a struggle now, "to become *Dragons*."

Part Four

The Deluge

The beasts were tended to by smaller creatures . . .

Chapter Thirteen

Reunion

It was a caravan of worlds, and it stretched across the dunes from one horizon to the other. The great creatures that carried the lands of the Archipelago and all the peoples who lived in them were perhaps distant cousins to the Feast Beasts that served meals at Tamerlane House, reimagined for a more massive duty. They resembled the offspring of camels that had been successfully courted by horned toads the size of elephants, and in place of humps were immense glass spheres, each of which contained the past, present, and future of a land from the Archipelago of Dreams.

The beasts were tended to by smaller creatures of the earth, who had been given the task by the leader of the caravan: the last true Caretaker of the Archipelago itself. When the Archipelago fell to Shadow, it was he who gathered up all the lands and peoples and transported them here, where they could make their way to safe haven until the world could be made right again. "Have they been given water?" he asked. "The heat is terrible today."

"Henry is takin' care o' that," said his First Assistant Dragon, a badger called Tummeler. "I've made him, ah, my assistant, if'n that's keen by you."

Samaranth looked at the badger in surprise. "The guinea pig?

Hrrrmm," he rumbled. "Is it really wise to entrust such a large task to such a small creature?"

"You of all, uh, people ought t' know," Tummeler said, admonishing, "that size is irrelevant. 'Ceptin' when it comes to stuff like actually hauling stuff, like entire islands from th' Archipelago. Then it pays t' be big—but we got creatures t' do that, so Henry is just perfect t' leave in charge as a supervisor. My point being—"

"I understand, little friend," said the great Dragon. "Better than you realize."

He looked back at the caravan and thought about the thousands and thousands of lives, and the history, and the culture, and most importantly, the stories that had been preserved by his actions. He looked at the badger, who had been a hero in the old Archipelago, and one of those a Dragon might actually call friend. And he remembered those who had been left behind.

"I wish . . ." Tummeler began, sensing the old Dragon's thoughts. He stopped, whiskers quivering, and looked up at Samaranth. "I wish we had been able t' bring Miss Aven with us," he said sadly. "I wish she didn't have t' stay behind, all alone."

"She wasn't alone," Samaranth replied, "but more importantly, she knew it was necessary. Someone needed to tell the Caretakers what had happened, so that events could proceed the way that they must."

"And have they?" Tummeler asked, looking back along the caravan of beasts. "We have been out here, wandering around with th' whole of the Archipelago on our backs, for . . ." He paused and did some figures in his head. "I really don't know. How long have we been out here, anyway? It feels like we been wandering for forty years."

Samaranth chuckled, but it sounded like the rasping of a rusty engine. "That was an entirely different exile story, little Child of the

Earth," he said. "We are no longer in any place that follows Chronos time, so it is all relative. But if I were to hazard a guess, I would say . . .

". . . that we have been gone from the waters of the Archipelago of Dreams for less than a month. Maybe two."

"Really?" Tummeler said, eyes wide. "If'n you'd asked me, I'da said we been taking care of th' Archipelago forever."

Samaranth made a rumbling noise in his chest and rose to his feet. "So would I, little Tummeler," he said, suddenly feeling the weight of his own history. "So would I."

Madoc being mistaken for a Nephilim didn't create more difficulty moving through the city; in fact, it seemed to be clearing a path for the companions as the flying goats drew the airship between the towers and deep into the heart of the city.

Angels with the ability to fly headed in the opposite direction as soon as the airship drew close and Madoc's wings became visible; and those below on the streets took shelter in whatever structure was closest and seemed to be avoiding even being touched by the *Indigo Dragon*'s shadow as it passed.

"They seem to be clearing a path for us," Quixote said as he peered over the side. "That is good, no?"

"No," said Laura Glue, pointing back in the direction from which they'd come. "It isn't us they're clearing a path for."

The giants had begun stepping over the river estuary, having crossed the miles of desert between themselves and the city in a matter of minutes. They seemed to be converging on a single huge building in the center of the city—and were leaving destruction in their wake as they passed.

"We never should have let Kipling go on his own," Madoc

fumed. "Now we have four missing people to find!"

"You forget," Fred said, removing his Caretaker's watch, "the Anabasis Machines may not be as useful for time travel these days, but I can still use mine to contact another Caretaker."

Swiftly the badger spun the dials in the necessary order, then waited. A few moments later it chimed. He read the message and frowned.

"He says that everything is fine, but he has t' run an errand before we can come get him," Fred told the others, "and he said we should go find Rose, Charles, and Edmund."

Uncas and Quixote exchanged puzzled glances. "What does *that* mean?" Uncas exclaimed. "'Run an errand.'"

Madoc raised an eyebrow, less concerned about the errand than his missing daughter. "He found them? He knows where they are?"

Fred shrugged. "He said we just need t' go where the biggest explosions are."

"Bangarang!" said Laura Glue.

"It figures," said Uncas, pulling on the reins to turn the airship. "Head for the smoke, girls."

Driven by no other compulsion save for the Summoning that drew them, the Corinthian Giants were destroying the City of Jade simply by walking through it. Towers were falling; entire boulevards were crushed. Everywhere angels were fleeing, not realizing that soon there would be nowhere to flee to. No shelter would be adequate to protect them from the coming flood. The elder angels realized this, as did one other.

Deucalion stood at the prow of his massive ship, watching the chaos from afar. The departure of the giants had created a frenzy among the refugees who had lived for generations in the encampments below. Thousands saw the removal of the wall of giants as an invitation to invade the city themselves. Others realized it for what it was: a shift in the world. A change of global proportions. And so they simply waited, and went about their business. Some were weeping; others sought solace in prayer. And all of them were doomed to die.

"Not this day," the old shipbuilder murmured to no one in particular as his youngest son came running up the deck.

"We've nearly secured them all, Father," Hap said, breathless. "All the animals are accounted for and in their places."

"Good," Deucalion said, still looking out toward the city. "Tell me, we still have a great deal of room herein, do we not?"

Hap nodded. "Lots. It's a very big boat, Father."

Deucalion turned and put his hands on his son's shoulders. "Do you know that boy we have broken bread with? The quiet one?"

Hap nodded again. "Enkidu. I know him."

"Find him," Deucalion said. "Find him, and tell him to run among the peoples of the encampment. Tell them something terrible is about to happen—but all those who wish it may take shelter on our ship. If they do not wish to come, or they have their own means to survive a great flood, so be it. But make sure the offer is known."

"To all the humans?" asked Hap.

"Not just the humans," his father replied. "There are other races as well—and I would not deny them if they chose to come.

"All who wish it will find shelter here," Deucalion said, turning back to the railing, "for as long as we can give it."

* * *

The elders of the angels, mostly Cherubim but also including a few Seraphim, were gathering together far from the center of the city, on the westernmost edge, where the terraces and towers looked out over the sea.

Rose, Charles, and Edmund followed Samaranth back to his Library, where he remained only long enough to retrieve a few items. It appeared to Rose that the objects he chose were more out of sentimental value than practicality—but then again, it was hard to imagine an angel being sentimental, so she assumed the things he gathered together had some sort of meaningful purpose.

"There is no stopping it now," Samaranth said, addressing those who had assembled at one of the towers. "The waters will come, and they will all but destroy this world. But they will also cleanse it and restore it to the state it was in before it was severed from the Un-Made World. But now," he continued, his face a mask of incredible sadness, "we must do what the Nephilim and the principalities had wanted all along, and separate the worlds as definitively as we can. If we can preserve as much from this world there as possible, then both may be rebuilt. And perhaps," he added, briefly glancing back at Rose, "someday both may be reconnected, and restored, as the Word intended from the beginning."

He turned to the angels. "Seven are needed for this. Seven, and the world will be divided—and protected."

There was no hesitation. Seven Seraphim—four female and three male—stepped forward and bowed their heads to Samaranth. He moved to each of them in turn, whispering words meant only for them, then embracing them. All the Seraphim appeared older than Samaranth, so it was an unusual sight to see grown men and women being comforted by a youth—but then again, Rose especially understood how appearances were not necessarily reality.

Samaranth stood back from the Seraphim and raised his hands. "I release you from your covenants," he said, voice cracking, "but not from this life. Go forth, and guard the Un-Made World, as your brethren guarded the Garden, and guard it still."

The Seraphim drew swords of flame and raised them to their lips. Then they began to expand. Swiftly the angels became giants, and as they grew they changed: They became less corporeal and more intangible, and they took on the appearance of massive thunderheads. The flaming swords became lightning; and the cries of the Seraphim as they left the life they knew became the thunder.

In moments the seven angels had become a dark wall of storms, which moved past the city and out over the water.

"The Frontier," Charles breathed.

"As good a name as any," Samaranth said. His face was red from the angst and great strain he was feeling, but his expression was once again resolute. "None will pass, save they are given the Mandate of Heaven. A vessel touched by divinity may cross, but none other. And no Fallen may cross over, unless given passage by one of us here. And that," he said with finality, "is *never* going to occur."

In the distance, more crashing and explosions could be heard, and the Corinthian Giants loomed over the eastern horizon like a counterpoint to the Frontier the angels had created. "They may survive," Samaranth said, "but their parents will not. Nor will any of the principalities who sided with the Nephilim. Fortunately, some have proven wiser than others."

He gestured at the assembly, and the companions realized he

was correct—a number of the younger gods were present, and appeared to have sided with Samaranth. Odin was there, and young Zeus, and the god Prometheus, who still carried the staff of fire.

"The Nephilim have gone," said Odin, "along with the star Rao, to do battle with the Jade Empress."

"I know where her power comes from," said Samaranth. "It will be a terrible battle, which she may lose. But it will give us the time we need. . . . Just enough, I think."

"There is one Nephilim still in the city," Prometheus said, "although he seems to be allied with at least one Seraphim and some members of an unknown principality. He is not flying himself, but is traveling in a flying vessel being drawn by goats."

A huge smile spread over Rose's face. "Does that sound like a Caretaker operation to you?" she asked, beaming.

"It certainly does," said Charles. "Look!"

The *Indigo Dragon* had just rounded one of the towers, avoiding flying directly through the smoke now billowing up from the giants' path. A shrill cheer sounded from Laura Glue as she spotted her long-missing friends.

Rose had expected some sort of rescue party and was not surprised to see Uncas, Fred, Laura Glue, and Quixote—but she was completely taken aback when the airship landed and her father stepped to the ground.

"Hello, Rose," he said, simply and plainly. "I've come a very long way to find you, girl."

Kipling looked up at the ornate sculpture standing at the intersection and sighed heavily. It was exactly where the note said it would be—which meant that any moment now . . .

His jaw dropped open as the Cherubim approached. He had not realized, had not understood until this moment, that he knew this angel—not in the same form, but close enough to be familiar. Close enough to recognize.

Close enough to feel regret, even as he stepped out into the street to do what he knew he must.

The Cherubim stopped, momentarily distracted by the markings that were still on Kipling's forehead.

"You are not of the Host," the angel said, confused. "Are you of one of the principalities?"

"I'm sorry," Kipling said, and without a pause, he began to recite the words on the note, beginning with the true name of the angel before him.

It took only a few minutes to complete his task, and when he was done, the Cherubim walked away, slightly dazed, to the spot three blocks away where he would be confronted by someone else, who would repeat almost the same process Kipling had performed. Just the thought of it made Kipling sick to his stomach, and he turned and vomited against a wall. Then he walked to one of the towers, away from the destruction being done by the Watchers and their children, and found a nice fountain to sit beside, and silently, he wept.

. . . his reflection was no longer that of a young man . . .

Chapter Fourteen

The First Dragon

The reunion was joyful, but brief. Rose hugged her father in astonishment as both badgers jumped gleefully on Charles, and Edmund wrapped Laura Glue in a passionate embrace, which he punctuated with a long kiss.

"I say," Quixote chuckled, "this is like witnessing the best ending to a fairy tale you never expected to finish."

"First things first," Charles said. "There's a lot happening that we need to tell you about."

"Like the flood about t' destroy the world?" asked Uncas. "We're on top of that."

"That isn't the most urgent business," said Fred. "Rose is."

"Me?" Rose asked. "What do you mean?"

"That," Madoc said, pointing to her shadow. "It isn't yours, Rose! The Echthroi have been following you everywhere!"

At the mention of Echthroi all the angels stopped, and their eyes glowed. "She is Fallen?" one of them asked, fearful. "There is a Fallen among us?"

"Not her," Fred said, moving defensively in front of Rose. "Just her shadow—which isn't hers."

Rose spun about to look and was horrified to see that her shadow did not turn with her. Instead it seemed to thicken, rising up and growing larger and larger, until . . .

A hand reached out to the wall and grasped the shadow.

"I'm sorry," the star Sol said to Rose. "I'm afraid this will hurt." He pulled, and ripped the shadow free from her with a single motion. Rose screamed and fell backward as her father leaped forward to catch her.

As if sensing its imminent end, the shadow thrashed about frantically, but Sol simply held it, watching.

"There can be no shadows without light," he said plainly. "So as there are shadows here, so let there be light." He flared, bright and brief, and the companions had to shield their eyes. When they could again see, the shadow was gone.

A few streets away, closer to the center of the city, Dr. Dee screamed and dropped to his knees. His primary link with this time and place had suddenly been severed, and the loss was taking a sudden and vicious toll.

He focused on breathing deeply and slowly, and in a few moments, he regained much of his strength, if not his composure. If the shadow—which had been Lovecraft's—had been destroyed, then he had enemies other than Kipling wandering through the City of Jade. But Kipling was still bound hand and foot in Hermes Trismegistus's study, and Dee knew from the Histories of the Caretakers that he would perish in the cataclysm, so it had to be someone else who'd destroyed the shadow.

No matter, Dee thought. He had what he came to the city to find. This had been the last moment in history where angels could be found walking the same streets as men—and now one of them had been bound to serve Dee.

Bound to serve the Echthroi.

Smiling wryly, Dee removed the black pocket watch he wore and spun the dials. An instant later, he was gone.

Rose looked down at her feet and exhaled, relieved. Her own shadow had returned.

"I'm sorry," Sol said again, this time to Samaranth. "If I could ascend, I would. But Rao . . ."

"I understand," said Samaranth. "You have done all you can. It is time for you to leave, Sol. Watch over us. Warm us. Be a guide to us. And never forget."

"I won't," Sol said. And then he was gone.

Other Cherubim had drawn closer to the companions to watch the star destroy the shadow, but one in particular, a stern-countenanced female, was whispering angrily into Samaranth's ear. He nodded once, then again, and whispered something back to her before they both turned to face the companions.

Rose suppressed a shudder when she realized who this angel was—and that they had met before.

"Yes," Charles said quietly. "I remember too, Rose."

Before the companions traveled further back in time to arrive at the City of Jade, they had been in ancient Greece, where they met Medea, the wife of the legendary hero Jason, and her familiar, a green-gold Dragon named . . .

"Azer," Samaranth said by way of introduction. "My wife."

"I beg your pardon," Charles said, trying to regain his composure, "but I had no idea that angels could marry."

"It is the way of things," Samaranth said, "to organize into families. In fact, we were thinking about having a child together, in another billion years or so. But," he added, with a sudden immeasurable sadness, "that may not be possible—not after this."

"I will never forgive you for this," Azer said through clenched teeth. "Know that, Samaranth. Never. You said descent would never be necessary."

The sadness in Samaranth's face was almost tangible. "We have a responsibility, my wife. One we accepted long, long ago. You, I, and . . ." He craned his neck, scanning the faces of the Cherubim.

"Who are you looking for?" one of the angels asked.

"Shaitan," Samaranth replied. "Among the Host, he is the one who is most like . . ." He turned and gestured at Charles and Edmund. "As these Sons of Adam and Daughters of Eve are. A . . . friend? I had expected him to be here."

"There have been a great many things happening today," the angel replied. "If Shaitan could have come, he would."

"No matter," Samaranth said. "We are out of time."

The angels gathered around an enormous circle of water on the terrace outside the tower. It extended out past the cliffs on which the city was built, over the ocean. "The Moon Pool," Samaranth said. "In it are the tears of the mother of us all, called Idyl, who gave birth to the world when the Word was spoken. With this pool of water, we can choose, and change, and descend."

"It's like a larger version of Echo's Well, on the Lost Boys' island in the Archipelago," Charles said to the others. "Jack used it once, years ago, to make himself younger," he explained, "because in his heart, he was still enough of a boy to become so in reality. He believed himself to be young, and young he became. I think this is something similar."

"It was touched by the Word," said Samaranth, "like the Creative Fire, and it changes not our Names, but our Being. Who we are is the same, but we will be Remade, so that the world may be saved."

He stepped forward and leaned over the pool. A lock of his red hair fell over his eyes, and he pushed it back as he stared at his own reflection.

In rightness's name
For need of might,
I thus descend
I thus descend

By blood bound
By honor given
I thus descend
I thus descend

For strength and speed and heaven's power
To serve below in this dark hour
I thus descend
I thus descend

Even as he had started to speak the words, the change had begun. Eddies of light began to swirl about the small, lithe form of the angel Samaranth, changing him as they watched. Without taking his eyes off his reflection in the glistening pool, he grew tall and broad; his flesh turned red, and wings sprouted from his back even as he was growing a tail. In short order, as the echo of the last words faded, his reflection was no longer that of a young man, but of the great Dragon Samaranth.

Of all the reunited companions, Uncas was the one who had known all the Dragonships in their glory, and he thrilled at the sight of those familiar visages appearing as, one by one, Samaranth's companions invoked the change.

"There's th' Red Dragon!" he said excitedly. "And th' Blue Dragon! And Green!" He turned to Quixote. "That one was all'ays a bit temper'mental."

"Amazing, isn't it?" Edmund said to Rose. "It's the most extraordinary thing I've ever witnessed!" He looked up at Madoc. "Uh, except your transformation. That was most excellent also."

Madoc didn't respond. He was watching Rose, and the tears in her eyes mirrored his own.

"This is where their lives as Dragons began," she said softly. "And I remember where they ended—I just wish I could forget."

Fred hugged her leg in sympathy. In one of the greatest battles of the Archipelago, all the Dragon shadows had been turned to serve a new master: the Shadow of the Winter King, her father, when he was known as Mordred. The only way to release the Dragons was for her to sever the shadows' link to the earth with the sword Caliburn—but that also meant the end of the Dragons' days as guardians of the Archipelago.

"It is not your fault," Madoc whispered to her as he hesitantly reached out to take her hand. "It was mine. My choices brought about their end. Not yours."

She didn't reply, or look at him—but she didn't let go of his hand, either.

It went more quickly than any of them could have expected, this transformation of angels into Dragons. But when it was complete, the terrace and the sky above the tower were filled with them.

"Uh, Samaranth?" Fred said, hesitant to address the Dragon directly, but doing so anyway. "I want to ask—out there, in the desert, there is a huge ship. On it are all the Children of the Earth."

"The animals," Samaranth rumbled. "We had made no provisions for them. . . ." He stopped, realizing what the little badger had actually said. "They are all on a ship, you say?"

Fred nodded so enthusiastically the others thought his head might fly off. "Several of every kind," he said, "gathered together by Ordo Maas. Uh, I mean, Deucalion. Or, uh, Utnapishtim."

"Ah," the Dragon responded, with what seemed to be a smile. "The old king from the Empty Quarter. I had wondered what it was he was building out there." He gestured with one hand and summoned another Dragon, a giant creature with the aspect of a cat in his countenance.

"Kerubiel," Samaranth told the Dragon. "Go, find the ship, and make certain it crosses over safely."

"Samaranth," the god Prometheus implored, "that . . . is my son. There are things he will need, things he must be given." He gestured at the flame. "May I accompany the Dragon?"

Kerubiel did not speak, but simply nodded at Prometheus. The god climbed atop the Dragon, who launched himself into the air and winged his way at top speed toward the desert.

"Thank you," said Fred. "That's very gentlemanly of you to do."

"It will take a long time for this world to recover," Samaranth told the companions, "but when it does, it can be as it once was, as the Garden was, in the beginning."

"Yes," said Madoc. "It will be the true Summer Country."

"The Summer Country," Samaranth said, growling in satisfaction. "So mote it be, little Namer. So mote it be, little king."

Madoc stared, shocked at the title. "I am no king, Samaranth," he murmured back, "as you will discover for yourself, in time."

At this, the Dragon rose up to his full, terrifying height and began to beat his wings to rise aloft. Even Rose flinched at the looming sight of the red Dragon. "I am a Namer, little king, and I know my own. You may not be a king in fact, but you have it in your countenance to be. You have it within you. Just remember—a king who commands by force may rule, but a king who is followed because he is loved, and trusted, will rule forever."

The Dragon turned to the rest of the former Host and indicated that it was time to leave, to attend to the responsibilities they had just taken on.

"Samaranth, wait!" Charles exclaimed. "I want to ask you something. Please!"

The great Dragon lowered himself to the ground and a growl rumbled deep inside his chest. "What is it, little Son of Adam?"

Charles shuddered inwardly and realized suddenly that this might not have been the wisest thing to do. This was not the old, tempered, world-wise Samaranth he'd met as a young Caretaker-to-be. This was a newborn Dragon, who had just sacrificed his life as an angel of the Host of Heaven in order to create the Archipelago and safeguard the entire world. Still, he couldn't help himself—he had to ask.

"The book," said Charles, "the one my colleagues call the *Telos Biblos*. It contains all the names of those angels who became Dragons—except for yours."

Samaranth leaned closer, exhaling hot breath into the Caretaker's face, and his eyes narrowed.

"To ask one's true name is to try to have power over them," the Dragon hissed, "and it is not advisable that you ask anything further."

"I don't mean to offend," Charles sputtered, slightly terrified but unwilling to let the opportunity pass. "I am a scholar of heaven, and angelic doings, and I know many of the names of the angels, uh, I mean Dragons," he corrected quickly, "but I never heard of any angel named Samaranth. And I know that that is not your true name."

"How can you know that?"

"Because," Charles said, "in another place, and another time, someone who serves the Shadows does something . . . something terrible, to your kind. And you are spared, because your name is not in the book. I don't want any power over you, of any kind. I just want to know. You don't know me now, but someday you will—and you will trust me. In the name of that trust, I—I just want to know."

Samaranth reared up on his hind legs and looked at the man before him. The Caretaker was afraid, but only because the aspect of the Dragon was terrifying—not because he feared Samaranth himself. There was trust, somehow.

"I will tell you," Samaranth said, again leaning close, "and with the name, a small Binding, so that it cannot be shared with another."

Charles nodded. "Fair enough."

The Dragon whispered into the Caretaker's ear, and Charles's eyes widened in surprise. "You—you . . . ?" he stammered as the Dragon moved back and prepared to take flight. "You are *that* angel?"

"I am not the eldest of the Host, but I am the eldest among those here, on this world," said Samaranth, "and my name has not been spoken since the dawn of creation. Even then, it was only to summon me to do my first task, which was necessary to do before anything else could be created or Named.

"Since that time, I had simply been known as the Lightbringer to those of my kind, and as Samaranth to those younger races of the earth. And now, as a Dragon, it is Samaranth I shall remain . . .

". . . until the end of time itself."

With no further farewell, the Dragon beat his mighty wings and lifted into the air. In moments, he was gone.

Chapter Fifteen
The Maker

As the Caretakers at Tamerlane House watched the great red Dragon soar away with the hundreds of newly born Dragons into the darkness of the newly made Frontier, the whirling pages of the Last Book began to darken and crumble apart. In moments, the images they had been watching so keenly faded completely, and once more the room went dark.

John turned to Poe, who had not moved from the doorway the entire time they had been watching the visions of Atlantis and the Dragons. "What happens now?" he demanded. "We need to keep watching!"

"We cannot," Poe replied. "The book gave us a window into the events that were witnessed by its author, and this was the end of his record. Thus, there is no more to observe."

"The author?" asked Jack. "But I thought the Last Book was written by—"

"The *Telos Biblos*," said Poe, "was written by Samaranth himself, in the days after the founding of the Archipelago, when one by one, he named all those from the Host of the City of Jade who followed him and became Dragons, but it is not the oldest history. There is one older still, which John Dee never acquired nor stole,

. . . everything around them glowed with pulsing, vibrant, living lights . . .

because it was never given to the safekeeping of anyone else other than him who wrote it."

"An older history?" John said, confused. "But I want to know what happens next! We know that our friends are safe—or at least, they were—but how can we discover what's become of them with an older history?"

"Because," said Poe, "their journey is not yet finished, and their quest to find the Architect must lead them deeper into the past before they can come back to the future."

"Hmm. All right," John said. "Is this book in the Repository, then? I don't remember ever seeing it."

"It has never been in the Repository," Poe said as he reached inside his breast pocket, "because it has never left my person."

The other Caretakers rose from their seats to look at the curious, small book that Poe was holding. It was very, very old, compact but thick, and resembled nothing so much as it did . . .

"The Little Whatsits." Twain chortled. "It looks like those bloody annoying books of genius and wisdom the badgers refer to all the time."

"The thing is," Bert said, "the information in the Little Whatsits is almost always spot-on."

"That," said Twain, "is precisely why those books are so bloody annoying."

"It is indeed much like the Little Whatsits," Poe said, "in that inside its pages is an accounting of all the knowledge of the world that once was. A world that was smaller, and seemingly simpler, and never to be known again except in stories."

"How did you find this book, Edgar?" Houdini asked.

"I didn't find it," Poe answered, "I *wrote* it.

"Now," he said, stepping out into the hallway and beckoning the others to follow, "gather everyone together. *Everyone.* All the Caretakers, and Mystorians, and Messengers; all the helpers, and apprentices, and associates. Everyone at Tamerlane House should attend, because I'm going to do a *reading*—one I have waited to do since the beginning of the world.

"It is time," the master of the house said, "for *all* the secrets of history to be revealed."

"What, pray tell," Charles exclaimed, "did you do to the poor *Indigo Dragon*?" He walked around the airship, fondly caressing the battered hull and once-living masthead he knew so well. He and his colleagues John and Jack had shared some amazing adventures aboard this ship, and it pained him to see it made so . . .

"Short," he said, bending over to examine it more closely. "And it's got wheels. Sweet heaven, old girl—what have they done to you?"

"It was kind of necessary," said Fred. "We needed something that could go anywhere, do anything. And the *Indigo Dragon* has been the greatest Dragonship there ever was."

"Meh," said Elly Mae.

"Mahhh!" said Coraline.

"Flying goats," Charles said, shaking his head. "The more things change, the more they, well, change."

"We need to get out of here," Rose said anxiously. "The city is coming apart, and the deluge can't be far away."

"Not yet," said Madoc. "Kipling is still—"

"Right here," a weary Rudyard Kipling said as he stepped off the staircase and onto the broad plaza where the companions were. "Sorry to have kept you waiting."

Rose ran to him, giving him a hug, and Edmund greeted him with a warm double handshake—but Charles realized immediately that something was wrong.

"Rudy, old boy," he said, his face showing open concern. "What is it? What's happened?"

Kipling sighed. "I'm not coming with you."

That stopped all of them, even the goats. "Muh?" said Elly Mae.

"I've been . . . compromised," said Kipling. "I can't—shouldn't—go with you."

It was Madoc who realized what had happened. "Your shadow," he said with a twinge of old sorrow in his voice. "It's missing, Caretaker."

Laura Glue and the badgers stared at him, dumbfounded. "What," the Valkyrie said, "did you *do*?"

Kipling looked pained, but he managed to smile anyway. "I did something terrible that had to be done. At least," he added, fishing in his pocket, "I hope it did."

He withdrew a small envelope identical to the ones that Deucalion had given to Uncas and Fred. The companions rapidly exchanged anecdotes and arrived at the same conclusion.

"Telemachus has made his choice," said Fred. "He's decided to join the side of the, um, angels. So to speak."

"Maybe not," said Charles, "if he's also giving instructions that cost Caretakers their shadows."

Rose, for her part, was still pained by what Fred and her father had shared with her about the true identity of their possible adversary. She still remembered the lost little boy prince, Coal, far too vividly to easily accept that he had been one of Verne's Messengers in disguise, was a possible apprentice to John Dee, and might be the Archimago destined to hand the entire world over to the Echthroi.

"We'll find a way to help you," she said, almost pleading. It felt terrible to contemplate leaving him there after finally seeing some hope—especially with what they all knew was going to happen. "Please, come with us."

"It's too risky," Kipling said. "Ask Madoc. He knows."

Reluctantly Madoc looked at his daughter and nodded. "If he is now shadowless, then he lost it by his own choice, by his own actions, as Jack once did," he explained, "and that leaves him vulnerable, as you were. If an Echthros somehow manages to use him as a conduit, then they can follow us anywhere. John Dee already gained access to the City of Jade because of the shadow that you didn't know had come with you. If we were to find the Architect, and an Echthros was with us . . ."

Madoc didn't need to finish the statement. Every one of them knew Kipling was right. He would have to stay.

"Edmund," Kipling said, "before you go, may I have a word?"

As the two men talked, the others readied the *Indigo Dragon* for the flight out and tried their best not to feel the despair that was all too present.

"All right," Edmund said when they stepped back over to the ship. "We need to leave now." This last he said with a wink at Kipling that only Madoc saw. The Dragon furrowed his brow but said nothing as the others all hugged Kipling and said tearful good-byes.

"One last thing," Kipling asked. "Fly me up to the tallest tower still standing. The show is going to be spectacular, and I'd like to have a really good seat."

• • •

As the reunited companions took flight up and out of the doomed City of Jade, Fred and Laura Glue explained how they had traveled there using Shakespeare's Zanzibar Gate, and also, less enthusiastically, explained what its limitations were.

"*Three trips?*" Rose exclaimed. "That's all we get?"

"Two now," said Fred. "We used up one to come find you."

"Just one, actually," Uncas said, trying to be helpful, "because now we have to go home before we can go out again. And whoever goes on *that* trip . . ."

"Will basically be in the same boat—so to speak—that Charles and Edmund and I were in the last time," said Rose. "But we aren't going to do that."

"We aren't?" said Fred.

"We aren't?" Uncas and Quixote said together.

"No," Rose said, a determined smile on her face. "After what you told us about Deucalion's great-grandfather, Enoch, I'm convinced that he is the man we're seeking. If we can get to him and restore the keep, then we won't need to worry about how to manage a return trip."

"One problem," said Edmund. "According to Verne, the rules of time travel say we must take a trip into the future to balance every trip into the past. Won't we be causing some kind of temporal problem if we don't do just that?"

"Verne lies," Rose replied. "I think the rules about time travel are more fluid than he'll ever tell us, if he can help it. Besides, we came further back again getting here without a counterbalancing trip to the future."

"Because we had help, remember?" Edmund said. "The old man in Platonia—the one who sent Bert back to Tamerlane."

Rose scanned the sky as if waiting for help from above. "I wish he'd step in to help us now—or at least, let us know we're moving in the right direction."

"Couldn't Edmund simply create another chronal map?" Quixote suggested. "That way, we wouldn't be using up the power in the gate."

"I tried it, back in the city," Edmund said sheepishly. "It didn't work. Whatever damage has affected the keep in this time is also affecting my ability to make chronal maps. If I have a machine to augment it, it could work. Hopefully."

"We do have the gate," Fred said helpfully, "and it's designed to use a chronal map. That's how we got here."

"That's the second problem," said Edmund. "I can program the gate, but I have no clue where we're going, since we don't even have a vague description of the City of Enoch."

"We have this," Fred offered, holding up the bronze bas-relief of Enoch. "It's a pretty good likeness, I think. You could make a chronal map to take us through the gate directly to him."

"I really don't know," said Edmund. "I've always created maps to places and specific times. I really have no idea whether it will work if we try to use it to take us to a specific person."

"I don't think we have much of a choice," Charles said, hooking a thumb over his shoulder at the city as they flew out over the desert. "Look."

The wall of water was more massive than anything they had ever seen before, taller even than the Corinthian Giants, the children of the renegade angels called Watchers. As they looked, it enveloped the City of Jade and moved past with no apparent loss of speed or power.

"Now, Edmund," Rose said, trying not to sound anxious, "I believe in you. This will work."

"All right," Edmund said as they approached the Zanzibar Gate. "I guess I'd better draw quickly."

"Well," Kipling said as he watched his friends through the spyglass. "I guess that's that, then."

He folded the spyglass closed and slid down the wall behind him, sitting on the smooth pavement. The buildings all around him and even the ground beneath him were vibrating constantly now, and in the distance, he could see cracks starting to form in some of the greater towers.

It would not be long now.

Outside in the city, those who still remained could be heard praying. Some were reciting histories; others, poetry. Each denizen who knew what was approaching had chosen to meet his fate in his own way, as Kipling had chosen to meet his.

He started to recite one of his poems, then paused before starting another, but he stopped reciting that one too. "Curse it all," he muttered to no one in particular, "I really should have written some less depressing poems."

He finally settled on "En-Dor," mostly because several stanzas were a comfort to him, even if the overall poem was not. Still, it was a good poem, and there, in that place, at that moment, that was as good a legacy as any, he decided. He had written a good poem, and he had done good things, and he thought if his son had been there, he would be proud of his father.

A loud rumbling startled him out of his reverie, and the light from outside dimmed, as if a cloud had moved in front of the sun. It wasn't a cloud, Kipling knew.

He closed his eyes and continued to recite the poem as the massive wave moved into the city, toppling towers and overwhelming everything in its path.

On their approach to the gate, the companions were relieved to see that the controls and aperture began to glow as soon as Madoc was near.

"That's what we like t' see," said Fred. "Dragon power! Boom!"

It took only a few minutes for Edmund to complete the drawing of Enoch. He added one or two more flourishes, then with Fred's assistance, he set it into the spot on the gate next to the control crystals.

"Hmm," said Madoc. "That visage looks terribly familiar to me, but I can't quite place it."

"As long as it gets us to him," said Edmund. "That's all I'm concerned about."

"I just hope," said Laura Glue, "that we don't end up parking the entire Zanzibar Gate right on top of him, like they did with that house the tornado dropped on the witch in Oz."

"I'm sure they didn't mean for that to happen," said Uncas.

"I'm sure they did," said Laura Glue. "The way I heard it, it took them three tries to actually get her."

"Well, we have one try to get this right," said Edmund. "We're good to go—all the settings are locked."

Madoc stood atop the deck, stretched his wings, and took a last look around. The refugees still in the encampments were either disassembling tents, or frantically running back and forth, or praying. In the opposite direction, Deucalion's great ark was sealed up and waiting to fulfill its purpose. And ahead of them, the future and the past were both waiting to be created.

"All right," he said finally. "Take us through, Fred."

The companions aboard the *Indigo Dragon* had no idea what to expect when they passed through the gate. There was no transition period, no time to adjust to a new environment. It was almost instantaneous, and very similar to walking through one of the doors at the keep.

What the *Indigo Dragon* moved into was a fairy forest.

It was night, and the skies were dark, but everything around them glowed with pulsing, vibrant, living lights that illuminated the airship and its occupants with greens and blues and other colors they would not have believed were possible on earth.

There was a ring of tall, mostly branchless trees that towered above a smaller grove of thicker, leafier varieties. The shrubbery was so thick that the ground was almost impossible to see, and everything seemed to glow of its own accord. Lights, like fireflies but not, floated lazily among the foliage, giving off more than enough light for the companions to see by.

"Oh," Laura Glue said as she reached for Edmund's hand. "Oh, it is so beautiful."

Uncas lifted his nose and sniffed. "It all smells like mint," he declared. "I like it."

"I thought we were coming to find a master builder. An architect," said Edmund. "Instead, we find this . . ."

"Garden," a voice said from the far side of the trees. "I know it must pale in comparison to the original, but I never had the pleasure of seeing that one in person, so I've simply done the best that I can."

They stepped off the airship and walked around the trees to better see who had spoken. There, sitting on a stool, was a man who very strongly resembled the drawing Edmund had done. He glanced briefly at the companions, then resumed his work, which was creating a city in the sky.

He was drawing with light, in the air.

A bright point of energy was emanating from his right index finger, and everywhere he touched, the light remained. There were squat, square buildings, but also majestic, soaring towers; and every inch of the miniature city glowed with the light from his touch.

"This is my next project," he said, turning around and sliding off the stool. "I thought I'd add a few things while I waited for you."

"You . . . have been waiting for us?" Rose exclaimed. "Are you . . ."

"My name is Enoch, the Maker," he said simply, "and I have been waiting for you to arrive for a very long time."

Chapter Sixteen

The Archons

After the initial astonishment at Enoch's statement passed, Rose regained enough of her composure to ask him how it was he knew to expect them.

"I was told," he said, folding his arms behind him and looking at them as if he'd actually said something useful.

"If he pulls a cream-colored envelope out of his pocket," said Laura Glue, "I think I might throw up."

"I was thinking the same thing," said Fred.

"We've come a long way to find you," Edmund said, trying to change the subject, but Enoch wasn't listening. He had stepped closer to examine Laura Glue's wings.

"These are constructs, are they not?" he asked. "Used for flight, but not a part of you."

"Yes," the Valkyrie answered. "They were made for me."

"But yours are your own," he said, turning to Madoc. "Intriguing."

Rose was about to ask another question when something she caught out of the corner of her eye distracted her. It was a column of swirling clouds, like an inverted tornado, far off in the distance.

"There. . . . Watch, as it turns to twilight."

"It looks like the Frontier that separated the Archipelago from the Summer Country," she said, pointing at the clouds.

Enoch looked at her in surprise. "Interesting," he said. "Few people can actually see the Barrier, and most of those see angels carrying flaming swords, the way the Adam claimed to. How unusual that you can see it for what it really is."

"Is that . . . ?" Charles asked, swallowing hard. "Is that the Garden of Eden?"

Enoch smiled wryly and shrugged. "It may be. The Barrier has been there since long before my time. Not many still live who remember the time of the Adam and the Eve, but one does. It may be possible for you to meet him. We shall see."

Edmund rubbed his chin, thinking. "You keep mentioning 'the Adam,'" he said to Enoch.

The Maker looked at Edmund, not understanding, then he realized what the young man was asking.

"It was his calling, not his name," Enoch explained. "No one living knows what his true name was—and I doubt that after what occurred with his sons, he ever shared his true name with anyone else, ever again."

"What does 'the Adam' mean?" asked Rose.

"As I said, it was his calling," said Enoch. He lowered his head, struggling to find the right words. "In the language of the Host, it means . . . purpose? Yes, that's it. To me, the Adam meant to have purpose in the world."

"That makes sense," Quixote said, nodding. "Given that he was the first man."

"But he wasn't," Enoch said quickly. "There were men and women here for thousands of years before he came, as there are many peoples here who have cultures and history far beyond my own. He was simply the first man with purpose. Regardless, it was his calling that mattered then, not his name. Names can be changed."

"My father has changed his name several times in his life," said Rose, taking Madoc by the arm.

"That would mean," said Enoch, "that either you are a great Namer, or you have not yet been completely made, and thus cannot be Named—not completely."

"We have come here seeking a Maker," said Rose. "And possibly a Namer as well."

Enoch nodded. "I know. He told us to expect you—or at least, to expect someone—who would be seeking him."

Charles stepped forward, eyes flashing with anticipation. "Someone else told you to expect us? But aren't *you* the Architect?"

Enoch blinked. "Is that a name?" He shook his head. "He never spoke that word. But he told us he had chosen to Name himself, and he was called Telemachus."

Rose's mouth dropped open in astonishment, and she turned to the others. It hadn't occurred to any of them that Telemachus, who had been manipulating events in time to keep them moving forward, might actually be the very being they were seeking.

"What did he say, exactly?" she asked.

Enoch shrugged. "He simply said he was the one who could help you, and that you would come seeking him."

"This guy," Uncas said to Quixote behind his paw, "is like the Zen master of not being helpful."

"He was here? You met him?" Edmund asked.

Enoch nodded. "He visited us here, long ago, in the days of

my youth, and learned many things from us. And in turn, we also learned many things from him, such as the art of making these."

He held out his hand and from it dropped a silver pocket watch, with an engraving of a Dragon on the case.

"Azer," said Rose. "Samaranth's wife. I never realized that was who was on Bert's watch—most of the Caretakers have one like Verne's. . . ."

"With the red Dragon?" Enoch asked. "I liked those less. There's something pure and geometrically pleasing about a simpler design. The original one he brought to me was broken, but it was simple to repair, and I think I improved upon the workings in the process."

Edmund suddenly brightened. "We have something similar in one of our bags," he said, grinning, "that was damaged beyond our ability to repair. But it may not be beyond yours. Would you mind having a look at him?"

"Him?" Enoch said in surprise.

In response Edmund simply walked back over to the *Indigo Dragon* and returned carrying the clockwork owl, Archimedes. He had been damaged on their trip into the future, where they battled the man who called himself Lord Winter. The agents of Winter had repaired the bird, but in doing so had taken away . . . something. He was now completely an automaton, with none of the fire of life he had possessed before.

Madoc sighed heavily when he saw the clockwork bird. "Ah, Archimedes," he said. "Perhaps my oldest friend, and one of my great teachers." He looked at Enoch. "Can you?" he asked. "Can you help him?"

The Maker gently took the bird from Edmund and examined

him closely. "It's possible," he said finally. "Physically, he is unharmed. But his aiua has been smothered, almost extinguished. I think you can call it back, though."

"Call it back?" said Rose. "What do you mean?"

"Just that," said Enoch. "His aiua is bound to yours, even after death. To restore him to life, all you need to do is call him, and he will respond."

"It's that simple?" asked Edmund.

"It's that hard," said Enoch. "The call must be with the full desire of your heart. Your aiua must draw his back. There is no other way."

"All right," said Edmund. "I'll give it a try."

"Not your aiua," Enoch said, pointing past Edmund to Madoc. "His."

Madoc stared at the Maker in surprise. "Why must it be me?"

"Your aiua is most intertwined with his," said Enoch, "so it must be yours that calls him."

Madoc took the damaged bird from the young man and cradled him in his arms. "That's all I have to do? Just believe him well?"

"Believing is seeing, Madoc," said Fred.

"No," said Enoch. "Believing is *being*. So believe."

The Dragon Madoc held the clockwork bird as gently as he could and closed his eyes. Instantly the choices and decisions of a lifetime flashed through his mind, filling him with regret, sadness, and then . . .

. . . happiness. And contentment. And a feeling of rightness about his place in the world. And as he focused on these thoughts, he realized how much a part of who he was could be attributed to the teachings of this cranky, crotchety, wise, and beloved old bird. And that was when he felt it happen—a change, like a blessing made tangible.

"What," Archimedes said, "did you do to yourself, Madoc? You have wings!"

Madoc opened his eyes. "I wanted to be more like one of my best teachers," he said, unable to suppress a grin.

"That's what it would take," Archie replied. "It certainly wasn't going to be through your penmanship."

The companions gathered around the newly himself bird, laughing and cheering in celebration. Enoch, however, simply stood apart from them, arms extended, with his eyes closed and head tipped back.

"What are you doing?" Fred asked him, curious.

"Communing with my father," said Enoch.

"Uh, you mean you're praying?"

"Hmm," Enoch said. "Yes, I think that might be the right word. It is how we Archons communicate."

"Archons?" asked Charles. "You mean as in rulers?"

"That word will do," said Enoch. "Look—they are there, above."

For the first time, the companions actually took their eyes off the entrancing scenery and looked to the sky—and they realized what it was that was creating such an ethereal glow over the landscape.

The Archons were immense personages, less giants than men and women seen through a lens of majesty. Five beings, floating high in the air, were sitting cross-legged in the center of impossible geometries of light. They were drawing in the air as Enoch had been, but where he was simply making shapes and figures, they were weaving tapestries that moved and flowed with life. It was creation itself painted in the air above them.

"Astonishing," Charles murmured. "And you can commune with them?"

Enoch looked surprised. "Of course," he said. "I am one of them. I simply wore this body to make it easier to commune with *you*."

As if on cue, the Archons turned their heads, noticing for the first time that they were being observed. The light around them brightened—and when it faded again, five men and women had joined Enoch.

"These are the other Makers," Enoch said by way of introduction, "at least, all of us save for one. This is Abraxas and Eidolon, and Sophia and Lilith, and this—" he gestured to the last man— "is Seth. My father."

"Seth," said Charles. "You are—you are a son of the Adam, then?"

The Archon nodded. "One of them, at least." He gestured at Rose. "Is that my father's box?" Seth asked. He was pointing at the Serendipity Box in Rose's bag.

"I believe it is," she answered, handing it to him. "Would you like to have it back?"

"I would," he answered, "if you have no further use for it."

"A shame," Laura Glue said. "I never actually got to use it."

"You should," said Seth, proffering the box to the Valkyrie. "The one mistake people always make with the box is waiting until the need is both mortal and immediate before deciding to open it—and ofttimes, that's the moment when they realize it's already too late."

Laura Glue grinned and flipped open the lid. Inside was a

space far larger than the box could have contained—an endlessly vast void.

"Ah," Seth said, nodding in approval. "A larger gift. Those are always interesting."

"Is that good or bad?" asked Fred.

"Neither," Seth replied. "It's merely interesting."

The young Valkyrie reached into the box to her shoulder. "I can just feel it," she said, screwing up her face with effort. "It's . . . just . . . out . . . of . . . my . . . Aha! Got it!"

Triumphantly she pulled out a tall, narrow hourglass. It appeared to have been made from bone, and had a valve in the center, where the glass was narrowest between the globes. The upper sphere was empty, but the lower was half-filled with a very fine alabaster-colored sand that seemed to glow in the waning light.

"Hmm," she said, frowning. "It's just an hourglass."

"Not just any hourglass," Seth said, reaching out to examine the device, "and not filled with any ordinary sand. These particles of dust were gathered on the shores of the ocean that reaches to heaven, and can forestall death itself for a full hour. If it's carried on a vessel, all who travel aboard it will be immune from the call of death until the last of the sand runs out."

"Holy cats!" Fred exclaimed. "That's like the best thing ever!"

"Except for lemon curd," said Uncas. "But yes, all things considered, it's pretty keen."

Laura Glue handed back the box, and Seth held it to his ear. "Hmm," he said. "It sounds as if there is one gift left to it." He handed it back to Rose. "You'd better keep it, just in case. Father would be happy to know it's been so thoroughly put to use over the centuries."

"You've given us great gifts," Madoc said as the Archons and companions seated themselves in a circle around the clearing. He looked up at Archie soaring happily around the treetops, and at the Valkyrie's hourglass and the Serendipity Box. "We have very little to offer you in return."

"I have a broken sword," Rose answered wryly. "It was a great weapon, once."

At Enoch's urging, she removed the shattered pieces of Caliburn from her bag and handed them to the Archon.

"It is great still," Enoch said. "It is Named—and it still has great power. It needs only to be repaired. Would you like one of us to do so? It is easily arranged."

"No need," Madoc said, rising to his feet. "Just show me to a forge, and I can take care of it myself."

He didn't notice the looks of approval that were traded among the Archons' faces, but Rose did.

One of the Archons, whom Enoch had introduced as Abraxas, led Madoc to a forge that was as fully modern as any he'd ever used. He had repaired the sword once before, at the beach of the Great Wall at the End of the World, but that time, he had the use of only one arm. This time, with both hands strong and capable, the muscle memory soon returned, and he was hammering away at the sword from underneath a cascade of sparks and steam.

The night passed, and then a full day, before Madoc rejoined the others. "It seems I am always repairing this sword," he said with a gruffness that wasn't entirely convincing. "Here," he said as he handed it to Rose. "Try not to break it this time."

Again, a gesture made by Madoc was met with approving

glances among the Archons, but this time they didn't escape his notice. "What?" he said with a note of real irritation in his voice.

"There are only ever seven Makers in the world," Seth answered, "and many years ago, one of our number, the first, the best, was taken from us. We have waited many centuries for another to take his place. And if you wish it, Madoc the Maker, you may join us."

He stared at the Archons in disbelief, not even entirely certain what he was being asked. But after a long moment, he shook his head. "I'm sorry," he said. "I'd like to pretend that it's at least a temptation, but it isn't.

"We have come a long way together, to try to make right some terrible wrongs, and I cannot step off that path, and away from my daughter. Not yet. Maybe not ever."

Instead of disappointment, this announcement brought still more looks of approval from the Archons. "Then tell us," Enoch said. "What can I do to help you? Why did you come here, seeking me out?"

"We came looking for the Architect of a great tower," Rose answered, "and we were told that you were the man who built the first city. If you could do that, then surely you might also know how to build—"

"The Keep of Time?" asked Enoch.

"You know it?" Rose asked.

"I do," he said, rising to his feet. "Come. Walk with me, and I'll show you."

The companions and the Archons followed Enoch as he took a small trail to the top of a nearby hill, where there was a clear view of the horizon, unimpeded by the great trees and mountains that ringed the valley.

"There," he said, pointing to the setting sun. "Watch, as it turns to twilight. Then you'll be able to see it clearly, even from here."

There were a few thin, high clouds, which followed the curve of the horizon, and the sky was denser, here in the distant past. Not thick, or cloying, but simply . . . *richer*. The fading light flowed through the sky in wave after wave of ambers and purples, and then, when it finally started to ebb, they saw it.

A pencil-thin line that stretched from sea to sky, lit brilliantly by the last rays of the sun.

"There is your keep," said Enoch. "It still stands, as it has always stood—and it was built long before my time. If it is the Architect of that tower you seek, you will not find him here."

Part Five

The Fall of the House of Tamerlane

"It's like a small Ring of Power," Charles said . . .

Chapter Seventeen
At the End of All Things

The desert crossing was terrible; the mountain crossing was worse. The great beasts that carried the Archipelago on their backs faltered often, and the great Dragon worried they would not last much longer—and then they were over, and the path eased.

While they crossed the long, narrow bridge that would take them to the Lonely Isle, there to wait again until called upon by those whom the old Dragon had entrusted to make things right, he told stories to his small friend, to better pass the time.

He had not been close to any of the Children of the Earth, not really, not as an angel, and not as a Dragon. But in times of need, the badger had always been there, with loyalty, and bravery, and heart. And the Dragon realized that in this one small example, he could demonstrate why an entire Archipelago was worth the effort to save. If there were five among all the peoples and creatures who were like the badger Tummeler, it would be worth it.

"There had been Makers, and there had been many, many Namers," the great Dragon explained, "but there is only ever one Imago, and one Archimago, walking the earth together at the same time. The Archimago had vanished into the mists of history—but the Imago, the first in thousands of years, was reshaping the world.

"There was a great battle between the first giants, who were the children of the angels called Nephilim and one of the Sisters of Eve called Lilith, and the Dragons. It culminated in a struggle between their greatest, Ogias, and the greatest of us, a she-Dragon called Sycorax, who finally subdued him with the help of the Imago, T'ai Shan.

"She was the youngest of a family of gods, who was judged to be weak and cast out of their house. What her name had been before no one knows, but she took her new name from that of an angel who saw her for what she was, and gave her introduction to the star Rao, who would give her his fire, and taught her to use it.

"But the angel Shaitan disappeared before the rest of his order descended to become the Dragons of this world; Rao betrayed his kind and was deemed Fallen; and T'ai Shan, after saving the world and returning it to the people she had loved and cared for, gave her armor and her power over to them for their use, and then left the world behind.

"First she crossed an uncrossable desert. Then she scaled an unclimbable mountain. And finally she reached an impassable sea, so she labored for the rest of her days to build a bridge of bone, so that others who followed behind her would find the path to heaven easier to walk."

"A desert, a mountain, and a bridge of bone over the sea," said Tummeler. "That sounds exactly like the path we've been walking."

"Yes," the Dragon said. "Exactly like that."

"That's impossible!" Charles declared. "The island the keep is built on is a long journey away, deep in the Archipelago. There's no way we'd be able to see it from here!"

"And yet, there it stands," said Madoc. "That *is* the true keep."

"Distance is less of an obstacle in this time," said Enoch, "and it is not so long since meaning was divided from duration, and time itself took two paths. The longer they remain split, the further what is meaningful grows apart from all else."

"If he in't a scowler," said Uncas, "he ought t' be. He sure talks like one."

"True that," said Fred.

"Have you ever seen it up close?" Rose asked. "Is it damaged?"

"It is," Enoch said, taken aback by the question, "although my father has told me stories passed down from the days of the Adam, when it was said the tower was whole, and unbroken. But no one living has ever seen it thus. I'm sorry I cannot help you find your Architect."

"What do we do now?" Edmund asked.

"The Zanzibar Gate has one more trip left in it," said Rose. "If we go home, we will be back at square one, or worse. But if we try to go out one more time, we may find what we need. I think it's worth trying."

"So those are our choices, then," said Charles. "Either we go home, or we take one more shot in the dark—literally—to try to discover the Architect."

"This *is* why we came," said Rose. "All the sacrifices, everything we've been through . . . It's all for nothing if we fail. And either we go home, or we take one more chance. I say we take it."

"Agreed," said Edmund.

"All right," said Charles.

"Ditto," said the badgers.

"In for a penny, night on the town," said Laura Glue. "I'm up for it."

Madoc turned to the Archons. "Is there anything you might tell us to help? We simply need to find out who first built the keep—and no matter how far back in time we go, we can't seem to locate him."

"Traveling in time is a difficult proposition," said Seth. "It flows in two directions, you know."

"This in't our first time at the Sweet Corn Festival, you know," said Uncas. "We've done this before."

"My point," Seth said, grinning at the badger, "is that time and history are two separate things. They have been since the time of the Adam. Before that, they were one, and mixed together freely. After that, they moved in divergent ways."

"What happened that changed everything?" asked Madoc.

"The moment when the Imago was slain by the Archimago," said Enoch. "That is the moment when history truly began."

The companions all went still. "What Imago?" Madoc asked slowly, putting a hand protectively in front of Rose. "And what Archimago?"

"The first Maker, and the first Namer," Seth said. "My elder brothers. That was the moment when time was divided. If meaning is what you seek, search out that moment above all others, and perhaps you will find what you need."

"That's part of the difficulty," said Edmund. "The way the Zanzibar Gate—the pyramid structure we came through—works is by programming a date or period into it, which we can refine with an illumination of whom or what we're seeking. But we don't know anything about the Architect, and if time is separate from history, that's even worse—because history is what gives us the markers by which we set the dates."

"It seems to me," Enoch said, "now that you have explained how your mechanism works, that the answer to your question is very simple."

"Simple?" Uncas all but hollered at him. "We've had the best scowlers and the best minds of all of history tryin' t' figure out how t' make this work for years now. How can it be simple?"

"Decorum, my squire," Quixote admonished him. "Always decorum, even at the end of all things."

"Exactly," said Enoch.

Suddenly the diverse pieces of the puzzle came together in Rose's head, as she realized what the Maker was trying to tell them.

"The beginning," she said, excitement rising in her face. "All this time we've been trying to figure out exactly *when* the Architect built the keep, and everyone we've met has told us the answer!"

Edmund frowned, still unsure of where she was leading them. "Except all anyone was ever told is that it was built long before their time," he said. "That it has always existed. Even the Caretakers have said as much—that it was there because it had always been there since . . ." His eyes went wide with the realization.

". . . since the beginning," he finished. "Can it be?" he asked Rose. "Can it really be that simple?"

"Nothing is *ever* simple," Fred said, looking at his father, "but sometimes, things are easier than we make them out to be."

"I'm afraid they've lost me completely," Quixote said, looking down at Uncas. "Are you following any of this?"

"I am," Laura Glue said brightly. "We've always worried about how to go back further and further, to find the right place in time when the keep was built, when what we should have been doing was trying to go back *before* it was built!"

Madoc threw his head back and laughed. "That's brilliant," he said, wiping tears from his eyes. "I am overcome."

Edmund jumped to his feet and pounded a fist into his hand. "It's too perfect not to try," he said, almost breathless with anticipation. "All we have to do is turn all the settings to zero and go through the gate. It should allow us to return, right here, at the moment of the keep's creation."

"I agree," said Rose. "We've been so worried about who built the keep that we've forgotten that it's just as important *when* it was built. And if we go to *when*, we'll finally find out *who* the Architect is!"

"*That's* what you've all been debating?" Archie said as he glided down and landed on Edmund's shoulder. "I could have told you that much." He looked at Madoc and made a clucking noise. "Did you learn nothing from my philosophy lectures?"

"This is all very exciting for you, isn't it?" Enoch said to the badgers.

"You have no idea," said Fred.

The companions bid the Archons farewell and prepared the *Indigo Dragon* for one final trip through the gate.

"Here," Enoch said as they climbed aboard. "The visitor, Telemachus, said that when you realized where you needed to go, I should give you this." He reached out and put the silver watch into Madoc's hand. "He told me that you had no watch of your own, and so this is yours."

"You don't want to keep it?"

Enoch smiled. "I'm a Maker, remember?" he said, stepping away from the airship. "I'll make more."

"All right," Edmund said, rubbing his hands together. "There is nothing guiding us but the settings on the gate, and I've set them all for zero. Everyone cross your fingers."

Fred engaged the internal motor of the airship and urged

the goats forward at the same time. Within moments they were going toward the gate, which glowed as Madoc came near, and in a moment more, they were through.

At Tamerlane House, the word quickly spread that Poe had some grand revelations to share, and no one wanted to miss out, so the great hall was quickly filled with all the residents and visitors it could hold. Caretakers Emeriti took most of the seats around the table, while the Mystorians filled in the standing room next to the walls. For his part, the detective Aristophanes brought in a couch from one of the other rooms for himself and the Messenger Beatrice, and, surprisingly, a chair for the shipbuilder Argus. Only the half-clockwork men called Jason's sons, known as Hugh the Iron and William the Pig, remained outside to guard Shakespeare's Bridge. Hawthorne and Irving went out one last time just to check on them before the meeting commenced, but otherwise, everyone at Tamerlane House was present.

A bright chime suddenly rang out from all the Caretakers' watches: once, twice, and then a third time. As one, they all stopped to look at the time, to see why the watches had made such an unusual sound, and that was when they all realized what had happened.

The watches were resetting themselves.

"What is this?" asked John. "What is happening here, Jules? Bert? They've never done *that* before."

"There is a new zero point," Bert said in amazement. "The Anabasis Machines have reset themselves to it. All of them. At once."

"That's not just any zero point," Verne said, peering at his watch. "They're resetting because it's *the* zero point. The prime zero. The moment in history when everything was connected, and the Keep of Time was built."

"Does that mean they've succeeded?" asked John. "Can this really be over?"

"I don't know," said Verne. "We should ask Poe about it immediately, though. This may preclude whatever he was planning to share."

"Not just yet," John said, holding up both his hands. "We're still waiting on a few fellows to arrive, and I think everyone should be here."

"I think they're coming now," Twain said, lifting a curtain to glance out the window, "and at top speed, apparently."

Hawthorne and Irving blew through the front doors with a bang, rounded the corner, and skidded into the room. Both their faces were ashen.

"Jack, you must come, quickly," Hawthorne said, ignoring all decorum in favor of urgency. "You, and everyone! Something's happened at the bridge."

"What?" Jack implored as the Caretakers all rose to rush outside with their colleagues. "What's happened, Nathaniel?"

"It's Warnie," Irving answered. "Dr. Dee has your brother, Jack. And he's going to kill him unless we give him access to Tamerlane House and the Nameless Isles."

It was dusk in the place and time where the *Indigo Dragon* emerged from the Zanzibar Gate. As they passed through, the glow that signaled it was functioning properly waned and died.

"Well, that's that," said Fred. "I really hope this works, or we may as well start building houses."

"I don't think it worked," Edmund said, unable to hide the trace of bitterness in his voice. "Look."

In the distance, dark against the fading light in the sky, was the swirl of clouds that made up the Barrier around the Garden of Eden. "We're still in the same place."

"But not in the same time," said Madoc. "The trees are different, as far as I can see. And those stones were not here."

In the center of the clearing, similar to the one where they'd met the Archons, was a small ring of stones, with a stone table in the center.

"It's like a small Ring of Power," Charles said, barely daring to breathe, "except for the table in the center. That's different."

Uncas and Fred both sniffed the air, as did the goats. "That's blood," Fred said with a shudder. "Fresh blood. Recent blood."

The companions all held their breath when they realized Fred was right—and that the dark stains covering the stone table still glistened in the waning light of day.

"Seth was right," Rose said, choking as she spoke. "We can't go back further in time than this moment, no matter how much older the keep is."

"A paradox," a young man said as he stepped around from behind one of the stones. "The keep is what binds the two worlds together, even though they are growing further and further apart."

Uncas, Fred, Quixote, and Laura Glue recognized him immediately. They had seen him in a battle on Easter Island only a few months earlier.

The others didn't know his face, but the Ruby Armor he wore was instantly recognizable.

"To restore what has been broken, you must travel beyond the point where the worlds have been split," he continued, "but to do so is impossible without the presence of the keep. It is, as I said, a paradox."

"If we can't go beyond this point in time," Edmund said slowly, not certain of the wisdom of speaking to this mysterious man, "then how are we possibly going to restore time? We've had two last chances to find the Architect, and now we're out of options."

The young man turned to Rose. "What do you think? Is your quest hopeless? Is it over?"

"There's got to be a way," Rose said, her voice low. "There is always a way. Always."

"Ah," said the young man. "*That's* what I was waiting for."

"Waiting for to do what?" asked Fred.

"Help you," the young man replied. "One last time."

In a trice, the young man in the Ruby Armor was replaced by someone Rose had seen twice before: a very ancient man, wearing a flowing robe. He nodded at them as if this were an entirely anticipated turn of events, then looked at Rose, smiling. "Hello, my dear," he said. "I have been waiting for you for a very long time, but I knew you'd show up again . . . eventually."

Without hesitation, Rose simply asked him the first question that came to mind. "Are you him?" she said. "Are you the Architect?"

"No," the old man said firmly. "I am *not* the Architect."

"Who are you, then?" asked Rose.

"You know, Moonchild," he replied gently. "You have always known."

"Coal," she said, her voice soft. "You're Coal."

He nodded. "I was. Am. Although I think I prefer the name I chose for myself. It suits me best, when I need a name, that is. You may call me Telemachus."

Chapter Eighteen
The Architect

The Caretakers of Tamerlane House gathered en masse at their side of Shakespeare's Bridge. There, just on the other side, they could see Dr. Dee and two tall men in black, who wore dark glasses and bowler hats. In between them was Jack's brother, Warnie.

"These are my colleagues, Mr. Kirke and Mr. Bangs," said Dr. Dee. "They have been trained to do many things, but what they most excel at is following my orders—and I have told them that unless you do exactly as I ask, they are to tear Major Lewis into pieces."

"Sorry, Jack," Warnie said. His military reserve and strength of character gave him the appearance of fortitude, but Jack could tell he was properly scared.

"You know me well enough, Jules," Dee said. "I'm not bluffing. And if need be, my colleagues can also kill Caretakers—no matter what form they've taken."

"What is it you want?" Verne asked, casting a quick glance at John to see if he would object. John nodded his head faintly, giving Verne the go-ahead to keep speaking. If Dee wasn't aware there was a new Prime Caretaker at Tamerlane, then John certainly wasn't going to correct him.

"These are my colleagues, Mr. Kirke and Mr. Bangs."

"There are guards set in these stones, and in the bridge," said Dee. "Runic wards. I want you to cancel them."

"I see," Verne said, stalling for time. "We use silver rings to bypass the—"

"I don't want a ring, Jules!" Dee all but shouted. "I want you to drop all the protection you have built up around these islands! Now!"

To punctuate his request, Mr. Kirke twisted Warnie's arm backward and up, dislocating his shoulder. Jack's brother let out a yelp of pain, then gritted his teeth and bore it.

"What if we decline?" asked Verne, trying not to look at Major Lewis. "What if we simply say no?"

"Mr. Kirke and Mr. Bangs are very, very strong," said Dr. Dee, "and we have silver sledgehammers that can shatter even cavorite."

"And?"

"And," said Dee, "as far as I know, this bridge is the only thing keeping Tamerlane House tethered to the Summer Country. If we smash it—and we will—then you suddenly get hurled into the heart of the Echthroi's domain. Forever. And then," he added, "we'll still kill Jack's brother."

"All right!" John shouted, realizing Verne was more likely to sacrifice Warnie than give up any tactical advantage. "We'll do as you ask."

Dr. Dee's eyes glittered as he looked from John to Verne and back again, processing this apparent breach of Caretaker protocol. "Good," he said, gesturing for Mr. Kirke to ease up on Jack's brother. "I see you are going to be reasonable men. Lower the wards."

"And then what?" John demanded.

"Then," said Dee, "I'm going to go *home*."

• • •

"You were taken from us, you know that," said Rose. "We've tried everything we could to find you!"

"I believe you," said Telemachus.

"So you've chosen?" asked Fred. "You decided to help the Caretakers after all?"

"I wasn't sure, not completely," he answered, "until I put on the Ruby Armor—and realized that I had more in common with T'ai Shan than I did with John Dee, or the Echthroi.

"T'ai Shan was born into a family of gods, but she was crippled, and so was cast out. She had to make her way in the world as a beggar, or perish. She survived in part because she was an adept—like you and I, Rose—but she thrived because she saw it as her purpose to serve others.

"She was given the power of a star, who then betrayed her. But she fought him and won. The giants, who were the children of angels, were subdued by her and made to serve the cause of the Dragons. She was betrayed, terribly and often, by those closest to her—and still, her purpose was to serve. And then, somehow, I was brought to this world through improbable circumstance, and given this miraculous armor, and with it, a choice. Do I serve the Echthroi, or do I serve the Light?"

"Is this one of those remoracle questions?" asked Uncas. "Because if it in't, I'm really afraid of what his answer is."

Telemachus smiled at this. "Don't worry, little fellow," he said. "With great power comes great responsibility, and an even greater awareness. I've made my choice, and I'm going to do what I can to help you set things right."

"That is exactly why I came to the end of time," said Charles.

He looked at Edmund. "Or is it the beginning? I keep losing track."

Edmund shrugged. "Where he's from, I don't think it matters."

"Wise boy," said Telemachus. "In Platonia there is no Chronos time, only Kairos time."

"Seth, the Namer, told us something similar about Eden," said Rose. "He told us time was different there, because it had only just been separated, and so both kinds of time still mixed freely, but I didn't really understand him. What did he mean?"

"Chronos time is merely about the progression of moments," said Telemachus, "but Kairos time is about the meaning held within those moments—and the meaning of a single moment can last an eternity."

"The killing," Charles murmured. "When Chronos—Cain—slew Kairos—Abel—it split the two kinds of time, because that murder was the first act of true meaning in the world."

"Yes," Telemachus said, glancing down at the stone table. "This is the moment when it all began, and so this is the moment when the keep must be built."

"But the doors," said Madoc. "I've been inside them, and time goes back much further than this. Eden, even the time of the Adam, is not the beginning."

"You're right, and wrong," said Telemachus. "The keep, once restored, will persist in time in both directions, forward and back. But history, and true meaning, began here, with this murder. The keep is what connected the Archipelago with the Summer Country, and Chronos time with Kairos time. It was not necessary before, because nothing was divided."

"So what happens now?"

"Now," Telemachus said, "the Architect must build the keep,

restore what was broken, and redeem the murder that split the world in two."

Nathaniel Hawthorne and William Shakespeare were in charge of the security of the bridge. It took only a few minutes to completely disable all the runes and lower all the wards.

"All right, Dee," John said. "Now what?"

"Watch and learn," Dee said, smiling. He was not looking at any of the Caretakers, but was instead looking past them. All of them willing to take their eyes off Dee turned to see what he was looking at.

There, on the largest of the easternmost islands of the Nameless Isles, the Nightmare Abbey, the dark, gabled house of John Dee, suddenly shimmered into view, solidified, and settled with a whisper into place.

"The Cabal," Jack said. "John, he's brought the entire Cabal to the Nameless Isles! The enemy is here at our doorstep!"

"Closer than that, I think," the Cheshire cat Grimalkin said as he appeared in the air over John's shoulder. The Prime Caretaker jumped away, but the cat merely smiled at him and scratched at himself with a wicked-looking claw. "We're in your house, eating your food, drinking your wine, and criticizing the decor."

"Grimalkin!" John exclaimed. "You aren't welcome here anymore!"

"Welcome or not, I'm still here, boy," the cat said, "although it seems not even my master needed me, really. I would have thought it would take more than 'Your shoelace is untied' to get all of you to take your eyes off Dr. Dee."

The Caretakers whirled around, but to their relief, Dee

was still there, along with Warnie and his henchmen.

"We've done as you asked, Dee," said John. "Honor your part of the bargain."

Dee looked at the cat. "Well, Grimalkin?"

The Cheshire cat licked a vanishing paw. "He tells the truth. The wards are down."

Dee nodded, and Mr. Kirke struck Warnie a vicious blow to the head. Without making a sound, Jack's brother fell to the ground, unconscious.

"I will kill you for that, Dee," said Jack. "You know this. Believe it."

"I kept my word," Dee said as he crossed the bridge. "He hasn't been harmed. Much."

The Caretakers drew their swords and readied their weapons. "There are three of you and a multitude of us," Twain said, leveling his *katana* at the former Caretaker. "We have you vastly outnumbered."

"Appearances, Samuel, can be deceiving," Dee countered. "You have numbers on your side, but this time I brought an ally whose loyalty cannot be questioned."

With a gesture, he signaled to the cat, who suddenly became completely visible—and who began to grow much, much larger. In seconds, Grimalkin was the size of a good-sized truck.

"Now we can talk reasonably, like civilized men," Dee said as he and his minions strode casually toward the house under the watchful gaze of the giant cat.

"I know you are bound," John said to Grimalkin. "I know that's why you serve him."

"Yes," Grimalkin said, with no trace of shame or embarrassment. "For a very, very long time now."

Twain shook his head in disgust. "I can't believe we've had a Lloigor here all this time."

"Not Lloigor," the cat insisted. "Echthros. A Lloigor is one who has given up or sold his shadow. But an Echthros is simply an Echthros."

"Echthroi are Fallen angels," said Twain. "Are you saying you're an angel?"

"Was," said the cat.

"A Binding is not the whole of your being, Grimalkin," said John. "People have resisted Bindings before! And you resisted enough to warn us about Rose!"

"What?" Dee said, startled. He turned to the cat, scowling. "You caused me to move my timetable considerably," he growled, "and there will be a price to pay, on that count you can be certain."

"Enough chatter, Dee," said Verne. "What is it you want?"

"There has always been one Imago and one Archimago on the earth," said Dee. "You chose your candidate for Imago, and I chose mine—and now it seems both have been lost."

"Ours is lost," said Jack. "Yours abandoned you out of common sense."

"Maybe," said Dee. "But I believe that yours may yet succeed in restoring the keep and the Archipelago. And when that happens, I would like to be present. That's why I have brought my house to the Nameless Isles—so that I can be here when the Imago and Archimago are together again in one place."

"You're out of your mind," John said. "There's no such person as the Archimago."

"It is one of the great secrets," said Dee. "One of the reveals the Prime Caretaker alone knows."

Several of the Caretakers automatically turned to look at John, and the Chronographer of Lost Times slowly realized that something significant had changed in the Caretaker hierarchy. He smiled wickedly.

"I see," Dee said, turning to look at Verne. "You haven't told him, have you? He doesn't know!"

"There are a lot of things I'm still learning, Dee," John said, "not the least of which is whom I should trust, and when."

"I was the Prime Caretaker before Jules was," said Dee, "until the Caretakers and I had a critical difference of opinion.

"The most significant reason it is the job of the Prime Caretaker to seek out and train the Imago," Dee continued with a flourish, "is because the Archimago resides here, with you, at Tamerlane House. He has been hiding in plain sight among the Caretakers ever since the first Imago was killed."

The Caretakers, all except for Verne, froze in shock.

"That's impossible," said John. "We would have known."

Dee shook his head. "It's not impossible. He's watching, and listening to all of us, right now," he said, looking up at one of the balconies.

As one, the Caretakers turned to look, some already realizing, and all of them already fearing what they would see.

There, watching in the shadows from between the parted curtains at his window, was Edgar Allan Poe.

"Rebuilding the keep," said Rose, "is exactly what we've been trying to accomplish. We just have no clue who the Architect is."

"You don't need clues," Telemachus replied, "because the answer you've sought has been staring you in the face all along.

"I was a good student," he went on, turning to Madoc, "and I knew well the history of the Archipelago. And I know," he continued, "that in your former life as Mordred, the Winter King, you once went to considerable lengths to try to destroy the original *Imaginarium Geographica*, am I right?"

Madoc reddened. "You are."

Telemachus shrugged. "So why couldn't you?"

"It had to be destroyed by the one who created it," Madoc replied, "and none other. No one else could even do so much as singe the pages, unless he permitted it."

"It is one of the first principles of Deep Magic," Telemachus said gravely. "The *Imaginarium Geographica* could not be destroyed save by he who had created it . . .

". . . and neither could the Keep of Time."

The understanding struck Laura Glue and Fred first, and they stared at the others in shock and amazement. Charles suddenly looked as if he had swallowed an oyster that was too large to choke down, and Rose simply gripped her father's hand more tightly. Of all of them, only Edmund beamed with delight at having an answer to the unanswerable question.

"Do I really need to clarify it for you?" asked Telemachus. He pointed at Charles. "You may have created the circumstances that led to its destruction, but you didn't destroy the keep." He continued, swinging his arm around to point at Madoc, "*You* did.

"You, Madoc. *You* are the Architect of the Keep of Time."

Chapter Nineteen

The Keystone

"Now, Grimalkin," said Dee.

Without another word, the Chronographer of Lost Times, the cat, and the two strange men called Mr. Kirke and Mr. Bangs vanished.

Before any of the Caretakers could react, two tremendous explosions rocked Tamerlane House and threw them all to the ground.

"What in Hades's name?" Verne exclaimed.

They clambered to their feet in time to see a small boat pulling up to the docks below. It was motorized but silent, so they had not heard it approach, and had in any regard been completely distracted by Dee.

In the boat were William Hope Hodgson, Aleister Crowley, and Nikola Tesla, who was wearing a device that resembled two massive engines strapped to his back. The engines were pointed forward, and Tesla smiled and pressed a contact. Immediately another explosion rocked the island, and one of the minarets crumpled in on itself.

"Sonic energy," said Shakespeare. "I'd bet my life on it."

"Oh, that is just not bloody fair," said Dumas. "Tesla always has all the best toys."

The shipbuilder had already completed the work . . .

"Split up!" Verne called out. "Our weapons won't be very effective against Tesla for long!"

The Caretakers scattered around the island as Tesla advanced, still firing at the house. As he fled to the north side of the island, John glanced up at the window where Poe had been watching. It was empty.

Madoc stared dumbfounded at the old man, too stunned to speak, but Rose found her words more easily.

"It makes sense," she said, still unsure of what this revelation meant, "but how could no one have known? No one in history?"

"Because," Telemachus said, "the only ones who were present are here now. We're witnessing it as it's happening. And history will move forward from this point, and no other."

"I know the structure well enough," Madoc said slowly, "but it's made of cavorite. Where am I meant to get the blocks to build it?"

"You brought them with you," Telemachus answered, pointing at the Zanzibar Gate. "They are precisely what you need, in the right size and shape. All you have to do is assemble them."

"That's not going to make a very big tower," Uncas observed.

"Many great things start small," said Telemachus, "and any seed planted properly can grow and flower into what it is meant to become."

Rose looked at her father. "What do you think?"

Madoc shrugged. "I think we have nothing to lose if we try," he said. "Let's get started, and see what happens."

"Tell me again what we're doing down here?" Shakespeare whispered. "I like to dabble in espionage, but I'm not very good at it."

He, Houdini, and Conan Doyle had taken a page from their adversaries' playbook—while Tesla, Crowley, and Hodgson were distracted by the other Caretakers, they had stolen the boat from the dock and launched their own assault on the Cabal's own headquarters.

"Haven't you studied warfare?" Houdini whispered to Shakespeare. "The single biggest advantage of being completely surrounded is that it gives you the opportunity to attack the enemy in any direction you choose."

"All right, fair point," Shakespeare whispered back. "So how do we go about breaking in?"

"This," Houdini said, "is the moment when I prove my worth to the Caretakers at large. Give me three minutes." He stopped, reconsidering. "No, make that two," he added as he scrambled up the embankment toward the house.

"Cocksure, isn't he?" Shakespeare whispered to Conan Doyle.

"Not really," Conan Doyle replied. "If he said two, that means he can do it in under one. Some of us got our reputations because we wrote good books or had clever publicists. He got his reputation through sheer hard work."

As if to underscore his colleague's sentiments, the double doors under the eaves of the house swung open on silent hinges and Houdini leaned out, winking at the others.

"See?" said Conan Doyle. "That's why he's my best friend. Never a dull moment."

The three men entered the house, prepared for a fight—but they met almost no resistance, not even the perfunctory kind, done for show. The house was practically empty—not even the servants were moving about.

Passing one gallery, Houdini noticed a former friend, and he paused. "Gilbert?" he said. "What are you doing?"

"Having a drink, for these are trying times," Chesterton said, not moving from the chair where he was sipping some sort of drink out of a small crystal glass. "Also, I wish to defect. I'm more of a strategist, not a fighter."

"Really," said Houdini. "What strategy are you advocating now?"

"Joining the winning side," Chesterton replied, "obviously."

"I can't argue with that," Conan Doyle said as he ran past with a blunderbuss. "I'll secure the south side, Ehrich."

As it turned out, without Dee driving them, not many of the Cabal were willing to put up a fight. Some, like Chesterton, who still possessed his own shadow, offered to join the Caretakers. Others, like Lovecraft, refused to even come out of their rooms. Even Tesla was finally cornered and subdued, overcome by sheer numbers. There were many Caretakers, and few members of the Cabal. From start to finish, it seemed to be a fool's errand. It was as if the entire effort to move the House on the Borderlands to the Nameless Isles was . . .

"A distraction," said Twain. "It was all just a distraction."

"I agree. I don't think the Cabal was prepared for this, at all," said John. "Other than Tesla, with his contraptions, and maybe Crowley, none of the rest of them seemed prepared for an assault. I think Dee brought them here without telling them anything about it at all."

"You don't think they might have been trying to storm Tamerlane House?" Bert asked. "There's a lot here that I know Dee would love to get his hands on again."

"This simply doesn't make any sense, Bert," John said to his old mentor. "They're just too outmatched. What can Dee possibly hope to achieve by literally bringing the fight to our doorstep?"

"I agree," said Twain. "There's some larger plan in the works here. Otherwise, he blows a few ventilation holes in Tamerlane, we eliminate a few of his Deathshead servants and knock Lovecraft and Crowley around for a bit . . . and everything remains as it is. No, there is something he can only get access to here, and we must discover what that is."

"The house is as secure as we're going to get it," Hawthorne said, grimacing as he joined the others near what remained of Shakespeare's shop. Tesla had gotten to it before he was subdued by Hugh the Iron and William the Pig, who were the only residents of Tamerlane House large enough to literally rip the engines off his back. "Any sign of Dee yet?"

"There aren't that many places to hide in the Nameless Isles," said John, "and we've already re-secured the access to Shakespeare's Bridge, so really, where can they go?"

"Did you notice?" Twain asked. "Dee has no shadow."

"I have some experience being shadowless," said Jack. "What I'm wondering about is that threat he made to smash the bridge."

"Be glad he didn't," said Twain. "I'm all but certain that would have thrown us straightaway into the realm of the Echthroi."

"That's my point," said Jack. "We'd be at the mercy of his masters. So why not do it? And if Rose and the others do manage to restore the keep, then the Echthroi would be driven out of the Archipelago. So isn't that a huge loss for him?"

"He has his own versions of our watches," said Twain. "He would have seen the same resetting of the prime zero point that we did."

"That's why he's here!" Jack cried. "He knows that it's about to happen. So where *is* he?"

"I'm just wondering," said Shakespeare, "but has anyone thought to check the boathouse?"

Quickly the Caretakers took a head count of themselves and their allies and realized that one of them was missing.

"Argus," Jack said, his heart sinking. "The shipbuilder is missing. And I think I know what Dee is going to try to do."

Waving for the others to follow, Jack grabbed up Hawthorne's sledgehammer and bolted out the door. John, Irving, Dumas, Verne, and Jason's son Hugh followed him, taking whatever weapons they could grab along the way.

Inside the south boathouse the Caretakers found Dr. Dee and the missing Argus—but minutes too late. The shipbuilder had already completed the work Dee had forced him to do.

Where there had once been a gaping, splintered hole in the prow of the *Black Dragon,* there was now the massive, regally maned head of a cat that aspired to be a lion. It was Grimalkin, the Cheshire cat of Tamerlane House, an angel become Echthros, and it was now part of a living ship. That gave it will, and power—and it was still in the thrall of John Dee.

Argus was half sitting, half standing on the dock alongside the ship. Even from a distance the Caretakers could tell he had been beaten, and badly. His shirt was torn, and bruises were visible on his shoulder and chest. Worse, there was a bandage over his left eye that was oozing with blood.

"Dee," Jack muttered. "I've had about enough of him."

Yelling and brandishing their weapons, the Caretakers charged into the boathouse, but Dee was prepared for them. He pressed a contact on the wall, and a sudden explosion threw all of them to the ground.

Splinters of wood flew everywhere, and the billowing smoke obscured their view of the ship—but when it started to clear, they saw there was a gaping hole in the wall of the boathouse. The ship was gone, and Dee and Argus were gone with it.

"I think this must have been part of his plan all along," said John. "We lost the only Dragon we had when Madoc left, and with him, any possibility of crossing the Frontier into the Archipelago. But if Dee has a living ship, bonded with a creature that was once an angel . . ." His words trailed off into a stunned silence.

"It can cross over," Jack said, "and I say we let it. Remember what is happening in the Archipelago? Or what used to be the Archipelago, anyway. It's all Echthroi. All Shadow. I say let them go and good riddance."

Once the extra material that Shakespeare had added was stripped off the Zanzibar Gate, the stone was easy enough for Madoc to pull apart. As he began to construct the base of the keep, Rose used Caliburn to cut branches into planks to use as support beams, while the rest of their friends busied themselves mixing mud to use for mortar.

"So," Fred observed as he dropped more straw into the pit where Quixote, Laura Glue, and Edmund were stomping it into the mud with their feet, "if the stones that Will used to make the Zanzibar Gate came from the original keep, but now we're back here helping t' build the original keep, then where did the original stones come from the first time? Isn't that one of those

. . . conundrum things Scowler Jules is always going on about?"

"A pair of ducks," Uncas said as he dumped his own armload of straw in, taking great care not to get wet. "That's what Mr. Telemachus said it was called."

"A paradox, you mean," said Edmund, "and no, I don't think so. Rose and I have learned that time only *seems* to move in two directions—but it really just moves forward, along with the events you perceive. So this is still the original keep, because we're building it for the first time. It's never been built before."

"But it'll still be there when we get back to our own time, because it's been rebuilt, right?"

"Yes."

"So," Fred repeated, "if the keep never fell in our timeline, then where did Will get the stone to make the Zanzibar Gate?"

Edmund frowned, and bit his lip. "Uh, hmm," he said. "I see your point. I'll tell you what. If it works, we'll never bring it up again. And if it doesn't, we'll have plenty of time to debate it. Agreed?"

"Gotcha," said Fred. "You don't know the answer either, do you?"

"Not the faintest clue," said Edmund.

"Oh, dear Lord in heaven," Shakespeare said, grabbing Hawthorne by the arm. "Look, Nathaniel!"

The small island where the Zanzibar Gate had been built was empty. The rickety bridge was still there, as was the path that had led to the gate. But the gate itself had vanished. It was simply *gone*.

Hawthorne waved over several of the other Caretakers and

pointed to the now empty island, and they quickly realized that something terrible had happened.

"It's supposed to continue to exist here, in the same way that the keep had duration, wasn't it, Will?" Dumas asked. "So how can a stationary object like that have simply disappeared?"

"I really cannot say," a bewildered Shakespeare answered. "The only way it could have disappeared is if it had been completely disassembled, but I don't know why anyone would even consider doing that, especially if it was their only means of coming home!"

"That's it, then," Verne said to himself quietly. "It's time to go."

As the other Caretakers debated what to do with the Cabal, and wondered what had happened to the Zanzibar Gate, none of them had noticed Verne slip away into the house—none, that is, except for one. Verne made his way to the lower stairs that led down to the basement and closed the door firmly behind him.

"What in heaven's name is he doing?" Bert murmured to himself. "There's no way out of that basement, and there's nothing down there except for"—he slapped himself on the forehead—"time-travel devices."

Bert dashed for the stairs and threw open the door. "Curse you, Jules," he muttered under his breath. "What are you up to now?"

Bert got his answer when he reached the bottom of the stairs. Verne was sitting in the time machine Bert had used himself so long ago to travel into the far future.

"Are you mad?" Bert exclaimed, rushing over to stop his colleague. "I can't believe you're just running away from this! You've never avoided a fight, Jules! And besides, this is not the way! You've used this machine before, so you can't use it again!"

"Oh, but I can," Verne said as he flipped the switches to line them up with the dials on his watch. "There's just a price to pay for doing so, and my bill is long, long overdue."

"It's suicide!" Bert cried, backing away as the wheel behind the plush chair on the device began to spin.

"No," said Verne, "it's the endgame, at least for me. And that means it is redemption."

"What do you mean?"

"The watches have all been reset," Verne replied, "but the keep has not yet reappeared, nor has the Archipelago been restored. Something is amiss. I think I know what is lacking—and none of our friends should have to sacrifice themselves. Not after all they have been through."

Bert stared at him, puzzled, and then he realized—somehow, this had been in Verne's plans all along.

"Yes, old friend," Verne said, nodding as tears began to well in his eyes. "I always knew. They have found the true zero point, and at long last, I get to be the hero of the story instead of . . . well, whatever I've been. Tell John . . ." He paused. The lights were spinning faster and faster now, and the edges of the machine were beginning to blur. "Tell him I said I'm very proud of him. It may not mean much now. But someday . . ." He flipped the last switch, adjusted the last dial. "That's it, then," he said with finality. "Time to go."

"Jules!" Bert cried, shielding his eyes from the light.

"Be seeing you," said Verne. And then, in a trice, he and the time machine were gone.

"All right," Madoc said, dusting off his hands. "I think we have it."

There, constructed around the stone circle and the stone table, were the first two levels of the Keep of Time. There had been just enough stones in the Zanzibar Gate for a structure that was tall enough to permit a doorway to be included, as well as the first floor of interlocking stairs, and a landing and framework for the first door up above.

"I'm afraid I don't know enough about how it functions," Madoc admitted. "Is there something we have to do to turn it on?"

"One last thing," Telemachus replied. "One last stone. That, and that alone, is what makes the tower a living thing."

Madoc looked around, puzzled. "We've used all the stones from the gate," he said, "and I don't see any more cavorite around."

The old man shook his head. "Not cavorite. The keystone of the keep must be a living heart, willingly given. Only then can the tower come to life, and grow. Only then will time be restored."

"Oh, fewmets," said Fred. "I knew there was going to be a catch in all this."

"If I must," said Madoc, before any of the others could speak. "It seems, dear Rose, that I am always sacrificing something for you. My younger self would never have believed it possible to love another person as I do you. But it's true."

"It's also the reason this is not your sacrifice to make, Madoc," said Telemachus. "You have already given her your heart, and she gave it to another."

"Curses," said Charles. "I knew Burton would find some way to give me a headache. Well," he added resignedly, "I suppose it falls to me."

Telemachus shook his head. "Your Prime Time has passed,

and you now exist in Spare Time. You cannot give your heart to this, Caretaker."

Fred stepped forward, whiskers twitching nervously. "I c'n do this," he said, trying his best to control the quavering in his voice. "I'll give my heart, t' rebuild th' keep."

For the first time, the companions saw Telemachus's features soften. He knelt and put his hand on the little badger's shoulder. "Your heart is big enough to contain a thousand towers," he said gently, "but it was not meant for this, little Child of the Earth."

Rose swallowed hard and gripped Edmund's hand tighter. She knew that he was about to volunteer, but Telemachus held up a hand. "Nor you, my young Cartographer. You have a great destiny ahead of you, and this is not it."

"Then who?" Quixote said, swallowing hard.

In just that moment, a blinding flash appeared on the hill just behind them, and an object appeared, throwing off sparks and belching smoke.

"I have always wanted to ride to the rescue," said a figure emerging from the smoke, "but I always entertained a vision of being able to enjoy having done so, afterward."

"Hah!" said Charles. "That may be literally the most timely entrance I have witnessed in my life—either of them."

"Well met, Caretaker," Jules Verne said as he extended his hand to Charles. "It seems as if I've arrived in the nick."

"Look," Telemachus said. . . . "See what your efforts have wrought."

Chapter Twenty

Restoration

"*Jules!*" Rose exclaimed, throwing herself at him with a giant hug. "How did you find us?"

"You made this a zero point when you came here, Rose," Verne said, smiling broadly. "All I had to do was set the dials and throw a switch. It seems as if everything that needed fixing has been fixed . . .

". . . almost."

Charles shook his head sorrowfully. "You came here for nothing, Jules," he said. "People like you and I don't fit the billing."

Verne's eyes narrowed. "What do you mean?"

Charles walked Verne around the nearly completed keep. "It needs a keystone—a living heart, to make the keep a living tower," he explained. "Tulpas exist in what this old fellow calls 'Spare Time,' and as such we aren't suitable candidates to—"

He stopped when he recognized the carefully neutral expression on Verne's face—and grew visibly angry when he realized what it meant. "You sorry son of a—"

"What?" Rose exclaimed, glancing anxiously from one Caretaker to the other. "Uncle Charles, what is it?"

"He's not a tulpa," Charles said, still glaring at Verne. "He never *was*."

"It's too high a price, Telemachus," Madoc said. "I won't allow another to sacrifice himself just for the sake of this keep."

"Telemachus?" Verne said, eyes widening in surprise. "Well, lad, you've, ah, aged a bit, since I saw you last."

"The sacrifice has already been made," Telemachus said softly, answering Madoc but looking at Verne. "All that remains is for you to make use of the gift that has been offered to you."

The companions turned as one to look at Verne, and gasped at what they saw. His hands were already the distinctive silver-gray of cavorite; tendrils of stone were already forming on his neck and were slowly moving upward.

"It's the price that must be paid for reusing a time-travel device," said Verne. "The universe can be fooled only so many times before she claims you, and pulls you to her bosom, and makes you one with eternity."

"You must decide quickly," said Telemachus, "before the process is completed. His heart will be cavorite soon, but it must be taken while it is still beating."

"Take his heart?" Fred gasped. "Out of his chest?"

"You must do it, Madoc," Telemachus said, with a trace of both sternness and finality in his voice. "You are the Architect, and so the placement of the keystone is for you to do."

Madoc nodded and turned to his daughter. "It's a fortunate thing that I repaired your blade," he said, reaching for her bag, "because it seems I'm going to need to use it."

Holding Caliburn in front of him with his right hand, Madoc strode to Verne and placed his left hand on the Caretaker's shoulder. "I cannot say whether I consider you an adversary or an ally," Madoc said, "but I do understand the value of this sacrifice. And I honor you."

"Believe it or not," Verne said with tears in his eyes, "that is all I needed to hear."

Madoc put his hand over the Caretaker's eyes and with a few swift strokes of the sword removed Verne's still-beating heart.

"Put it there," Telemachus instructed, "where the two stairways meet."

Madoc did as he was told, then covered the heart with one of the standing stones they had found when they arrived. "Blood for blood," he said to the keep. "May it be worth the price we have paid this day."

Madoc stepped out of the keep to where Quixote, Fred, and Uncas were covering Verne's body. "We'll bury him here," he said. "If something goes wrong, we shouldn't be carrying around his body."

Reluctantly, and with great sorrow, the companions agreed. Verne had been such a presence in all of their lives that it was almost too much to bear that his own had ended so abruptly.

"Look," Telemachus said as they were finishing the burial. "See what your efforts have wrought."

Laura Glue was the first to see it and could barely contain her expression of delight, even though the sadness she felt at Verne's death was still visible on her face.

The tower had grown by several feet as they worked. And now, as they watched, it grew taller still.

"It's done, Father," Rose said, her voice barely audible. "You have come full circle at last, and restored what was broken."

• • •

"The keep has been restored," said Madoc, "but the question still remains—how do we get back?"

"It's the Keep of Time, and there's only one door," Telemachus said simply. "That means when you go through it, you'll be going into the future."

"In the old keep, only the uppermost door went into the future," said Charles, "and this one has a doorway, not an actual door. How do we know it will go to the future?"

"That's just it," said Edmund. "From here, there isn't anything *but* future. It's *all* future. So we simply have to focus on the point in the future we want to arrive at, and we should go directly then." He stopped and swallowed hard. "I hope."

"You're entirely right, young Cartographer," said the old man. "It's just as if you were standing at the South Pole—the only direction you could go would be north.

"When you walk through the doorway," Telemachus explained, "it will give significance to the moment, but also duration. You will have begun the process that links the beginning of all things to the future. Here, in this place, it will begin to grow, and it will anchor Chronos time and Kairos time once more—and by connecting this moment to your own future, you will ensure that the connection between the Archipelago and the Summer Country will be restored."

"So theoretically speaking," said Rose, "after accounting for the actual days we've been gone, we should end up right about the time we left, right?"

Telemachus consulted his watch and his face paled. "Oh dear," he said softly. "I didn't realize . . ."

"What is it?" Madoc demanded. "What kind of game are you trying to play now?"

Telemachus held up a hand in supplication and shook his head. "You misunderstand. It's the avoidance of game playing that has become my purpose, and many years ago . . ." He paused, looking at Edmund. "Many years ago, in my own timeline, I made a promise not to manipulate events if it was in my power to do so. I have helped, encouraged, and prodded at times, but I have never deliberately tried to shape a particular outcome, nor will I do so now."

"Are you saying that going through the doorway won't take us home?" asked Rose.

"Not at all," Telemachus answered mysteriously. "I'm absolutely certain that it will. But it will not be the end of your challenges. There is still one trial to come, and you may have to pay your way through it with dearest blood."

She looked at him curiously. "You say that *we* have to pay, but you are coming with us . . . aren't you?"

He shook his head. "I cannot come with you, I'm afraid," he said. "This is the only place in time where the two of us can exist together, at least in the Summer Country—and that's where you're going. There can only ever be one Imago and one Archimago on earth at the same time—and until now, I have been the Imago. But when you step through the doorway, that burden will shift over to you, and someday you will be the Imago, Rose."

"Not to argue," said Edmund, "but isn't she the Imago already? Or at least, since she's the best candidate, won't that simply just make her the Imago by default?"

Telemachus's response was unexpected. His eyes welled up with tears, and silently, he began to weep.

"Here, Mr. Telemachus," Fred said, offering him a handkerchief. "Take a minute, why don'tcha."

When he had regained his composure, he took Rose by the hands. "No," he said, answering Edmund's question. "It is not as simple as being Named. It is not even as simple as taking the responsibility by choice. It is something that must be hard fought for, and hard earned. And there will be times when you want to cast it off, but you won't. Because you know it is your purpose to one day be the Imago, and purpose is invincible.

"One day you will have done enough, and learned enough. It grieves me that there is still so much living that you must do before that day. But it will be worth it, my dear Rose. . . ." This last he said as he transformed once more from the ancient sage into the young man wearing the Ruby Armor. "It will be worth it. Because the Imago protects life. And as long as there is life . . .

". . . it is such a wonderful world we live in, after all.

"And Rose," he added as they waved farewell, "if things go well for all of you, you may see me again, after."

Madoc had deliberately made certain the entrance of the keep was wide enough to accommodate the *Indigo Dragon*, but he had neglected to do the same for the door inside. They were debating whether to leave the airship behind when Fred suddenly noticed that the inside of the tower had expanded. Suddenly there was more than enough room to maneuver the ship inside and through the doorway.

The little badger stroked the stones on the outside of the keep. "Thanks, Scowler Jules," he said with earnest humility. "We appreciate it a lot."

"All right," Rose said to the others. "Let's see if we can go home one more time."

Together, the companions climbed into the airship, and Fred guided it through the doorway.

The *Indigo Dragon* entered the doorway of the keep, which disappeared as they passed through. On the other side, it was night, and the airship slid quietly onto the East Lawn of Tamerlane House.

"We did it," Laura Glue said, squeezing Edmund's hand, then reaching out to hug Quixote and the badgers. "We found them, and brought them home."

Growing happier by the moment, the companions leaped out of the airship and raced for the front door of the house. Throwing it open and dashing inside, they were greeted by the very familiar face of a dear friend who was taking his tea by the hearth.

"Rose! Edmund! Charles!" Jack exclaimed as he leaped from his chair, scattering tea and cakes all across the room. "Uncas! Laura Glue! Fred!" He stopped, eyes wide. "And Madoc! You are all returned, finally! At last! At last!"

The Caretaker rushed to embrace the companions, and could not hold back his tears. He wept freely, in both joy and relief, as did all the newly returned companions, including Madoc.

"I can't believe it!" Jack exclaimed. "Somehow, I knew deep down you'd return, but it's been so long. So long!" He embraced Rose again, then shook Edmund's hand. Fred and Uncas, however, both held back. Something was wrong.

Laura Glue caught the same whiff of uncertainty. "You look . . . younger than I remember," she said, not bothering to conceal her suspicion. "How do we know you aren't an Echthros?"

Jack chuckled, but Charles knew him well enough to note the fleeting expression of pain that danced across his features, as well as to realize what Laura Glue and the badgers only suspected, and the others had no clue of at all.

"I'm not the enemy," Jack said blithely, "but yes, things have changed. After all, you have been gone a very long time."

"How long?" asked Charles. "And what, specifically, has changed about you, Jack?"

"Nothing about him is different than you remember," another Caretaker said as he stepped into the room. "He's just been youthened."

It was James Barrie—one of the portrait-bound Caretakers who resided in the gallery at Tamerlane House. He spoke directly to the young Valkyrie and grasped her shoulders with an affectionate firmness. "I don't yet know how long it has been for you, Laura-my-Glue, but for us, here, it has been almost twenty years since you went on your little rescue mission into the Zanzibar Gate. And it has been almost three years now since Jack came to join us in the gallery."

As one, all the companions gasped and looked in astonishment at Jack. "You're a *portrait?*" Rose said breathlessly. "That means you're . . ."

"Dead," Jack said matter-of-factly as he stepped to her and kissed her on the forehead. "I waited for you to return for the rest of my life, and then some. And it was worth the wait—because at long last, you have come back, dear, dear Rose."

As Barrie went to alert the other Caretakers, Jack and the companions settled in around the table in the dining hall so that he could begin to tell them about what had happened in the years since they'd left.

"I married, and adopted a son," Jack told them, "as unlikely as either seemed to be in the years when you knew me. I lost her soon after, but it was still a thrilling, heartbreaking, wonderful part of my life."

"That reminds me," he added, turning to Charles. "I've also had to continue taking care of the Magwich plant, which has progressed in size from shrub to tree. Karmically speaking," he continued, "you now owe me several lifetimes' worth of favors."

"I thought Warnie was helping take care of him, at the Kilns?"

"He did, for a time," said Jack. "The problem was that Magwich would never shut up, and he was starting to attract attention, so we had to relocate him here."

"Here?" Charles said, unable to keep himself from cringing. "You brought that Maggot to Tamerlane House?"

"Not Tamerlane specifically," said John. "We planted him on one of the outer islands, where Jason's sons go to play their war games. He gets to talk to someone, and they completely ignore him. It's an entirely amicable arrangement."

"What happened here?" Charles asked as the other Caretakers began to arrive. "The house looks as if it went through some major renovations that were either poorly planned or badly executed."

"There was a battle," Dickens explained as he took a seat next to Charles, "between the Caretakers and Dee and his minions, and Tamerlane House paid the greatest price, I'm afraid."

"Several of the towers and minarets had been toppled, and almost the whole of the north wing was destroyed," said Hawthorne.

"We did add to our collective real estate, however," Twain said as he entered the room and kissed Rose on the top of her head. "The House on the Borderlands is now our neighbor."

"What?" Charles and Fred exclaimed at once.

"Yes," Bert said as he joined them at the table, eyes filled with tears. "The Cabal, or most of them, anyway, have established a truce with the Caretakers."

"Where's John?" Rose asked. "Is he . . . ?"

"Oh, he's still among the living," said Jack, "and still the Prime Caretaker. He just has a great deal of business to tend to at Oxford these days. We've sent for him, and he should be here at any—"

"Where are they?" John exclaimed as he burst through the door. "Are they really . . . ?"

"Hello, Uncle John," Rose said, jumping to her feet. "You've gotten older!"

"I have," he said, hugging her closely, "while you have stayed exactly the same, just as I'd hoped."

Part Six

Beyond the Wall

. . . the island where the last inn stood . . .

Chapter Twenty-One

Tabula Rasa Geographica

The great bridge of bone reached across almost the entire width of the ocean, but stopped just short of the Lonely Isle.

Poets and painters had dreamed about the island, which stood at the farthest reaches of existence, and which was the last haven for travelers before they reached the shores of eternity. And in truth, dreaming was the simplest way to reach it, and the only way most ever would.

For the great Dragon Samaranth, it meant using the last relic of the life he had lived before this one, when he was a Maker in a wondrous green city at the edge of an ocean far, far away.

It was a chest made of amethyst, and it was meant to contain worlds. Slowly, carefully, he placed all the lands of the Archipelago of Dreams into it, and then released the great beasts to return to the deserts and mountains where he had gathered them.

To his smallest, last friend, he offered a choice, and was not surprised by the badger's answer, but was surprised by his own gratitude at receiving it.

Together, they made their way through the storm-tossed sea to the island where the last inn stood, where they would be greeted by the last of the angels from the City of Jade, and where they would wait, for as long as they were able.

At their knock, an old woman opened the door. Her expression was one of joy, then of sorrow at seeing her old friend. "To cross the threshold requires a price," she said. "Will you pay it willingly?"

"I shall," the great Dragon rumbled, "for myself, and my friend, Tummeler."

"Then enter and be welcomed, Samaranth, and Master Tummeler," she said. They stepped across, and she handed them an hourglass made of bone. "You have until the last sand runs out," she admonished. "To the last grain, and no more."

Samaranth nodded. "I understand. Thank you, Sycorax."

She closed the door behind them and went to set their places for tea. If she had paused a moment more, she would have seen the black ship not far behind. Soon there would be more company. Very soon.

The companions and the Caretakers spent the entire night telling and retelling stories, to catch up the companions on twenty years of missed history, as well as to tell the Caretakers about the unknown history of the keep itself—and about the sacrifice that had made restoration possible.

They bowed their heads, and there was a long, respectful moment of silence for the man who had been one of the greatest Caretakers of them all.

"To Scowler Jules," Fred said, raising his glass.

"To Scowler Jules," the Caretakers chorused.

"And what of Poe?" Charles asked. "What happened to him?"

John's expression darkened, and he glanced at both Bert and Twain before he answered. "We haven't seen him again," he said, choosing his words carefully, "and I'm not certain that's a bad thing."

"I still don't understand," Rose said, "why we lost twenty years in passing through the doorway."

"I think I know," Shakespeare offered. "My gate was made from the keep, but it was not the keep. Not the same. It still relied on technology and mechanical programming more than simple intuition, and thus could be more precisely programmed. Whereas the doorway in the keep could not."

"Wasn't that the original reason the Dragons added doors to the keep?" Edmund asked. "To better focus the chronal energies?"

"I think so," said John. "At least, that's my understanding of how it worked for traveling in time."

"That may also be the difference between the time-travel devices and mechanisms and your own uses of chronal maps and trumps," Shakespeare said. "Those latter draw very strongly on will and intuition, and rely less on mathematics and science, and so I think they are subject to fewer laws."

"Limitations," Twain said, puffing on his cigar. "When you use science, you by definition put things in boxes. You create limits. And thus it follows you would be bound by those limits. But doing what these young'uns do," he added, gesturing at Rose and Edmund, "that is, literally and in every other sense of the word, *art*. And art has no limitation."

"So did it work?" Rose asked. "Has the keep been restored? Is the Archipelago back?"

"The keep, yes," said Twain. "The Archipelago, no."

"When it was being taken over by the Echthroi," John explained, "we know from the message Aven left on Paralon that Samaranth somehow . . . removed all the lands and peoples of the

Archipelago and took them somewhere safe. The problem is, we have no idea where."

"Have you tried summoning him, from one of the Rings?" asked Madoc. "I'm not so good at it myself, but then again, I never had permission."

"We have all tried it," said John. "Every man and woman among the Caretakers, and a few associates and apprentices besides."

"He was waiting," a new voice said, "for the Imago to return, so that she would be the one to restore the Archipelago."

It was the Watchmaker, the ancient being who resided on the island to the northwest of Tamerlane House. But the companions who had just returned from the deep past now knew him by a different name.

"Enoch," Rose said as she and her companions moved forward to embrace him. The Caretakers were fairly stunned—the Watchmaker had never left his cave, as far as they knew. Ever.

"He had a name?" John said to Bert. "I never knew that."

"The Summoning was not going to be sufficient," Enoch said, ignoring the curious stares from the Caretakers, "not until the keep itself was restored. And now that has been done, you're going to have to go find the lands of the Archipelago and bring them back."

"Back from where, Enoch?" Rose asked. "Where did Samaranth take them?"

"Beyond the End of the World," the Maker said, "past the Great Wall, and to the shores of heaven itself."

"Is that even possible?" Madoc asked. "Mind you, I speak from experience at having tried."

Enoch nodded. "You are a Dragon, and those such as you are permitted to pass, as are those with you. But," he added cautiously, "your adversary has the services of one of the Host, who is bound to serve him, and he is already speeding his way toward his destination. If he reaches Samaranth first, then the Archipelago may still be lost."

"We have not seen him in twenty years," John explained. "Not since he forced Argus to bond Grimalkin to the hull of the *Black Dragon*."

"The cat?" Charles exclaimed. "What was he expecting to come out of that?"

"Not just a cat," John said heavily. "Grimalkin is a Fallen angel, who is bound to serve John Dee. And he can go everywhere a Dragon can go—including past the End of the World. Worse, they have a twenty-year head start."

"Perhaps not," said Enoch. "Time operated differently past the wall. What seemed to us to be years can be a far shorter time to someone on the other side."

"Great," said Fred. "That's just what we need—more time-travel issues."

"You misunderstand," said Enoch. "The moment you came through the door of the keep, you realigned Chronos time and Kairos time. It is now the same on both sides of the Frontier, and that includes the flow of time past the wall. So while years were passing here, your adversary has been in flight only a short time."

"Which means we can still catch them!" John said, rising to his feet. "What are we waiting for? Let's go!"

"Please, tell me that we are not actually this insane," Jack pleaded. "I know we have had our differences, John, but—"

"What he means to say is we have really missed you, Charles," John said, giving Jack an exasperated look. "You were a tempering agent between us, and you were sorely missed. Especially since he died. There's been no end to the arguments after that."

"What I'm trying to say is that you aren't as young as you used to be, and this is a task for others to do."

"I understand your reservations, Jack, but this is not a negotiation," John said. "I'm going to go."

"I'm sorry, John," Twain said, his voice filled with honest regret, "but you cannot go. You are the Prime Caretaker in fact as well as name, and your choices guide the path of this group. You must remain here."

John glowered at the others for a moment, then sat down, sighing heavily. "I suppose you're going to want to go with them," he said to Jack.

"It's been a long time," Jack said. "I haven't left Tamerlane House much, and, not to put too fine a point on it, I am now younger than you."

"Hah," John said. "That's just because Basil painted you younger."

"Look at it this way," Jack said, winking at Rose as he got up from the table, "someday you'll die too, and then you can go save the world with us."

"Oh, shut up," John huffed. "Go do what must be done. And then," he added, "hurry back."

It didn't take long for everyone at Tamerlane House to realize that save for the loss of Kipling, the current crew of the *Indigo Dragon* was the perfect team to undertake difficult tasks. "The Young Magicians," Jack said as he climbed aboard. "You are the future of both worlds, you know."

"I'll be content enough just to save one if I can," said Edmund. "Let's go."

After the *Indigo Dragon* left the Nameless Isles, there was one place Rose required that they go first, before she would even contemplate pursuing the trail of Samaranth and the missing Archipelago.

"Of course," Madoc murmured. "Of course that's where we should go." Jack, Charles, Edmund, and the others all nodded in agreement. Rose blushed when she realized that she had simply given voice to an assumption they all had made before they started.

They had to see the tower first. They had to make certain the Keep of Time had indeed been restored.

"It isn't difficult to find," said Jack. "It's just about all that is left of the Archipelago."

He was right. They came upon it in a matter of hours. It was both comforting and heartbreaking to see the stark gray outline of the tower in the distance—but just seeing it was enough.

"I recall it taking far longer to get to the last time," said Charles. "Is the airship just faster, or did the Archipelago shrink?"

"Probably both," said Jack. "I think the Archipelago grew in accordance with how many lands were added, or discovered, or invented, or even imagined. And," he said, surveying the bleak, open ocean, "with no lands to fill it up, it simply got . . . smaller."

It took considerably less time for them to arrive at the only other island that couldn't be removed by Samaranth, because it was the very island that marked the edge of the original Archipelago.

"Terminus," Madoc said as he leaned heavily against the railing. "I never expected to see it again."

"Father, are you all right?" Rose asked.

"I am . . . remembering," Madoc answered slowly. "The last time I went over the side of this waterfall, it wasn't in a ship."

"Wait!" Charles exclaimed. "What about the different gates, below," he said as the ship flew down the face of the waterfall. "Aren't there dangers abounding here?"

"I don't think we'll find any," said Jack. "It's been twenty years since you restored the keep, so we've had a little time to look around. As far as we could tell, when the Echthroi occupied the whole of the region, they completely absorbed or destroyed all the gates. It's all free passage to the end now."

"That's sort of a good-news, bad-news scenario," said Charles. "It's the first thing that the Echthroi have ever done that I was actually happy to hear about."

It was dark by the time the ship reached the bottom of the waterfall and began sailing over open ocean again.

"When we came this way before, there were thousands of lights above," Rose said wonderingly, "and the Professor said they were Dragons. I wonder where they've gone?"

"I thought you had, ah, released all the Dragons with the sword," said Edmund, "and that there weren't any left."

"Those were all who descended from angel to Dragon at Samaranth's urging, when the City of Jade fell," said Madoc, "but they were not all the Dragons there are, nor were they the first Dragons of creation."

"Where have they gone?" asked Rose. "What's happened to all of them?"

Madoc shrugged. "I can't say for certain. Samaranth taught me that this plane borders heaven itself, and so that may be where they have returned to. Why, I have no idea."

"It was the Echthroi," said Fred. "The entire Archipelago was lost to shadow. I don't think any Dragon would stick around to watch over a world that we screwed up that badly."

"Maybe when we put everything right," said Rose, "the Dragons will return again." She looked up into the darkness and sighed. "Maybe."

"It shouldn't be too long now," Madoc said as he and Rose consulted the *Imaginarium Geographica*. "We're almost there, at the End of the World."

"There was a time not long ago," said Uncas, "that we believed Terminus and th' waterfalls was the End of the World, but then we found out it went beyond that. And now, we're finding out that the boundary is even farther away. I'm starting to think there's no end to anything!"

"There was also a time," Jack said wryly, "when you would have taken my shadow for the chance to have that book, Madoc. And done many other terrible things besides."

"Jack!" Rose exclaimed. "I can't believe you said that!"

"It's all right," Madoc said, shushing her. "It's better that I know these things, if he feels they are worth saying."

"This will be difficult to hear," Jack said. "You are not the man now that you were then."

Madoc considered Jack's words, then slowly nodded his head. "True," he said at last, "I am not. I have been several men since that time, and a Dragon besides. But I think I am better than I was. I hope I am. And if that is true, I should be able to bear an accounting of my own darker choices."

"Fair enough," Jack said, turning to the others. "During our first great conflict with, ah, the Winter King, we discovered something that chilled us all to the core. We were focused on safeguarding the *Imaginarium Geographica* and by extension the Archipelago, but Mordred knew how connected this world was to our own. And he knew that as devoted as we had become to seeing through what we had promised Bert and Professor Sigurdsson we would do, we might abandon our responsibilities as Caretakers if something we cared for more was threatened."

"Something?" Rose asked, looking at her father.

"Someone," Madoc replied, meeting his daughter's gaze.

"Several someones, actually," said Jack. "Mordred had dispatched several Shadow-Born to the Summer Country, to seek out and . . . murder our loved ones. Charles's wife. My mother, and best friend. And John's young wife, Edith, as well as his eldest child, then newly born."

Uncas glared at Madoc with barely contained fury. "That in't right," he said, his voice low and trembling. "Goin' after younglings . . . That in't right."

Strangely enough, it was the badger's anger that affected Madoc most of all. Everyone else—every human—he faced squarely, fully accepting that his past sins were choices for which he would continue to pay. But he struggled to meet the badger's eyes.

"Charles never knew," Jack continued, "and I was still young and brash enough not to understand the gravity of the situation. But John knew, and understood. And he realized that if we abandoned our duties here to try to race back to save our loved ones, then both worlds might be lost. So the decision was made to soldier on and try to find a way to defeat the Winter King. It was the only way we could save them."

He paused, and put a hand to his forehead. "I . . . I found out later, through James Barrie, and some of Verne's Mystorians, that the Shadow-Born came closer than we realized to killing our families. In fact, two of them were right outside Edith's door—close enough to hear her singing lullabies to young John, the baby, in his crib.

"It was in that moment that Charles and Tummeler figured out how to use Perseus's shield to close Pandora's Box and reseal all the Shadow-Born within it. At once, all the—the Shadow-Born vanished, including the assassins that had been dispatched to the Summer Country."

"I never heard that story," Uncas said, eyes shining with pride. "Your grandfather was a credit to badgers everywhere," he said, clapping Fred on the back. "A credit, I tell you."

"The reason I wanted to share that story," Jack continued as he leaned against the railing, "is so that you understand that all our choices are cumulative—and we must always keep the bigger picture in mind. Sometimes . . . sometimes the stakes that are more personal can distract us from the goals that are more necessary to achieve. And that's—that's when you must be resolute. . . ."

The Caretaker's voice trailed off as he rubbed his temple. "I—I think I need to sit down."

Before any of the companions could assist him, Jack's eyes rolled back in his head and he pitched forward, already unconscious.

Standing atop the rocks before them . . . was a Cherubim . . .

Chapter Twenty-Two

The Lonely Isle

"*It's happened several times,*" Jack admitted as Laura Glue dabbed at his forehead with a damp cloth. "Mostly just headaches, but they've been increasing in frequency and intensity over the last few years. And in the last several months, I've started having blackouts."

"And no one at Tamerlane House noticed?" asked Rose.

Jack shook his head and propped himself up to a sitting position. "I'm good at hiding the headaches," he admitted. "That's what a lifetime of British reserve will do for you. And only Dumas ever saw me black out, but I managed to explain it away. I didn't want any of them thinking something was amiss."

"You're already dead," Charles said bluntly. "You're technically a portrait, Jack, and I'm a thought-form given flesh. People like us don't *get* headaches or have blackouts. It simply doesn't happen."

"If he's stable for the moment," said Edmund, "we can discuss it later. I think we've arrived."

The wall at the End of the World stood above a shallow beach, which was barely wide enough to pull a boat onto, but the wall itself rose so high that not even the keen-eyed Archie could fly high enough to see the top of it.

"Is it even possible to get over or through?" Jack asked. "Can it be done, Madoc?"

"I could not have done it then," said Madoc. "That is indisputable, because heaven knows I tried. I walked the length of the wall in both directions until my strength gave out, and the only way to restore it was to return here, to the center. The compulsion was unbearable, but crossing was impossible. And thus is hell on earth attained. But now, yes—it may be possible."

"Because you're a Dragon?" asked Fred.

"A Dragon *can* cross," said Madoc. "A true Dragon, at any rate. I have been one in the past, and the Zanzibar Gate proved that I carry with me some of the aspect of a Dragon still. But this is different."

"How is it different?" asked Charles. "It's just a wall, isn't it?"

"On this side, yes," said Madoc. "But behind it is the true Unknown Region. It is the source of the Dragons, and all the magic that is in the Archipelago. It is the true beginning of the world, and whatever lands we may find might very well be within sight of the shores of heaven itself."

"So how do we get over it?" asked Charles.

"We don't go over," said Madoc. "We go *through*."

Two great doors, hundreds of feet high, with sculpted angels on either side, suddenly materialized out of the mist and gloom as if they had been there all along—which, the companions realized, they probably had been.

"It's like with the Zanzibar Gate," said Laura Glue. "Your presence alone activates whatever is needed."

"Such is the power of a Dragon," Madoc murmured. "If only I had known then . . ."

He took the reins to the goats from Fred and urged them onward with a gentle shake, and quickly, they crossed the wall into the Unknown Region.

"It's an old children's poem, I think," Madoc said as they surveyed the landscape past the Great Wall. "Something about an impossible desert, or something like that . . ."

"I can tell," Archie said, dropping from his perch atop the airship's balloon, "that you have sorely neglected your studies while I've been away."

"Is that what you call it?" Madoc replied with a grin. "'Away'?"

The clockwork bird ignored him and instead began to recite a poem. To his delight, Laura Glue joined in, chanting the verses along with him.

Cross the uncrossable desert, tally-yee, tally-yay.
Climb the unclimbable mountain, tally-yee, tally-yay.
Swim the impassable sea, tally-yee, tally-yay.
Find the house that angels made,
On the isle of bone.
Pay the price that angels paid,
On the isle, alone.
Choose the Name that shows your face,
Drink your tea and take your place.
At Hades's gate or heaven's shore.
There to live, forevermore.
Tally-yee, tally-yay.

"There, Caretakers," Madoc said, winking at Rose. "Find that bit of wisdom in your little *Geographica*."

"It isn't *in* the *Imaginarium Geographica*," said Fred. "That's what the Little Whatsits are for. Page two hundred ninety-six." He looked up at Archimedes. "I see what you mean about his education."

Madoc laughed. "Point taken, little fellow."

"So what does it all mean?" asked Charles.

"It's our map," said Jack. "All the wisdom in the world can be found in fairy tales and nursery rhymes. And, it seems," he added, scratching Fred behind his neck, "in the Little Whatsits."

"I see the end of the desert already," Laura Glue said, shading her eyes, "and beyond that, the mountain."

"Surely Samaranth passed this way years and years ago," said Charles.

"Perhaps," Rose said. "But remember what Enoch told us—time has been flowing differently here. It changes with one's own perception."

"And," said Madoc, "we aren't carrying the history of an entire world on our shoulders. It's going to go much more quickly for us."

As Madoc predicted, the passage over the mountain and then across the sea went quickly; in a short while, the airship passed over the last of the bridge, where it was tossed about by the storm clouds that circled the island.

"The Lonely Isle," said Fred. "The last haven in all the world."

"There's an inn on top," Charles shouted over the wind. "Aim for that, and let's see if we can't land without crashing."

They needn't have worried—once they were close to the inn,

the storm stopped. It was around the island, but in the center, it was calm. Outside the inn were some scrubby trees where they could tie up the goats and leave the airship.

"We're either just in time, or barely too late," Jack said. He pointed to the other side of the island, where a familiar black ship, also converted to an airship, had been moored.

"The *Black Dragon*, or, ah, *Black Cat*, or whatever it is now," Charles sputtered. "They're already here!"

Quickly the companions rushed up to the door, which swung open at their approach. A tall, stern-looking woman with a frazzle of graying hair spread out behind her stood there, appraising the newcomers.

"Do you know where you are?" she asked. "This is no place for visitors. There is a price to pay to sup at this inn."

"What price is that?" Madoc asked.

"One life, for one hour here," she said. "One of you must give themselves to death, or none may enter."

"All of us are coming in," Laura Glue said as she rummaged through her bag. "I've got a pass."

She pulled out the bone hourglass that the Serendipity Box had given her, turned it over, and twisted the valve. Slowly the grains began to slide through the neck of the glass.

"This is acceptable," the woman said, "as long as you understand that all of your party must abide by the glass. If any still remain on this island when the sand runs out, then all are forfeit, and if you cross the threshold again, you will die the final death, and not return."

"I understand," said Laura Glue.

The woman could barely suppress her expression of surprise

and delight. "Then you are welcome here on Youkali," she said, "but there is one more caveat—whatever you are Named, you must cross this threshold as you really are. None can be here in this place except as they truly are, and not as they appear."

"We know who we are," Rose said. "And we're not afraid to pass."

The woman stood aside, and one by one, the companions entered. Rose and Edmund simply walked across the threshold, unchanged, as did Uncas and Fred.

"We animals in't very complicated," Uncas explained as they passed.

Charles also passed unchanged. "I do feel a bit more like a writer than an editor," he said, "but I don't know if that's a good thing or a bad thing."

Quixote, however, youthened considerably as he entered the inn. "To be young in one's heart is the greatest achievement," he said.

"Good work," said Uncas.

Jack's change was much more dramatic, as was Madoc's.

On entering, Jack became a boy again, as he had once been on the island of the Lost Boys. And Madoc lost his wings, and much of his age, becoming a fresh-faced youth not much older than Jack.

"Ah," said Charles. "So now we see the truth of things. And our Madoc truly is Madoc again."

"Come," the woman said as she ushered them into the next room. "You may join our other guests for tea."

In the main room, the companions were astonished to see the tea party taking place. Sitting around an elaborately set table were five guests: a very young man with red hair that kept spilling into his eyes; a very young woman who was demurely nibbling at a cookie; an older, bearded man who wore an expression of such sadness that it was almost palpable; a very aged man, who was so old that his skin resembled the most fragile parchment, and whose eyes radiated hatred; and a badger, who immediately leaped up to greet the newcomers.

The reunion of Tummeler with his son and grandson, and with his old partner Charles, was so filled with joy and happiness that even the old woman started to tear up. The three badgers and the Caretaker whooped and hollered and hugged one another until it seemed they would burst.

"To see that, something so wonderful, I would pay almost any price," the young man said.

"Samaranth?" Rose exclaimed. "Is that you?"

"It is," the young angel replied, nodding, "but you've come just moments too late. I've already lost the Archipelago to Dr. Dee."

The companions all suddenly realized that there were hourglasses of bone identical to Laura Glue's in front of each of the guests, but only one, in front of the old man with the terrible visage, was still trickling sand through the glass.

As if in confirmation of Samaranth's words, he reached out and grasped a crystal box, which was glowing a soft purple, and pulled it across the table closer to him.

"The Archipelago," said the man they now realized was Dee, "is *mine*."

"How did you cross the threshold?" Charles exclaimed. "You would have to sacrifice a life to—"

"That's exactly what I did," Dee said, gesturing at a

sorry-looking shadow in the far corner. "What do you think I brought Crowley for?"

"My time ran out, all too quickly," Samaranth said, "and as Sycorax can confirm, I cannot take the Amethyst Box with me without destroying the entire Archipelago."

"But the time limits," Jack began.

"The box is protected," the woman Sycorax said, "but it must be taken elsewhere, away from this house, before it can be opened."

"We can take it!" Rose exclaimed, reaching for the box.

"No!" Dee shouted. "I have already claimed it! By the rules of Deep Magic, it is mine!"

"Is that true?" Rose asked Samaranth as her face fell. "Is it his?"

"Yes," said Samaranth. "It is. But the box can only be opened with a Master Key, and the Master Key may only be turned by an angel, or," he said, pointedly not looking at Madoc, "by a *Dragon*."

"Hah!" said Uncas. "You really blew it then, Dee. We got the only Dragon left, an' he'll *never* help you."

Dr. Dee ignored the badger, instead focusing his attention on Rose.

"I was there, in the City of Jade, before the deluge," Dee said, his voice soft, and his eyes glittering. "I went there for two purposes. The first was to find a Master Key—one of the keys the angels used to unlock anything in creation—and the second, to find, and bind, an angel."

He stood and picked up the box. "Time to go," he said, smiling at Samaranth, and then at Rose. "Be seeing you."

Madoc, Charles, and Edmund all started to move for Dee at once, but a shout stopped them in their tracks.

"No!" Sycorax said sternly. "This is the last of the Free Houses, and no violence may be committed here."

"In other words," said Charles, "'take it outside.'"

"Just so," said Sycorax. "He still has sand in the glass and may do as he wishes."

Rose looked at the other three glasses on the table. "But you can't, can you?" she asked, already knowing the answer. "I think I understand. All of you here—you're already . . ."

"Yes," Samaranth said, nodding. "We are already on our way to the final death, where we will cross over into the next stage of being."

"I waited," the girl said, speaking for the first time, "so that I could meet you, the daughter of my heart."

"Who are you?" Rose asked.

"The one who built the bridge, but could not finish it," the girl replied. "Perhaps someday, you will finish it for me. I hope you will."

"I just didn't want to be alone," the bearded man said. "I have been here a very, very long time."

"I can tell," Jack said, looking more closely at the man. "Someone hurt you, didn't they? Hurt you badly."

"I don't think he meant to," the man said. "He was my brother. I think he was just sad, and I think it was my fault. I've waited here, in case he comes, so I can tell him I'm sorry."

Jack didn't respond, but instead reached out and gave the man a hug, which, after a moment, he returned.

"Oh . . . oh no," Uncas wailed, looking at Tummeler and suddenly understanding the meaning of the empty hourglass in front of Samaranth. "Does that mean . . . ?"

The old badger nodded. "It's all right, young one. I did good, helping Mr. Samaranth. And I got t' see you, and Fred, and Scowler Charles. That's a lot. In fact, that's everything."

"Not everything," Dee said as he stepped out the door, "as everyone in your precious Archipelago is about to discover."

Before anyone could stop him, Tummeler let out a loud howl and threw himself at Dee.

Samaranth jumped to his feet. "Tummeler, don't! Don't cross the threshold!" But it was too late.

The little badger fell to the ground, just outside the door. His eyes rolled back in his head, and his breathing stopped.

As the companions all cried out and moved to attend to Tummeler, Dee walked across the front of the island to where the black ship waited. Outside the inn, he returned to his usual appearance, but his face was still a mask of hatred.

At his approach, Mr. Kirke and Mr. Bangs stood and lifted the shipbuilder Argus roughly by the arms.

"Now," Dee said to the shipbuilder, "do as you did with the *Black Dragon,* and release the Cherubim from the vessel. And then we will unlock the Archipelago and reshape two worlds in the image of order. In the image . . .

". . . of the *Echthroi.*"

By the time the companions who had arrived on the *Indigo Dragon* approached Dr. Dee to reclaim the Amethyst Box, Argus was nearly finished with his task.

When the shipbuilder bonded him to the hull of the *Black Dragon,* Grimalkin had still resembled a Cheshire cat. But when the process reversed, Grimalkin emerged, shaken but whole, as a very different sort of creature.

In the same way that releasing Madoc had reverted him to a more human state, the way he had been before he became a Dragon and then allowed himself to be bonded to the ship, releasing Grimalkin reverted him to being what he had been before he was bound by Dee to serve the Echthroi.

Standing atop the rocks before them, drinking in the energies of the storm swirling above, was a Cherubim—one of the oldest angels from the City of Jade. And he was not happy.

The Caretakers and the companions who had been in the city and witnessed the transformation of angels suddenly realized that the aspect of children, of youth, that angels like Samaranth wore so easily was simply so they could more easily commune with mortals. Here, now, Grimalkin had shed that aspect of himself completely.

Around his neck was the collar he had worn as a cat—but everything else had changed. He stood nearly twelve feet tall, and had four feathered wings that stretched out behind him like a wall of steel feathers. He had great claws and wore armor that was stretched tight over muscles that rippled with the power of heaven itself. But most significantly, he now had four faces: the face of an ox, the face of an eagle, the face of a lion, and the face of a man, which bore some of the aspects of the Cheshire cat that so many around Tamerlane House had seen so often.

"Fear me, little thing," the angel rumbled, looking at Dee. "You have summoned your own doom."

"I'm not afraid of any Dragon who ever was," Dee said menacingly, "or of any *angel*. And I am prepared for you . . . *Shaitan*."

Shaitan, far from being cowed as Dee expected, merely smiled and spread his arms. "I am not a Dragon, as you can plainly see," he said, his voice a soft purr that nevertheless carried echoes of thunder in it. "I never descended, and so I am *still* an angel, still Cherubim, exactly as you intended for me to be."

"And still able," Dee said, "to do everything that a Dragon could do here, in this place. That is why I have released you now. To do my bidding one last time."

"Stop!" Rose shouted as she drew Caliburn from its scabbard. "Stop, Dee! You know what I can do with this."

"Little Imago," Dee sneered. "It is far, far too late."

He turned back to the angel, arms spread. In one hand, he held what looked like a green crystal. It was glowing, just like the buildings in the City of Jade. "Shaitan! The time is *now*!" Dee proclaimed, his face a mask of triumph. "Take the Master Key, so we may release the Archipelago and deliver both worlds to the eternal rule of order—so we may deliver them both to the Echthroi."

"Excuse me," Edmund said, raising a finger, "but I don't think that's going to happen."

Everyone turned in surprise to look at Edmund McGee. He seldom took point in a battle, and none of them could understand why he would challenge Dee in such a manner.

The young Cartographer was holding up a trump. It depicted the towers of the City of Jade, along with a familiar face.

"Hello there," Kipling said. "I was beginning to wonder if you'd get around to saving that world before this one meets its doom. I can see the water from here."

"Save the commentary," said Edmund. "Do it!"

"Grimalkin, called Shaitan, called the Cheshire cat," Kipling said, "I release you from your Binding. Thrice I bound you; thrice I release you. I release you. I release you. I release you."

There was a clap of thunder, and a rending of the sky as the angel's collar flew apart and shattered into fragments of light.

"Impossible!" Dee cried. "He was bound to me! To the Echthroi! He is all but Echthros himself!"

"Bound by *you*?" Kipling asked through the trump. "That's what *he* thought too. But a creature who is bound to one cannot be bound to another. And I got to him *first*."

Dee looked dazed. "B-but all these years, he has served *us*!" he said, confused. "He has been a spy in the House of Tamerlane! He has killed agents of the Caretakers!"

Kipling's expression darkened at this, but he merely nodded. "All at my direction, I'm afraid. When I bound him, that was the one thing I ordered him to do—to serve John Dee, and follow his orders as if he were bound to him, until the day when I released him. Which," he added, smiling more broadly now, "I just *did*."

"Over?" Jack snorted. "It's never over until you win . . ."

Chapter Twenty-Three
The Last Battle

The angel Shaitan looked down at John Dee, who suddenly seemed a lot smaller. "Little thing," Shaitan said, "you have caused my countenance to be darkened. You denied me the opportunity to serve the Word by becoming a protector of this world. And there is a price to be paid."

"Not me!" Dee shrieked, pointing at the trump in Edmund's hand. "I never bound you! Kipling! He's the one!"

"Intention counts," the angel replied, "and I can see past his countenance into his heart, just as," he said, moving closer, "I can see into *yours*."

Dee shrieked as the great angel moved down to embrace him with wings and arms and eyes of fire. "I'm sorry!" the Chronographer of Lost Times cried out as he burst into flame. "Forgive me! Please forgive—!"

The angel began to glow, brighter and brighter, and suddenly Dee burst into a thousand shards of shadow, all scattering in an effort to escape the purifying light—but it was impossible. For an instant, the island glowed like a star, and the shadows evaporated in Shaitan's light.

When the companions could see again, the great and terrible

creature that had been the angel had been replaced by a young man, dressed simply in a tunic, who had curly black hair and a look of horrible sadness.

"It's over, isn't it?" he said, to no one in particular.

"No," Samaranth said from the doorway of the inn. "It is just beginning, my friend Shaitan."

The young angel's expression changed from one of sadness to joy, and he ran to his friend. When Sycorax explained the price of entry, he didn't even hesitate.

"Quickly," Edmund said to Kipling. "The flood hasn't hit the city yet. I can still pull you through!"

But to the surprise of all the companions, the Caretaker refused.

"I'm done, I think," he said. "This was my last mission, my last hurrah for the Caretakers. It's time for the—what did you call them, Jack? The Young Magicians? It's time for you to take over now."

"But why?" Rose exclaimed, suddenly understanding where Kipling was, and what kind of price he paid and was paying still to give them this opportunity. "You can still save yourself!"

Kipling smiled. "I think I already have, dear girl," he said, stepping back, away from his own trump. Charles saw it first. "Your shadow!" he exclaimed with relief. "It's come back! Good show, old fellow."

"That's why I'd like to stay," Kipling said. "I lost my shadow by doing a terrible thing for the best of reasons, and then I earned it back by giving you a chance to save the world."

"Also, you got to stick it to John Dee," said Laura Glue.

"Yes." Kipling chuckled. "That too.

"Regardless," he went on, "I've lived two good and worthy

lives now, and I get to finish this one watching the destruction of Atlantis. And when that's done," he said, wiping a tear from his eye, "I'll get to see my boy again. Can't say fairer than that."

He turned away from the trump. "I can hear it now," he said. "Time to go."

"Thank you!" Rose shouted over the increasing noise of the approaching flood. "Thank you, Caretaker!"

Kipling winked at her and turned away as the card faded and went black.

"Oh no," Laura Glue exclaimed. "My hourglass! It's almost run out. We have to go!"

"I'd love to," Quixote said, "but our transportation seems to have disappeared."

The companions' hearts sank as they realized what must have happened—while the angel was dealing with Dee, his henchmen Mr. Kirke and Mr. Bangs had taken the *Indigo Dragon*.

"It's worse than that," said Rose. "I think they took the Amethyst Box as well."

"We still have the Master Key, though," said Charles. "And we have Madoc. We just don't have any way to get back."

"The *Black Dragon*?" Laura Glue asked. "It might work!"

They rushed over to the ship, but all they found was an unconscious Argus, and a massive, gaping hole where the masthead of the angel had been.

"It's no use," Madoc said. "We'll never be able to repair it enough to fly. Not so quickly."

"We should have left a guard," Jack moaned. "What happened to Archie?"

"They must have done something to him," said Madoc. "He would have alerted us otherwise."

"Still," said Jack. "We should have taken more precautions."

"We're at the end of all things, Jack!" Charles sputtered. "Heaven itself is a stone's throw out the back door! Why would we *possibly* have worried about someone stealing the *Indigo Dragon*? Where would they possibly go with her?"

"Back to the Archipelago, for one place," said Laura Glue.

"You are *not* helping things," said Charles.

The Valkyrie turned to make a sarcastic comment to Fred, and for the first time they realized that the two badgers and Quixote were still close to the inn, sitting with Tummeler. Even during Dee's confrontation with the angel, they hadn't left him.

Suddenly Tummeler inhaled a massive breath, and then began to speak. "I am a commander, first class, in the Royal Animal Rescue Society," he said, exhaling as hard as he could, ". . . retired."

"He's still alive!" Charles shouted, half in astonishment and half from joy. "Come quickly! We have to help him! Tummeler is still alive!"

"How?" Jack asked, looking at Samaranth, who shook his head in response. "I don't think there's anything we can do, Don Quixote," the Caretaker said softly.

"A portrait?" Uncas said. "At Tamerlane?"

"There are no portraits of . . . well, any animals in Basil's studio," Jack said, casting a sorrowful, apologetic glance at Tummeler's son and grandson. "Uncas, Fred . . . I'm so sorry."

"A tulpa!" Fred exclaimed, clutching at Charles's coat. "Y' did it once before, with someone else, t' make th' tulpa of Jack!"

"And look how that turned out in the future," Charles answered bitterly. "He became Lord Winter and turned the whole world over to the Echthroi. No," he said, shaking his head, "I'm partly to blame for what's happened here, because I did that foolish, foolish thing—and I cannot countenance doing it again, for anyone."

"It only went badly because Jack was still alive," said Rose. "Can't you make one for Tummeler, for his aiua to enter?"

Charles shook his head. "There simply isn't enough time. It would take a miracle to save him now."

Uncas leaped to his feet. "Brilliant, Scowler Charles! That's it exactly!" The little badger dashed away to where Rose had dropped her bag when she drew her sword, and returned bearing a box.

It was the Serendipity Box. And he presented it not to Charles . . .

. . . but to Don Quixote.

Uncas trembled as he proffered the box to the wizened old knight, who knelt to receive it.

"I know I'm just a squire," Uncas said, voice quavering with emotion, "an' squires is supposed t' help their knight, not ask for boons. But . . ." The little badger risked a glance at the barely breathing Tummeler. "He's my pop. Will you . . . Will you please make a wish, and open th' box?"

"Of course I shall," said Don Quixote. And with no hesitation, he opened the box—but all that was within was what looked like an oversize playing card.

"A trump," said Jack. "It's a *trump*! And look," he said, gesturing at the illustration on the card. "It's the waterfall, at Terminus. We can escape before the sand in the hourglass runs out!"

No one else was listening. Instead they were watching in sorrow and disbelief as the Serendipity Box fell to pieces in Uncas's paws. There was nothing else inside, and now the box itself was crumbling to dust before their eyes.

"There *has* t' be something else!" Uncas cried inconsolably. "There's no time t' take him back for help!"

"No," a very weak voice answered. "But there is time for you to go catch the *Indigo Dragon* and save our world. The box knew. It gave you what you needed most. And that wasn't t' save me."

Tummeler lifted his head, trembling. His strength, his life, were nearly gone. Charles clung to him more tightly as tears streamed down his face.

"I did what I was asked," the old badger said, "and Samaranth and I saved the Archipelago. . . ."

"Balderdash," Charles said. "We know it was really you who did all the work."

"But it will all be lost," Tummeler continued, "if you don't go, now, and do what y' have t' do."

Uncas knelt next to his father. "But you . . ."

Tummeler shushed him. "I got what I wanted, my boy," he said, looking at his son and grandson, and up at Charles. "I got t' be a hero, at last."

"You were always a hero, Tummeler," said Charles, but his old friend didn't hear him. Tummeler was dead.

"We will mourn him after," Madoc said, "but he was right—the hourglass is nearly empty, and we have to leave now."

Quickly Rose and Edmund focused on the trump, and it began to expand. In minutes they could clearly see the rocky outline of Terminus above the great waterfall, and soon it was large enough for all the companions to step through.

Fred and Uncas were still reluctant to leave Tummeler, but

Samaranth assured them that he would not leave his friend alone. "Where he went, I'll soon follow," the angel said. "He is not alone."

"That's all I needed to hear," Fred said, wiping the tears from his face. "Let's go."

With one last farewell to the two angels, the reunited friends standing in the doorway at the inn on the shores of heaven, the companions stepped through the trump just as the last grain of sand circled the neck of the hourglass and fell.

"All right, what now?" Rose asked.

"Now," a voice said from above, "we are going to change history."

The companions all spun about as the *Indigo Dragon* rose up behind them. Mr. Kirke was at the wheel and held the reins.

"Curse it all!" Charles spat. "With the airship, they have the high ground!"

"Not all of it!" Laura Glue exclaimed as she spread her wings and leaped into the air. No one was surprised by the Valkyrie taking to the air—but all of them were surprised when Madoc beat his wings and rose into the air next to her.

"That won't help you," Kirke shouted over the din of the waterfall. "I still have the advantage."

"That's what you think," said Fred. He stuck his paws in his mouth and whistled shrilly, twice, then again. "Coraline! Elly Mae!" he shouted. "To the moon!"

Instantly both goats shot straight up into the air, pulling the airship with them.

"Good girls!" Fred shouted. "Left rudder! Right rudder!"

At the commands, the goats spun about and flew in opposite

directions, flipping the airship upside down and releasing their harnesses at the same time.

"Oh, hell," said Mr. Kirke.

The airship crashed to the ground and exploded into shards of wood and metal, which sent the companions flying for cover and threw Kirke and Bangs into the rocks at the edge of the island.

Instantly Dee's henchmen were on their feet and rushing at the companions, who were still regaining their composure after the crash of the *Indigo Dragon*.

Kirke ran first to Rose and grabbed Caliburn out of the scabbard. He circled the others warily, holding the sword menacingly in front of him.

"You're outnumbered," Madoc warned him, "and if you try to use that sword, it will break on you. I promise you that."

"Not if I'm worthy," said Kirke as Bangs circled around in the other direction. "And a part of me must be, or I wouldn't be holding it now."

"Who are you?" Rose asked, eyes narrowing.

"My friend, Mr. Bangs, was a tulpa," Kirke said. "The first Dee ever created, from a shadow of a whisper of the last words spoken by the first Imago, who was murdered by his elder brother."

"Abel," Jack whispered. "Dee made a tulpa out of Abel."

"Indeed," Kirke said. "But he was imperfect. I, however, am not. And I intend to claim my due, and inherit the earth."

"You're a tulpa too, aren't you?" asked Rose. "So who are you, really?"

"You should know," Kirke said, looking at Charles. "As should you," he added, looking now at Jack. "Having any headaches lately?"

"Oh, dear Lord in heaven," Charles exclaimed, growing pale.

"Why do I have to be in the middle of every awful thing that happens in the Archipelago?"

"Who is it?" Jack asked.

Kirke took off his glasses, and suddenly they all recognized him.

"You, Jack," he said, smiling. "I'm *you.*"

Before the companions could react, Kirke leaped out at Rose, but it was only a feint—one he had been taught by Laura Glue and Hawthorne. Madoc immediately leaped to protect her, and Kirke cut a vicious stroke across one of his wings, dropping the Dragon to the ground in agony.

"I know everything you know, Jack," Kirke said, still smiling, "and I know all your moves before you make them."

Suddenly Bangs jumped forward and struck Laura Glue a terrible blow on the head, and she fell unconscious. Edmund let out a cry and swung a fist at Bangs, who countered it easily and then pinned the young Cartographer to the ground.

"One by one, you are losing allies, Jack," Kirke said menacingly, "and with every second that passes, I grow stronger while you grow weaker. You've lost," he continued, his voice triumphant. "You've lost everything now. All that remains is for you to kneel at my feet and acknowledge the truth of things—that this world belongs now and forever to the Echthroi."

"That," Jack said, suddenly calmer, "is the first mistake I've seen you make, 'Mr. Kirke.'"

"Mistake?" Kirke said, momentarily confused. "What mistake?"

"You're not Echthroi," said Jack. "Not if you can wield Caliburn. And that means you are more like me than you think. And you may know how to beat all my friends, but I," he said, feeling more confident with every passing second, "know how to defeat *you*."

Kirke's face drew into a rictus mask of anger. "Just try it, Caretaker," he hissed. "I am going to rule this world."

At this Jack stepped forward, and to the others' astonishment, he was smiling. "That," he said, rolling up his sleeves, "is *never* going to happen."

Kirke frowned, and his eyes narrowed. "You have nothing left, no allies who can defeat me. It . . . is . . . *over*."

"Over?" Jack snorted. "It's never over until you win—and for you to do that, all we have to do is stop. Defeating you might just be impossible—but as long as we continue to fight, you can't win. You'll *never* win. And if it takes an eternity, I swear by all that's holy on earth and in heaven, I will never stop. Never. Never. Never."

"Jack, this is the moment!" Charles exclaimed. "The one written about in the Histories! The fate of the past, present, and future of the world is at stake! If he defeats you, you'll die—and he will become Lord Winter in the future! This is the moment when the Echthroi take over! You can't just—"

His friend cut him off with a calmly upraised hand. "It's all right, old fellow," Jack said as he moved to engage Kirke.

"I got this."

"We are the same," Kirke said, stepping back but still brandishing the sword. "We share the same aiua, you and I—and I am growing stronger. Soon I will have it all, and you will be dead."

"The headaches!" Rose exclaimed as she tended to the injured Madoc. "That's why Jack has been getting sick! There have been two of him this whole time! One, the living, breathing Jack in Prime Time, who then became the portrait at Tamerlane, and the other, the tulpa that Charles made and Dr. Dee corrupted!"

"Exactly so," said Kirke. "But I wasn't corrupted, I'm who Jack really is. Your father saw that in me the first time we met, all those years ago."

"You're a part of me, yes," Jack said. "A part, but not all."

"This is reality, Jack!" Kirke exclaimed. "You cannot defeat me, because I am your opposite number. I am the player on the other side, and we are as evenly matched as any two men in history—except I am stronger."

"No," Jack said as a sudden realization flooded through him. "You *aren't*."

He put down his arms and simply looked at Kirke.

"We can never stop fighting against our own nature," Jack said softly, "but we can accept it as a part of who we are, and embrace it. Look around you," he continued. "Your masters have abandoned you. It is your allies who have been defeated, not mine. And the Archipelago is about to be restored to the world, in service of the Word."

"Nnnnnaaaaghhhhh!!!" Kirke screamed. "I won't permit it! You cannot do this, Jack! I . . ." He stopped, then dropped to his knees, and the cries of defiance turned to plaintive whimpers.

"I don't want to go!" he exclaimed, almost pleading. "I want to live! I deserve to live!"

"Yes, you do," Jack said, kneeling in front of the tulpa. "And you shall, as a part of me. The part I could not deny when I was young, and cannot deny now."

"Mr. Bangs!" Kirke cried, more weakly now. "Help me!"

But the other tulpa had already stopped fighting and was simply standing apart from the others, watching.

"Don't worry," Jack said as he reached out to embrace the tulpa. "I know who you are, and I accept you, and you are not alone."

The Caretaker wrapped his arms around his shadow-self and pulled him close. The tulpa resisted a moment more, and then gave up his resistance. Kirke started to fade, turning back into the smoke from which he was made, and in seconds, he was gone.

Jack stood up and brushed off his trousers, then walked to the edge of the waterfall and simply stood there, looking out into the abyss.

"That's all well and good," Fred said as he, Uncas, and Charles helped their injured friends, "but what's to be done with Bangs there? I don't think any of us is equipped t' hug *him* into smoke."

Rose picked up Caliburn and strode over to Bangs, but he offered no resistance. Instead he dropped to his knees and bowed his head.

"Please," he said, his voice raspy from sorrow and centuries of pain, "release me."

"I don't want to kill you," Rose began, but he cut her short.

"Already dead," he said, "oh so long ago. The man I was is sitting with the angels at the end of all things, but cannot go on until you release the aiua from this body that was created. And only an Imago or an Archimago can release their own."

Rose closed her eyes in sudden understanding and nodded her head.

"Thank you," the tulpa said. She nodded again, and the sword Caliburn rose, and then fell, and the tulpa dissolved into smoke.

"Now," a voice whispered into her ear from across the eternities, "you are truly the Imago."

Chapter Twenty-Four

The Reign of the Summer King

It took some time for the companions to recover from their ordeal past the wall at the End of the World, and the events on Terminus, but eventually they all healed, and soon preparations were made for the restoration of the Archipelago of Dreams.

The Caretakers Emeriti insisted on a ceremony, with a lot of pomp and circumstance, and speeches, and of course, a massive feast. But when all the ceremony was done, in the end all that was left to do was for the last Dragon, Madoc, to open the Amethyst Box with the Master Key.

It was as simple as it seemed. He inserted the key, and the lid of the box exploded with light, and color, and sound, and life. The torrent from the box filled the sky overhead in an ever-expanding curtain of strange and wonderful geometries.

"Does that look familiar to you?" Edmund asked.

"Yes," said Rose. "It's the tapestry the Archons were weaving in the sky, with light and color and all those impossible gestures they made."

"This is better," Charles said to them both. "You get to design everything about the Archipelago that the angels intended to

“It seemed like the place I should be.”

create when they were planning it in the City of Jade—only there's no impending flood to hurry things along."

Edmund and the badgers were put in charge of island placement, using Tummeler's editions of the *Imaginarium Geographica* as a guide.

"I have to say, this is the most unusual cartographical job I've ever undertaken," said Edmund. "I've used many maps to find lost islands, but this is the first time I've ever used an atlas to tell me where the island should be returned to."

"That's kind of how things work around here," said Fred.

"Here!" Uncas exclaimed excitedly. "I found what we was lookin' for, Rose!"

He turned the atlas around and pointed at a map of a very large, very green, and very undistinguished island.

"This would work just dandy," Uncas continued. "It has mountains, but not too many, beaches and harbors, nice trees, and a huge, honking cave that we can use t' build a new Great Whatsit."

"If it's so undistinguished, then why did Tummeler include it in the facsimile *Geographicas*?" asked Charles.

Uncas shrugged. "We had to fill out a printing signature," he said matter-of-factly, "and it was either a map of this boring ol' place, or another muffin recipe. And we had four in there already."

Charles slapped his forehead. "I should have known," he said, rolling his eyes.

"It looks perfect, Uncas," Edmund said. "Absolutely perfect."

"What is it you're doing, Rose?" Charles asked.

"I'm going to summon the Corinthian Giants," she answered. "We're going to use this island to create a place that we should have never lost, and give it a name that makes certain we always remember.

"We're going to build New Paralon."

The new Cartographer of Lost Places declined to keep the rooms he had been given in Tamerlane House in favor of something that felt more fitting for his calling. Once he had moved all his maps, charts, and equipment to his new workplace, Rose and Madoc took the *Indigo Dragon, newly restored by the shipbuilder Argus,* out to go visit him and give it their blessing.

"It seemed like the place I should be," said Edmund. "Once the Caretakers explained to me fully who the Cartographer of Lost Places really was, and how significant he was to everything that happened in the Archipelago, I thought that there would be no better place for me to work than here, in his old quarters."

Rose looked around the room and realized that it was smaller than the space he had used at Tamerlane, but somehow, this was more fitting. The second-to-the-last room at the top of the Keep of Time had housed a Cartographer for a very, very long time—and it seemed fitting that it did so again.

"But," said Rose, "without the lock on the door."

"Never with a lock," Madoc said, shaking his head. "Never again."

"We're building a small cottage on one of the other islands," Edmund said. "This room is the only one that's in the present, and I need to have someplace to retreat to from time to time."

"'We'?" asked Madoc.

Edmund blushed and smiled. "I've asked Laura Glue to marry me," he said, slightly embarrassed, "and she said yes."

"That's wonderful!" Rose said, rushing over to hug the young Cartographer. "The first wedding in the New Archipelago."

"Thanks," said Edmund, "but it's the same Archipelago, isn't it? We just brought everything back."

"No," Madoc said firmly. "It's not the same. It's better—because wiser people are making better choices about it this time around, and," he added, putting his arm around Rose, "I hope that this time, I will be one of them."

Back in her quarters at Tamerlane House, Rose flopped down on her bed, exhausted, and realized there was a parcel sitting on one of her desks. Wearily, she got back up and turned on a light. What she saw made her gasp.

It was the Ruby Armor of T'ai Shan.

There was also a note, addressed to her, but unsigned—although she knew without any doubt whom it was from. She carried the parcel back over to her bed and opened up the note, which was written on the now familiar cream-colored paper. It read:

My dear Rose,

This armor belongs to you now. I have no further use for it, but you may still do some good in the world. I hope that I have as well, though I cannot be sure. I tried to help when I could, and I hope it was enough. I know that there are still many questions, and I'm afraid you'll have to answer them on your own. That is part of the path of the Imago. But I know you, Rose, and I believe in you. And if anyone ever questions you, if they question your motives, or your choices, you can point to me as an example. I had every reason to fall into shadow, but when I had the opportunity to choose, I chose the light. Not because of some noble cause, or for any great purpose, but because, when I was a child, and I was afraid, the Caretakers did not leave me behind.

Small gestures can change the world. Never forget that, my dear Rose. And never forget me.

Tears began to well up in Rose's eyes again as she read and reread the note, and then her breath caught when she realized that there was someone in the room with her, sitting quietly in the shadows.

"Telemachus?" she said. "Is that you?"

Her silent visitor stood up, and she realized it wasn't the boy prince—it was Poe.

He walked to the door, beckoning for her to follow.

The corridors and hallways were empty—all the Caretakers were keeping themselves busy with the restoration project, and so they were spending as little time as possible cooped up inside Tamerlane House. So Rose simply followed Poe as they walked silently to the uppermost minaret of the house.

Poe walked to the balcony and pushed open the doors, letting in the sea air. Then, with no preamble, he began to speak.

"The Archimago came first into the new world," Poe began, "because that was the way of things. Without darkness to penetrate, light would have no meaning. And so he came to make his way, and find his purpose. The Imago followed after, but the light was too much for the Archimago to bear. He was merely a Namer, whereas his younger sibling, the Imago, was a Maker.

"He didn't realize that there could be as much meaning in Naming as in Making, and in his jealousy, he . . ." Poe stopped, his voice trailing off into silence.

"From the moment I raised my hand and struck him," Poe said, still not turning from the balcony, "and he fell to the ground . . . there was sorrow. And regret. I—I need you to know that.

"He was meant to be the Imago. The protector of the world, and I took that from him. I didn't understand what I had done, until it was too late."

He dropped a small ring to the floor, and it dissolved in smoke and ash. "A Binding," he said, "of my own devising. I could not bear to speak of it, and so I made certain I never could—not until he was truly freed, and the damage I caused was undone. It was the best I could do to live here, in Kairos time, and try to restore that which I had destroyed, and to help those who cared for the Archipelago to try to find another Imago to take his place."

At that he turned to look at her. "I am grateful that we have. I am grateful to you, Rose Dyson."

"I—I don't know what to say," she answered truthfully. "I'm not even certain what I should call you."

"I have gone by many names, and lived many lives, over these thousands of years," said Poe, "and the one that suited me best was the one given to me by my father—Cain. But the one that I think I shall return to is the one my mother called me—Chronos. I think it suits me better now, don't you think?"

"Yes," said Rose. "I do."

He didn't say anything after that, but merely turned to look out over the sea, so after a few moments, Rose turned and left, closing the door behind her.

As the restoration of the Archipelago continued apace, a meeting was called among the Caretakers to address something being asked by the reemerging peoples of the lands: Who would rule?

"I think 'govern' is a better word," Madoc said as he and the Prime Caretaker made their way to the great hall. "Ruling is an anachronism, I think."

"That's just modesty talking," said John.

"Not modesty," said Madoc. "Caution. It was my ambition to rule the Archipelago that created most of the problems to begin with, remember?"

"And it was your eventual wisdom that resolved them," John said. "You mustn't forget that, either."

"I wasted my youth." Madoc sighed. "I could have done so much better, for so many around me."

"You were a good boy, who never had the opportunity to become a good man," said John.

Madoc shook his head. "I had opportunities—I just allowed the bitterness to dominate my choices. That, and deciding to listen to John Dee instead of . . ." He sighed again heavily. "I've made a lot of mistakes in my life—and it has been a very long life."

Madoc and John had decided that the best approach would be the most direct one, and so at John's urging, the son of Odysseus stood to address the Caretakers.

"We are going to dissolve the Frontier," he said simply. "Before today is ended, the Archipelago of Dreams and the Summer Country will once more be one world."

At hearing this, da Vinci choked on his wine, spraying it across his hapless colleagues at the end of the table. "Are you mad?" he said, barely containing his anger. "If you do that, then anyone can simply cross over! It's madness!"

"Anyone who has a guide," Madoc said, gesturing at the stack of *Imaginarium Geographicas* piled on the floor next to Fred. "A guide, and the purity of heart to see the invisible world that our magic has restored."

Twain nodded in agreement. "Most humans wouldn't be able to find the Archipelago if we strapped them to a Dragonship and dropped them onto Tamerlane House," he said as he lit another cigar, "but there are some who would be able to find a way here if they were blind, deaf, and dumb. They would still feel the magic, and heed its call. And for those people, it should be as open as possible."

Da Vinci scowled. "This has all gone exactly as you wanted, Mordred," he said, deliberately using the name that had at one time struck fear into the hearts of all the Caretakers. "You wanted to rule the Archipelago, and you shall. You wanted to open the Archipelago to the world, and you will. And after all our efforts trying to defeat you over the years, and all the lives that were lost in the pursuit of that goal, you have won everything after all. Well. Done."

"I am no longer Mordred," Madoc said, his words measured and cool, "and I am dictating terms to no one. I have the support of the Prime Caretaker"—he gestured to John—"the Caveo Principia," he continued, gesturing at Jack, "the other Caretakers of this era"—he nodded at Charles and Fred—"and the Imago herself. This is the best plan we can try, and it will be worth our efforts."

"It also supports what I established with the International Cartological Society, back in the Summer Country," said Jack. "We already have dozens of apprentices, and hundreds of associate Caretakers, and we hope that number will soon grow."

"Grow?" da Vinci said, incredulous. "At this rate, anyone in the world who wants to will be able to find their way into the Archipelago of Dreams!"

"Yes," Madoc said, smiling. "If we do our jobs right, that's exactly what will happen."

It was dusk when John, Jack, Charles, and Madoc made their way to Terminus for a private discussion they had wanted to have for a very long time.

"You realize," Madoc said as they stepped off the new boat Shakespeare had built to be pulled by the flying goats, "the last time all four of us were together was here, on this island."

"So many graves here," Madoc said. In addition to Captain Nemo and Artus, they had also added markers for Kipling, Tummeler, and Samaranth. "It's a good place to think about the future. A good place to remember the good choices, and the bad ones."

"It's easy to see the good and bad in others," said Jack. "It's much harder to see it in ourselves."

"Is it?" asked Madoc.

"You knew about me," Jack said. "When we first met, all those years ago, when I was still a child, you knew. You saw the shadow-side I didn't even know I possessed."

"I was a different man then—" Madoc began, before Jack cut him off.

"You keep saying that," the Caretaker told him, "but that's not actually true. You are the same man, Madoc—you've just been Named differently. Sometimes of your own volition. Sometimes by others. But still the same man.

"When I was young, and brash, and full of good trouble," Jack went on, "you saw the potential in me to have a darker side. That was very difficult to accept. But when I finally did, I was able to do things others could not. I was able to restore a Shadowed Archipelago not because of my purity, but because I had faced my own shadows—and accepted them. That's all I did when I faced my shadow-self here on Terminus. And if it hadn't been for the lessons you taught me all those years ago, I never would have been able to do it."

"We wanted to bring you here," Charles said, "to tell you about the new History I've just begun. It's a history that starts here, today, with the four of us—just the way the last one ended."

"That one was a prophecy, though," said Madoc. "It was all about the things that happened—the things I caused to happen—that only the three of you were able to stop."

"This one is going to be a self-fulfilling prophecy, then," said John. "It's going to project all the things we want to have happen, and will make happen, because we choose for them to happen."

"Yes?" Madoc said. "And what are you going to call this work of fiction-made-real?"

"Rose suggested the name. We're going to call it *The Reign of the Summer King*," John said as the three men put their hands atop one another in front of him. "May you live forever, Madoc. Forever."

Epilogue

The old man was dying. He had, however, lived a very long and happy life, and he had accomplished many things. He had a loving family and colleagues who respected him, and he wasn't in pain. All those things were important to him.

Two years earlier, when his wife passed away, he had returned here to his Oxford, to live at Merton College. It was a balm for him, to live in familiar surroundings.

It was, in truth, his second-favorite place in the entire world. He blinked his eyes in the soft light—someone, several someones, had entered his room.

"Who's there?" he called out. "Who is it?"

"Uncle Hugo let us know it was time," said Rose, "and we've all come to be here with you."

"Rose! Charles!" he exclaimed, rising up on his elbows. "And Jack! You shouldn't have left Tamerlane House! What if . . ."

Jack simply smiled and helped him lie back down. "Now, John—you know I've left Tamerlane a hundred times in the last ten years. Just as long as I'm not away more than a week. You know that."

"I know," John said, breathing heavily. There was a rasp in his

lungs. He was not long for this world. "So has Basil painted my portrait, then?" he asked. "Please tell me he thickened up my hair and tightened up my belly."

"No portrait, Uncle John," said Rose. "You would never be content being so tied to Tamerlane House."

A look of alarm crossed the old man's features. "But I haven't prepared a tulpa! And there isn't time, unless someone else has already . . ." He looked at Charles, who raised his hands in protest.

"Not I," Charles said. "I learned my lesson the last time, remember?"

"Then what?" asked John. "What's to become of me?"

"Something you earned, Scowler John," Fred said, stepping out from behind Charles. "Something special."

"The lands of the Archipelago are restored and flourishing once more," Rose said as she removed a small pendant from around her neck, "but the restoration is not yet complete. One thing remains to be done. The Archipelago of Dreams must have a protector."

She held up the pendant. John could see it was made of clear crystal, with some kind of fluid inside that caught the light and made it dance.

"Water from Echo's Well, which is the same water from the Moon Pool of the City of Jade," Rose said, smiling even as tears began to streak her cheeks. "Just look into the water, and speak the words."

A momentary thrill crossed John's features, only to dim a moment later. "It's . . . a great, great honor," he said, "but to suddenly vanish from the Summer Country . . ."

"Your family knows," said Fred. "Your son is an apprentice Caretaker, after all. It's all been arranged."

"Well then, it's all fine and good," said John, "but I was hoping . . . I mean to say that I wished that Edith . . ."

Jack leaned forward and put a gentle hand on his friend's shoulder. "Edmund made a chronal trump, and he and Hugo are with her now, two years behind us. She will meet you on New Paralon."

"Two hearts are as one, Uncle John," said Rose. "Of course we wouldn't give this to you, without offering it to her as well."

A great breath escaped John's lips, as if that was the only thing that had held him to life. "Then yes, please. Yes. I accept, gladly, happily, joyfully, yes."

"Just look at your reflection in the water," Rose repeated, leaning close, "speak the words . . .

". . . and ascend."

When the huge, violet-colored Dragon arrived at New Paralon, his mate was already waiting. She flexed her own great wings and lifted up to meet him as he plummeted faster and faster toward her, and to the reunion he had hoped for since her death. They had been apart for two years, but now they would never be apart again. Without speaking a word to any of those assembled on the newly built docks, the two Dragons soared up into the clouds and disappeared.

Occasionally someone would report a sighting—never of one, always of both—and the peoples of the Archipelago knew that they were close, and if they were needed, would be even closer. These were not tame Dragons, but they were Dragons nonetheless, and they knew their purpose—to protect those who needed protecting, and offer guidance when it was needed. Everything else was flying. Together.

No one was on Terminus, at the waterfall at the Edge of the World, to see it happen, but in the moment the Dragons returned to the Archipelago, a star appeared in the darkness beyond. Then another. And another. And another. And soon the sky was so full of stars that no one would ever imagine that it had ever been a place of darkness at all, or a place where anyone in need might cry out and not be reassured with the response that was carried in a whisper across the sky. . . .

. . . Here, there be Dragons.

Author's Note

One of the drawbacks of blazing a new trail, which writing a book always is (especially if it's part of a series), is that you can't really tell how successful your choices are going to be looking forward. You have to blaze the trail first, so that you can look back and take an accounting of how well your choices worked.

A great many things changed between the time I wrote my original series outline and the publication of *Here, There Be Dragons*. When plans went forward to do *The Search for the Red Dragon,* the outlines changed even more; and when I jumped full-bore into writing the third, fourth, and fifth books, there were not only points where I veered a long way off from what the original plan was, but also points where I wondered if the whole thing hadn't just gone completely off the rails. But that's the nature of the beast: Fiction, especially in an extended form, is more than just a narrative. It's the recording of the lives of the characters within it—and sooner or later, everyone's lives become complex and complicated. That's what makes things interesting.

I had always had the general endgame in mind—but the exact nature of the players involved changed over the course of the series. Some bad guys became worse; characters who started out as rogues transformed into friends; and the character who changed the most revealed himself to be far, far greater than I ever imagined—and in the process, gave me a big part of the ending that pulled all the threads together into a tapestry. The idea that something can be destroyed only by the one who created it was set up with the first book, and the nearly indestructible *Imaginarium Geographica*. It was a perfect circle to close to realize that I had set things up for that to apply to the Keep of Time as well.

The original outlines are really interesting to look over (to me, anyway), and might be worth doing an essay about sometime. I had envisioned three main books under the series title Here, There Be Dragons, and a second set of smaller books, to be called the Chronicles of the *Imaginarium Geographica*, which would tell the history of the Cartographer—the notes for which were used almost in their entirety in *The Indigo King*. The three primary books were to involve the three main conflicts with the Winter King and were going to be very much more straightforward adventure stories than these books turned out to be. But once I realized that merging the Cartographer's story into the main narrative made everything more fun to write, that meant that Madoc was going to play a more complex role in the stories as well. After that, the series took on a life of its own.

Someone said the best way to make a story interesting is to have a good character do something bad, or have a bad character do something good. I think that's the sort of thing that makes the best stories resonate with readers long after the cover of the book is closed: because we all have those elements within us. We all have the potential to make mistakes—and the potential to learn from them, and to try to choose better.

I am not ashamed to admit that in writing this book, I wept more than once. The characters I spent eight years writing were changing, so it was a very emotional book to finish. Most of the book had to be written to line up with everything that had gone before; but I wrote the epilogue, with only a few changed details, over five years ago.

There were times in writing these books where I felt like I was losing my way, but in the end, I think I pulled it all together and made it read as if I knew where I was going all along. And maybe, just maybe . . . I *did.*

James A. Owen
Silvertown, AZ